# TRAJECTORY

**Also by**
**CAMBRIA GORDON**

*The Poetry of Secrets*

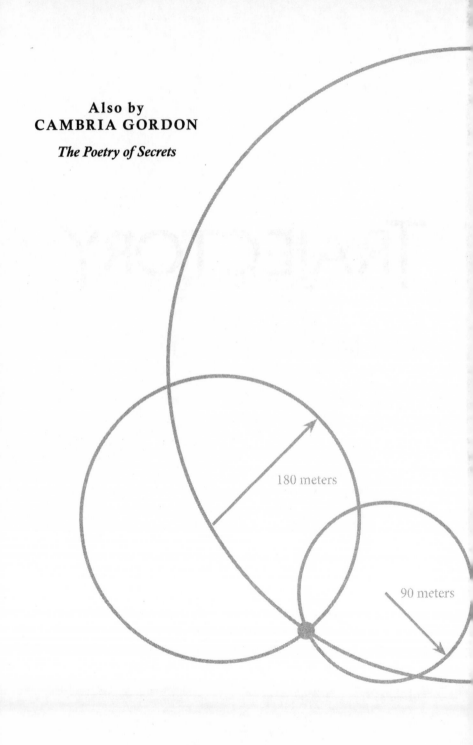

180 meters

90 meters

# TRAJECTORY

## CAMBRIA GORDON

meters

SCHOLASTIC PRESS / New York

Library of Congress Cataloging-in-Publication Data

Names: Gordon, Cambria, author.
Title: Trajectory / Cambria Gordon.
Description: First edition. | New York : Scholastic Press, 2024. |
Audience: Ages 12 and up. | Audience: Grades 10–12. | Summary: As the United States enters World War II, seventeen-year-old Eleanor wants to do something to help her Jewish relatives in Poland, so she puts her brilliant math skills to work for the US army to fine-tune a top-secret weapon that will help defeat the enemy.
Identifiers: LCCN 2023015636 | ISBN 9781338853827 (hardcover) | ISBN 9781338853834 (ebook) |
Subjects: LCSH: Jewish teenagers—United States—Juvenile fiction. | World War, 1939–1945—United States—Juvenile fiction. | Holocaust, Jewish (1939–1945)—Juvenile fiction. | Mathematical ability in children—Juvenile fiction. | Bildungsromans. | CYAC: Jewish youth—Fiction. | World War, 1939–1945—Fiction. | Holocaust, Jewish (1939–1945)—Fiction. | Mathematicians—Fiction. | Coming of age—Fiction. | BISAC: YOUNG ADULT FICTION / Historical / United States / 20th Century | YOUNG ADULT FICTION / Historical / Holocaust | LCGFT: Historical fiction. | War fiction. | Bildungsromans.
Classification: LCC PZ7.G65435 Tr 2024 | DDC 813.6 [Fic]—dc23/eng/20230501
LC record available at https://lccn.loc.gov/2023015636

10 9 8 7 6 5 4 3 2 1    24 25 26 27 28

Printed in Italy 183

First edition, April 2024

Book design by Elizabeth B. Parisi

For my parents

*Girls can be made proficient and give good service as human computers*

*in the year before they graduate to married life and become experts*

*with the housekeeping accounts.*

—Astronomer L. J. Comrie
*"Careers for Girls" from* The Mathematical Gazette, *1944*

**To the tune of Gene Autry's "(I've Got Spurs That) Jingle, Jangle, Jingle"**

*I've got differences that wiggle, waggle, wiggle*

*As I go smoothing crazily along.*

*I've got factors that make me wanna giggle*

*As I inverse interpolate along.*

*Oh, Gregory–Newton, oh, Gregory–Newton*

*How we love your coefficients—*

*Yes, we love them for computin'.*

*I've got ranges that wiggle, waggle, wiggle*

*And my φ's waver crazily along.*

*But if Hitler's nerves begin to jiggle*

*Then our tables can't be very far from wrong.*

—circa 1943, by the women of the Philadelphia Computing Section

*My dearest Sky,*

*You know that letter I gave you for safekeeping to send to my parents in case the worst happened? I'd like you to replace it with a new letter I'm enclosing here. It says basically the same thing I'm about to tell you, but without the classified parts.*

*Here goes.*

*I'm going to join the 5th BG on their mission. I know what you're thinking. You don't want me to risk my life. Someone else can work the Norden.*

*You must trust me when I say this: There is no one else. And time is running out.*

*I want to be able to say I did everything I could to end this devastating war. Even if where I'm going is over the Pacific and not Nazi Germany. Everything is connected. But you already know that.*

*By the time you get this, I'll be airborne. Of course, I'm terrified. But I have a special good luck charm. I've written this quote from Eleanor Roosevelt on a small piece of paper, which I will carry with me:*

You gain strength, courage, and confidence by every experience in which you really stop to look fear in the face. You must do the thing you think you cannot do.

*Finally, I feel worthy of my guardian angel.*

*Yours always,*
*Eleanor*

# I.

## May 1942

I used to think that only Catholics could have guardian angels. Then my uncle Herman told me that Jews believe in them, too. I decided that mine would be Eleanor Roosevelt, for reasons way beyond our shared name.

Unfortunately, she has yet to show up.

"Eleanor, can you season the chicken?" calls Mom. She pokes her head into the study, where I'm arranged in my usual spot: sitting on the love seat, pretending to read a magazine. Today it's an issue of *Life*. One of Dad's math textbooks is hidden behind the pages so that anyone looking at me from the outside would think I was reading about summer playclothes instead of doing calculus.

Mom continues. "I can't be expected to cook the whole Shabbos meal by myself"—I whisper this last part with her—"after being on my feet all day." It's her refrain every Friday evening.

When she leaves, I lay the magazine on the small coffee table and replace the math book on the shelf. Tangent vectors will have to wait. Then I follow her into the kitchen.

Near Mom's feet, my younger sister, Sarah, sits on the floor with a screwdriver and rusty baby carriage.

"Why can't *she* season the chicken?" I ask, annoyed.

"Because I'm earning money," says Sarah. "The government is paying for scrap metal. This old thing might become a hand grenade."

"Season it generously," Mom tells me. "God knows it cost me enough ration stamps." She chops carrots lickety-split, then starts to measure out the rice. "You need to find a way to show your patriotism, Eleanor. You're seventeen, for heaven's sake. Your sister is only twelve."

"She's too timid to do anything," pipes in Sarah.

"That's not true," I say. Even though it is.

When Eleanor Roosevelt was young, she was painfully shy and felt like an ugly duckling. I've been told I look like Maxene, the middle singer of the Andrews Sisters, so I don't think I'm an ugly duckling, but like a young E.R., I prefer to go unnoticed. Somehow she managed to overcome those obstacles, become the First Lady, and use her voice to fight against injustice. I guess I keep hoping that, short of showing up on my doorstep, E.R. will send me a sign that I, too, have a powerful woman inside me.

I hear the *thump drag, thump drag* of Dad's cane and bum leg coming down the stairs, reminding me of yet another connection I have to Eleanor Roosevelt. We both love men who are disabled. I pull out Dad's special chair at the dining table, the one with the higher cushion so he can get up from it easily. I give him a kiss on the cheek, stick a straw in his water glass, and go back to dinner prep.

A half hour later the doorbell rings. Aunt Jona swoops in to hug me like a diving pelican, squeezing my ribs against the pillow of her breasts. Uncle Herman goes straight to the liquor, and cousins Jacob and Lila, seven-year-old twins, duck under their mother's arm and run inside. They make a beeline for the radio. *The Lone Ranger* is just beginning.

"Hi-yo Silver, away!" squeals Jacob, galloping with his sister, making a loop of the downstairs area, through the kitchen and into the study, where he and Lila crash into a side table, causing a lamp to teeter. I get there just in time to prevent a disaster. Dad's study is a sacred space for me. Besides doubling as my secret math hideout, it's also where his typewriter lives, the same page yellowing in the cartridge from his unfinished book on transcendental numbers. After a line, he gets tired and falls asleep. I don't think his sentences make sense anyway.

We light the Shabbos candles and say the blessings. The chicken is roasted perfectly, the rice has soaked up all the juice, and our victory garden carrots taste like candy. Everyone's talking at once. I'm quiet, which is not unusual, but all the more noticeable in this boisterous family of ours. Uncle Herman tells a joke about an old man who goes to the doctor because he can't pee. The doctor asks how old he is. The man says ninety-three. The doctor says, You've peed enough.

"New fr Pol?" asks Dad.

"Dad wants to know the news from Poland," I say. This is how I usually participate in dinner conversations. Translating Dad's slurred speech.

Uncle Herman hears all the gossip from his Polonia Society meetings. Even though most of the members are Catholic, the Poles stick together here in Philly—many of them live in row houses on Manayunk Avenue, like my aunt and uncle. Unlike Mom, who married a third-generation American Jew and moved to the suburbs as fast as she could, her brother Herman is still tethered to the old country.

"Shreklekh," he answers in Yiddish. "Terrible."

"Azriel, Roza, and Batja?" asks Mom, her voice fading, not wanting to ask the real question: Are they alive?

Uncle Herman shrugs. "God only knows." He looks at me. "Have you received anything, shayna maidel?"

"Not in months," I answer.

My cousin Batja and I have been writing letters to each other since my fourth-grade teacher wanted us to know there was a world beyond Jenkintown, our little suburb of Philadelphia. She had us correspond with a pen pal in another country. At the time, I vaguely knew about our relatives in Poland, first cousins of Mom's and Uncle Herman's—Azriel and his wife, Roza, and their daughter, Batja, born around the same time I was. When Mom suggested Batja for the assignment, I jumped at the chance to get to know her better. She wrote in Yiddish

4

and I wrote in English. Uncle Herman translated for me, and her teacher translated for her. She's never gone this long without writing.

Uncle Herman continues. "The only thing I know is what my neighbor told me. His brother is a deputy of the Jewish Council and managed to smuggle out a letter." He pauses, sipping his martini, as if to gird himself for what's about to come. "All the Jews have to wear white armbands with blue stars of David to identify themselves when they're outside the Stanislau ghetto. Three gates are guarded by German Schutzpolizei and the Ukrainian militia on the outside, and by the Jewish police on the inside."

"Jesh poli?" asks Dad.

"Jewish police?" I say.

"One hundred Jews serve in the ghetto police. Can you imagine? Having to rat on your own kind?"

Mom's water glass trembles when she rests it on the saucer. "The world needs to know about this. I'm going to speak to the Joint."

That would be the Joint Distribution Committee, where Mom used to volunteer, raising money for Russian and Polish Jews who lost their homes in pogroms after the Great War. Her involvement in the organization is yet another casualty of Dad's illness, but she's still on their mailing list. Recently, I saw a Joint newsletter on our kitchen counter. It showed a Nazi propaganda poster advertising that Jews are lice and cause typhus.

"Vat else the letter say?" asks Aunt Jona.

"Twenty thousand souls are living there, smashed together in a few city blocks. Sometimes twelve people sleep in a room smaller than this." Uncle Herman gestures around our dining room walls. "Everything is dirty and rat-infested and most people are sick. Those who aren't sick are forced to work in German arms factories. Many are beaten if they can't keep up the ten-hour day with no lunch, no breaks."

Aunt Jona leans into her husband. "Vat they do vith the sick ones?"

I've never seen my joke-telling uncle look so sad. "This wasn't in the letter, but I've heard talk. About selections. During these aktions, no one knows who might be useful and who might be sent to die. The mechanics? The doctors? They certainly don't need the ones who worked in offices or the old and the sick." We all bow our heads, thinking of Azriel, who is a lawyer.

"How does a human do this to another human?" asks Mom.

It's a question without an answer.

I picture Batja's small hands, the ten-year-old ones that drew me a picture of her farm, milking goats the only labor those fingers had ever seen. In return, I sent her a drawing of our dog, Felix, in his doghouse, with a talk bubble that said *I woof you*. I think of her now, trying to fall asleep on an empty stomach, sharing stale air with eleven others in one cramped room. The food in front of me is no longer appetizing.

"Whaa abo sen monnn," says Dad. "For bri."

"What about sending money," I repeat. "For bribes."

"Do you see a money tree growing in our yard?" Mom throws her napkin down and rises to clear the plates.

Silence around the table.

Uncle Herman turns to Dad. "What do home mortgages and trigonometry have in common?"

I know he's trying to be funny, making light of our debt, needing a humorous release from this whole tragic situation in Poland. Dad can't formulate the answer to the riddle. I see his lips moving, but no sound comes out. It's painful to watch.

"You have to sine and cosine," I blurt out.

Aunt Jona pats my hand. "Zei gezunt. She's a math genius like her father."

I stiffen. "It's just a dumb joke, Aunt Jona. Anyone could answer it." I lean over and hug Dad around the neck. "This big guy is the only mathematician in our family."

Satisfied that Dad won't need any more defending tonight, I slide my chair out. "Good Shabbos, everybody. Trudie's waiting for me."

At 8:30 p.m. it's still light out. The sky is the color of a soft gray sweater. I meet my best friend at our usual corner, halfway between our houses.

"What took you so long?" Trudie tucks her halo of pin curls behind her ears. "I told Don we'd be there fifteen minutes ago. He can be so impatient."

"We got to talking about my cousins in Poland."

"My father says now that America has entered the war, it's going to be over in a few months."

"I don't think so. The Great War lasted four years and this one's been going on since 1939 with no signs of letting up. The Nazis are evil incarnate."

"Aren't you the Sad Sally. Brighten up. It's the weekend, for Pete's sake." She hooks her elbow through mine. "I hope Don invites me to go to his parents' lake house this summer. Do you think he'll pop the question there? Or maybe he won't wait that long, and he'll get on his knee at graduation? Better yet, he might do it at Tommy Dorsey's show next week. Can you imagine, getting engaged in front of Frank Sinatra?" She smiles at me. "I don't think I've properly thanked you for being my partner in crime. Don and I would never have gone steady if it weren't for you coming to Oswald's with me every Friday night this year."

Trailing after her is more like it. I'm no good at parties and I don't know the first thing about flirting. But I'd never leave the house if it weren't for Trudie. So I suppose being her sidekick is the price I have to pay for having any kind of social life.

"Any new jokes?" she asks.

I tell her Uncle Herman's joke about the old man who can't pee. She doubles over in hysterics. I always like making her laugh.

Oswald's Drug Store is six blocks away from my house. For twenty years, the red neon sign has become a lighthouse of sorts, guiding young people to its sweet-filled shores. Trudie pinches her cheeks and waves at Don through the glass. Then she struts in and settles on his lap. I take the empty stool between them and one of Don's friends, a skinny kid named Ricky.

The bored soda jerk wipes down the counter in front of us while the boys argue about the Phillies. They always talk sports. Never world events. Never the draft. Come next fall, they'll all turn eighteen. Maybe they're avoiding the subject on purpose.

Trudie starts to retell my uncle Herman's joke, but when she gets to the part after the man says he's ninety-three years old, she pauses. She can't remember the punch line. Ever so casually, I lean over and whisper it to her.

"The doctor says you've peed enough!" she exclaims.

The guys crack up and I do, too, knowing I've made her look good. It's been that way since we met in grade school. She gets the big laugh and I get the assist without having to actually do any talking.

"I got center-field seats for tomorrow's game," says Don.

"Too bad I can't go. It's the MathMeet," says Ricky.

I stop sipping my malted. "The MathMeet?"

"She talks!" says a third boy.

"Don't tell me Nervous Nellie's going to enter and actually shout out the answers?" quips Don. I redden, hating the nickname.

Trudie pokes her boyfriend in the arm. "Don't be mean, Don."

"I just wondered where it was being held," I say.

"The Women's Club. Eleven a.m.," replies Ricky kindly.

They go back to their conversation. Trudie goes back to the messy work of stroking Don's Brylcreemed hair. I go back to my straw. I definitely do not, absolutely, under any circumstances, think about the MathMeet.

# 2.

I lied. I'm standing in front of the Women's Club, a two-story brick building downtown. High school students from all over Pennsylvania—from Erie to Bucks County—compete every year in the MathMeet. I can't believe it's being held right here in Philadelphia. A boy bumps my shoulder as he runs inside, his notebook banging against his leg.

I step into the building. A gray-haired woman sits at a desk, trying to sign in each contestant. Teenagers, mostly boys, swarm around her like ants on a watermelon. Alas. This event may be sponsored by the Women's Club, but it seems most girls are still afraid to admit they love math. Beyond the desk is a large auditorium, already crowded with families jockeying for seats.

"Form a line, please!" yells the woman with surprising grit.

I hesitate a moment, watching her slip papers onto clipboards, handing them out efficiently. Then I walk past her into the auditorium. I squeeze through a row of adults, trying not to bump too many knees, until I reach the last seat in the last row.

I'm not here to enter. I'm just going to do the problems for fun.

Up onstage, someone adjusts a long blackboard on wheels, making sure it faces the audience just right. Someone else taps a microphone on a dais. "Is this on?"

A screeching feedback comes out. "Testing, one two three."

The din around me is loud with nervous excitement.

Then a woman in a tweed suit walks onto the stage and the room quiets down.

"Welcome to the Pennsylvania State MathMeet," she says. "I won't take much of your time. The rules are quite simple. I'll write an equation on the board and when you have the answer, you shout it out. We will give out two awards: one for the school and one for the individual who answers the most questions correctly. Individual winners can be from any region. Pencils ready?"

I rest the point of my Dixon on page one of my notebook.

It's standard stuff. Cubic equations like:

$x^3 - 8x^2 + 19x - 12 = 0$ and $4x^3 + 16x^2 - 11x - 3 = 0$

and this one:

Find the particular solution $y = f(x)$ to the differential equation $\frac{dy}{dx} = e^y\,(3x^2 - 6x)$

with the initial condition $(1,0)$.

So far, I'm finishing faster than everybody else. It's great fun and I'm glad I came. The woman continues writing problems and kids continue to shout out answers.

"Four pi."

"Wrong."

"One-seventh."

"Correct."

It goes on for forty-five minutes. Then she scritch-scratches this onto the board:

$$\int \frac{3(x+1)}{x^2 \left(x^2+3\right)} dx$$

Immediately, I know how to find the antiderivative. You do it by using partial fraction decomposition. The original fraction is converted into two smaller fractions that are easier to integrate. I start writing.

$$\int \frac{3(x+1)}{x^2 \left(x^2+3\right)} dx = \int \frac{Ax+B}{x^2} dx + \int \frac{Cx+D}{x^2+3} dx$$

It takes five more steps in my notebook to find the answer.

$$ln|x| - \frac{1}{x} - \frac{1}{2} \, ln\left(x^2+3\right) - \frac{1}{\sqrt{3}} tan^{-1}\left(\frac{x}{\sqrt{3}}\right) + C$$

Meanwhile, no one is shouting out anything. People rustle in their seats. Next to me, someone murmurs, "What if no one figures it out?"

The moderator waits fifteen whole minutes before she calls it. "Time!"

Moans and groans from the audience ensue.

"That's it for today."

Certificates are handed out to the winners and then people begin to make their way to the exit. I wait in my little corner for the crowd to thin out.

"Eleanor? Is that you?"

"Mrs. Obermeyer. What a surprise." (Not a happy one.) I rest my notebook on the seat behind me and stand up to greet my mother's friend. Her hat has so many flowers on the side, it's a wonder her head isn't permanently tilted.

"Isn't this exciting! Last time we had a full house at the Women's Club was the Red Cross art auction and cake tasting. How's your mother? We miss her at our meetings."

Mom hasn't participated in the Women's Club in years, though she does speak wistfully of the strolls she and Mrs. Obermeyer use to take. Things just got too busy with her sudden need for a new job and all the time it took to care for Dad. Unfortunately, the way Mom chooses to deal with Dad's situation is to keep up appearances, which leaves encounters like this fraught.

"And has your father been able to get any work done since the, well, you know . . ."

"Oh, don't worry about him. He's nearly finished with his book!"

Mrs. Obermeyer takes stock of the empty auditorium. "Goodness. We closed down the place. Come. Let me give you a ride home. I'm going right past your house."

I don't want to sit in a car and have to make small talk with her, but I don't want to be rude, either. She was once a dear friend of Mom's, in another life. I'd get home twice as fast if I accepted the ride, and I do have those cognitive exercises to work on with Dad. I nod and we go outside to the sidewalk.

"My driver should be around here somewhere . . ." she says, walking down the block a short way.

I feel a tap on my shoulder. It's the MathMeet moderator, the smart-looking woman in the tweed suit. "I'm so glad I caught you," she says breathlessly. "You forgot this."

My notebook. I reach out to take it, but it drops on the pavement, splayed open with all my calculations visible. I scoop it up before she can see.

A green Cadillac pulls to the curb in front of us and the passenger-side window rolls down. "Hop in," says Mrs. Obermeyer.

I hesitate, glancing back to the woman in the suit. I haven't even thanked her for returning my notebook. "You go on ahead, Mrs. Obermeyer. I'll take the train home."

"If you're sure now. Give my regards to your mother!"

Up close, the woman is younger than I thought, probably early thirties, with rimless glasses and short brown hair held off her face by combs behind her ears.

"Thank you for chasing me down," I say. "I really appreciate it."

"Did you compete today?" she asks me. I get a faint whiff of her perfume. Coty, what Mom wears.

"Um . . . no, I didn't enter."

"Too bad." She glances at the notebook, guarded tightly against my chest. "Since no one else was able to figure out the answer to that last one."

So she did see.

She reaches into her pocketbook and hands me a business card. *Mary Mauchly. Moore School of Electrical Engineering, University of Pennsylvania.* This surprises me. "I didn't know MathMeet was associated with U Penn . . ."

Her lips part in amusement. "MathMeet is a ruse, dear."

I don't understand.

"For me, at least. When we entered this war, the math organization agreed to let me be a moderator. It's one of the ways I find jewels in the crown. Female jewels."

"Just women?"

"All the men are heading overseas. And the people I work for need brainpower. Lots of it. To make lots of computations."

I don't know what to say. Is she recruiting me to be a coed? "I haven't applied to college," I confess. "My family needs me."

"Well, the US Army needs you."

My eyes flick to her lapel; I wonder where the military badges are.

She catches this. "I'm a math instructor. I just work for the armed services. We're starting a new team. You'll be the tenth girl."

"I couldn't possibly . . ."

"Think about it over the weekend."

"I don't need to think about it. I already know the answer. I'm sorry."

The woman opens her mouth to say something, but I don't let her. "Thank you again for returning my notebook."

I run to the train station and don't look back.

# 3.

On Sunday, Mom has enough energy to push Dad in his chair and walk through the Morris Arboretum. We go early so as not to run into anyone we know and endure the pitying looks directed toward the once-vibrant man of our house. In the chill of the morning, I tighten my sweater and replay yesterday's conversation with the woman in the tweed suit. It killed me to say no to her, but I needed to be truthful. I can't take the math job. I made a promise to myself long ago. And just thinking of breaking that vow sends my heart bouncing around my rib cage like a rubber jacks ball.

I'm still agitated on our drive home from the park. Mom pulls the car into the open garage, and I go around to the trunk to retrieve Dad's cane.

Sarah points across the street. "What's that?"

We all squint at the FOR SALE sign. "Looks like the Rushes are selling their house," replies Mom.

"Why does it say 'restricted section'?" asks Sarah.

Dad swivels his head out the passenger window to try to see for himself. "Is co. Cauc buy on."

16

"It's code," I repeat. "Caucasian buyers only." I knew this was popular in real estate lingo now, but I hadn't seen an actual sign with that wording before.

"It's despicable," says Mom, slamming the driver's-side door. "How would we like it if they applied the same standards to Jews?"

"That's what the Germans are doing right now. Kicking people like Aunt Roza, Uncle Azriel, and Batja out of their own neighborhood, treating them like they don't belong."

"Th Bib sa yo shou no opprs the strag fo yo wer strag i lan o Egp," says Dad. We all know what that means. The Bible says you should not oppress the stranger for you were strangers in the land of Egypt. It's one of his favorite quotes.

After we get Dad settled in the study, happily listening to Walter Winchell, Mom takes out the vacuum. Sarah tackles taking apart an old radiator. I head upstairs to stew. Clearly, the MathMeet is not out of my system. I sit on the edge of my bed, my knee bouncing in pent-up energy. I count the folds in the blackout curtains on my window, starting from the outside in on both ends and meeting in the middle. Seven folds on either side. Fourteen total. Finding patterns always calms me down.

Only it's not working.

My eyes drift to the closet and it all comes back to me. Actually, it never left. The memory is always there, like a scar.

I'm six years old, Dad thirty-nine. It's a muggy August day. I'm bored and want to make brownies with my Sears electric oven. I haven't played with it for a while and the baking utensils—trays, rolling pin, beater, and all the other necessary tools—are in a box on the highest shelf of my closet. I need the tallest person in the house to get it down.

Mom is feeding Sarah in a high chair as I dart into the kitchen. "Where's Daddy?"

"Don't bother him when he's working," says Mom. "He needs to concentrate."

I ignore her and fly into his study. It's a crowded space, filled with dusty books on shelves and stacks of math journals on every open surface. A Penn State pennant hangs at an angle on the bulletin board over his desk.

"Not now, sweetie," says Dad, his red pencil poised over a page. "I've got too many tests to correct."

"Pleeeeaase!" I beg. "No one else can reach it."

He rubs his eyes, then smiles at me. "I never can resist you, can I?"

I flip the sign on the door from THE PROFESSOR IS IN to THE PROFESSOR IS OUT.

"Betcha can't beat me," I say, dashing past him up the stairs.

"Eleanor!" scolds Mom. "I told you not to interrupt him!"

"It's all right," Dad assures her, running after me. Halfway to the top of the stairs, he stops, holding his forehead.

"Come on!" I call from above.

"Just a second. Daddy's head hurts."

But I'm impatient. "Hurry! I need to bake!"

18

Slowly, he takes the rest of the stairs. He goes into my room and reaches up toward the shelf. Then he lets out a moan. Five seconds later, he collapses on the ground.

When Mom returns from the hospital to tell me Dad had a stroke, my first thought is that it was a stroke of good luck. But when Dad is wheeled home in a special chair because one half of his body doesn't work and the only word he can say is *mi* (short for *minus*), I know it's bad luck.

I also know it's my fault. I was a bad girl and didn't listen to Mom. I made him stop working. I chased him up the stairs. I pestered him to hurry. I asked him to reach up too high.

I took away his brilliant brain.

Mom got a part-time job to help pay the medical bills. And she became perpetually tired. No more dressing up for faculty banquets. No more parties at our house with sparkly friends and laughter that wafted upstairs. No more volunteer charity work. Our own household was too needy. The only socializing we did was with Aunt Jona and Uncle Herman for Shabbos dinners. The vibrant life she and my father had had together was now lost forever. I ruined everything for her as well.

I started kindergarten in a state of bewilderment. In the classroom, there was a big orange-and-red carpet in the center of the floor. Each child had to find a circle and sit down. Before everyone sat, I stared at the circles. My left eye began to twitch and some of the circles lifted up from the carpet and started dancing in front of me. I blinked and they returned to just being spots on the ground.

When I opened my eyes, I said to my teacher, "So there are thirty kids in the class, Miss Eloise?"

"Yes, that's correct. Did you count all the circles?"

"No, I just counted the six going across and the five circles going down."

Her eyes got big and round, like the circles on the carpet. "How did you know that six times five equals thirty?

"I don't know. I just saw the circles."

"You figured out the magic of multiplication, Eleanor! Your father's a math professor, right? You've inherited his genius! I'm going to let your parents know. They will be so excited. We'll have to get you more advanced worksheets, maybe even bring in a private tutor."

No, Daddy is the genius, I thought. Not me.

She wrote a note for Mom and Dad on a purple piece of stationery, folded it up, and slipped it into my lunch box.

But after the bell rang at 3:00, I went into the bathroom and ripped up the letter into tiny pieces. I buried the bits of purple under some paper towels in the trash can so no one would ever find it. I vowed to keep the secret forever. My parents would never know about my math brain. They would never discover that I was blessed with the very gift I took away from Dad.

I became known as the quiet girl. I purposely threw math tests. It wasn't easy for me. The wrong answers looked like grease stains on a white dress. When the teachers did call on me to give the answer to an equation, I went outside my body. How was I sounding? Too smart? Too dumb? I got so exhausted with worrying how to be that I ended up fumbling the words, stuttering. Then in the middle of a book report presentation in first grade, I froze up entirely. Someone yelled out "Nervous Nellie" and the whole class laughed, repeating it over and over. "How perfect!" they said—Nellie is, after all, a nickname for Eleanor. It comes from Old Nell, or a worn-out horse.

The awful thing about being called a name that appears to be true is that if you act that way again, it confirms everyone's expectations. And then eventually, you keep doing it more and more until you believe it, too.

So obviously I can't sign up for this army program. Not only am I too shy to walk into the room, I could never pursue my own dreams when I've thwarted both my mom's and dad's.

I go back to patterning. Through the floorboards of my room, I can hear the clanging of metal, the radio, and the sweep of the vacuum. Two clinks, four words, six motorized back-and-forth motions. A nice even-number sequence. The phone rings, breaking the pattern.

The vacuum stops. "Eleanor, it's for you!"

"Hi, Trudie," I say, winding the cord around my fingers.

"Actually, it's Mary Mauchly. From the MathMeet."

That woman in the suit? "How did you get this number?"

"I have a photographic memory. If found, please return to Eleanor Schiff, JEN 2730."

I feel my cheeks get hot. For the childish way I wrote my phone number on the cover of my notebook. For my unworthiness at having this important woman calling my house. For my regret at having to say no yet again.

"I hope I'm not interrupting anything," she says. "I thought I'd try and convince you one last time. I don't think I stressed how important this job is. You'll be a real Rosie the Riveter, Eleanor, only with a pencil in your hand, doing advanced math for our country."

Like that song on the radio. Rosie is a make-believe woman who works in a factory, drilling metal plates onto airplane wings. She represents every American woman doing her part for victory.

I feel Mrs. Mauchly tugging at my heartstrings. Of course I want to do my patriotic duty, especially if it could help Batja in some indirect way. But this math job isn't the answer. "I can't accept your offer."

"Did I mention that the pay is $1,400 a year? Plus overtime?"

My jaw drops right there in the upstairs hallway. $116.66 a month in income. $50.00 a month to pay for a private nurse for Dad. That leaves $66.66 a month to buy extra ration stamps so we don't blow them all on Shabbos chicken.

It's tempting, for sure. But impossible.

"I'm confident you'll fit right in with the group," says Mrs. Mauchly, dauntless. "We start tomorrow at eight a.m. The basement of the Moore School of Electrical Engineering at the University of Pennsylvania."

"Tomorrow's a school day."

"I have relationships with all the high school principals and college deans. Let me take care of it. Where do you attend?"

"Jenkintown, but—"

"All right then, Eleanor from Jenkintown. We'll see you tomorrow. Oh, one last thing. Please don't talk to anyone about this program. Other than the other girls, that is. It's top secret."

The telephone receiver dangles from my hand. I'm flabbergasted. Did my guardian angel finally decide to show up? Because it feels like someone really wants me to take this job. I don't know if it will be a pathway to discovering my inner Eleanor Roosevelt, but it does sound extraordinary. I would get paid to do what I love while helping my country at the same time—and no one would have to know. Keeping Mom and Dad in the dark is the only way I'd ever consider doing something like this.

I could just try it once. Yes. That's what I'll do. I'll go tomorrow and see if I like it, see how it feels.

There's no harm in that.

# 4.

Monday morning, I stare at myself in the mirror. From the neck up I look fine. My shoulder-length dark brown hair is wavy in the right places and not going haywire, which it can do sometimes. My eyes are clear and blue. It's the neck down I'm worried about. My gray jumper is cutting under my arms, bunching up my white blouse. Even though I'm barely five feet one, I've outgrown this outfit. My saddle shoes and bobby socks make me look like a schoolgirl, when I need to look more like a young professional. I remove my good temple dress from its hanger and fold it carefully into my book bag, along with some low heels. I'll find someplace to change clothes later.

Mom doesn't look up from packing Sarah's lunch as I walk into the kitchen. She lets out a weary sigh. I linger for a moment, having second thoughts. Then I dispel them. I'm only going this one day anyway. I kiss her on the cheek and head out, turning left toward the train station instead of right toward school.

The platform is crowded with commuters. I settle into a seat, put my nose to the glass, and watch the row houses glide past. A commotion makes me look to the front of our car.

"Find another place to sit!" shouts an older gentleman, his finger pointing at a young mother and her son.

The mother wears a scarf around her head and has two shopping bags from Germantown Market in the crook of each elbow. Her son, about three years old, cowers behind her leg, his sweet roll uneaten in his hand. I can't see what's wrong, why the older gentleman wouldn't want to let them sit near him. The train is crowded, and his row has the only seat left in our car. The boy's going to have to sit on his mother's lap anyway.

Next to me, a businessman stands up, getting in on the action. "That's right. Go back to Germany!"

Stricken, the mother takes her son's hand and walks down the aisle, wobbling with the motion of the train, until they exit to the next car.

"Serves them right," murmurs my seatmate, adjusting his briefcase at his feet. "Enemy aliens aren't welcome here." He's looking at me like we're in cahoots. I stare down at my lap.

I don't understand this "alien" term. My grandfather crossed the ocean from a tiny town in Poland called Stanislau. Philadelphia's filled with immigrants. In fact, most people from Germantown have been here longer than most other immigrants. William Penn invited the Germans to settle in his colony in the 1600s. Those first Germans were escaping religious persecution. Someone should tell Hitler how unoriginal he is.

I look up to see if anyone feels the way I do, but most passengers have their noses in the *Inquirer*. I feel sorry for the mother and her son, but I don't want the attention turned on me.

Before I know it, the brakes are squealing. I use the station bathroom to change into my nice clothes, hop on a trolley, and cross the river to University City.

University of Pennsylvania and Drexel aren't the typical isolated college campuses. They're planted in the midst of the city, so regular traffic goes right through them. I've only ever driven in a car through the area, so walking down the pedestrian paths and seeing the trees and the giant brick buildings up close is quite different. The summer humidity hasn't arrived yet and the fresh air hugs my bare legs. The clock tower reads 7:50. If I were in school, I'd be removing my English book from my locker right about now. Trudie and I would be sprucing up in the bathroom, or rather she would be, and I'd be standing there antsy to get to class, but dutifully waiting for her. What am I going to tell her? I'll have to figure that out later. I have ten minutes to find where I'm supposed to go.

I flag down a passing student. He stops, but the words coming out of my mouth are a whisper.

"I can't hear you," he says, impatient.

I'm out of practice for basic stranger interaction.

He steps closer. "Are you lost?"

I nod.

"What building do you need?" he asks, friendlier this time.

"The Moore School of Electrical Engineering."

"Can't help you there. I only go back and forth between the two arts and sciences buildings. You'll have to ask an upperclassman."

"How can I spot one?"

He shrugs. "Good luck. They're all enlisted."

In front of a bronze statue of Benjamin Franklin, I stop to check my heel. Swell. A blister is already forming.

Just then some boys come jogging by, all dressed the same, in blue shorts and white T-shirts. They're probably in an ROTC program. I can't lose this chance.

"Which way is the Moore School?" I ask, feeling like I'm shouting when it's probably how the rest of the world speaks normally.

One of the boys trailing the pack points to his right. There are two walkways in that direction. After a couple more wrong turns and a now bona fide blister, I eventually find it. Another imposing brick building, this one four stories high, with sixteen windows across. Sixty-four ways to look out from the west side alone. Once I'm inside, the marbled floor makes my pumps click with confidence that I don't have. Again, there's no one around to help me. The basement, however, is easy to find. I just follow the stairs down toward the sound of chattering girls.

I count eight gathered outside a closed door. No sign of Mrs. Mauchly. A ninth girl stands off to the side, reading a letter and crying. She's petite, with a dark headband keeping the tight curls from her face. I hand her a hankie from my pocketbook.

"Thanks," she mumbles, wiping her nose.

She seems so sad that I forget my shyness. "Maybe you can apply for the math team again in a few months?"

She shakes her head. "These are happy tears. This letter is from the kids at my school. I had to say goodbye to them to be part of this team."

I flush. "I'm so sorry. I just assumed—"

"That a colored girl like me wouldn't be smart enough in math?"

"No! It's that *I'm* the kind of person who laughs when I'm supposed to cry and cries when I'm supposed to laugh. I've never met anyone else who does that."

She hands me back my handkerchief.

"That's okay," I tell her. "You keep it."

She flinches for a second, then straightens out her narrow shoulders. "Sure, I understand."

This is going terribly wrong. Now she thinks I don't want it because a Negro has touched it. "Jeepers. It's because it was in your nose. I'd tell anyone to keep it."

Then we both laugh.

"I'm Eleanor."

"Alyce. With a *y*."

"For someone so tiny, you're pretty fierce," I say.

"I'm four feet eleven and I've been told I pack a wallop."

"I'm five feet one on a good day, which means we have to stick together," I declare. "Next to you, I'm a giant."

I size up my fellow cohorts. One wears glasses over large, round eyes and plump cheeks. Two carry notebooks, looking prepared and secretarial, making me relieved I decided to bring my notebook as well. One pale, willowy girl clutches her purse to her chest like a security blanket. Another powders her cheeks using a compact mirror, though who she needs to polish up for is unclear. Coty perfume pulls me away from taking inventory. Mrs. Mauchly is dressed as smartly as she was on Saturday, with her hair pulled tight into an upsweep in back.

"Follow me, ladies."

We head into a classroom. There's a blackboard on the wall and three long wooden tables with matching chairs around them. In front of each chair rests some sort of machine with yellow, red, and green push keys, like a colorful place setting at dinner. Alyce and I choose the middle table.

I shouldn't be here. It feels forbidden yet thrilling at the same time, as if I were standing on the precipice of a cliff and I will either fall in or expand like the ocean toward an unknown horizon. I look at Alyce and her eyes are as wide as mine.

Two girls join our table, identical twins it seems, mirror images of each other's features in matching plaid jackets. I force myself not to stare.

Our teacher stands in front, making eye contact with each of us. "I'm Mrs. Mary Mauchly. Welcome to the Philadelphia Computing Section, or PCS. As you know, this is a secret unit of the US Army. Look around you. These girls will be your family, your confidantes, your bunkmates. If you get into a fight, you'll have no one to complain to but another PCS girl. So think twice before you steal someone's rag curlers. This afternoon, you'll be getting a tour of your living quarters: the Sigma Chi House, empty now because"—a pregnant pause—"well, all the fraternity boys are gone, defending our country."

We all fall silent for a moment. But in the quiet it hits me. We have to live on campus? No one said anything about that. Who's going to help out with Dad?

"We work six days a week, sometimes up to sixteen hours a day. That's why you'll be boarding nearby. All meals are paid for unless you go out on your own." She clears her throat. "Now, a word about free time. PCS is part of the army and therefore the WAAC."

I'm reminded of one of the handclap chants Sarah and I made up. *FDR flies T&WA, lands at PMA, visits PSFS.*

Mrs. Mauchly continues. "WAAC is the Women's Army Auxiliary Corps. You now represent the United States of America and will be expected to behave respectably. Curfew is eleven forty-five p.m., even on weekends." Her eyes sweep the room. "Any questions so far?"

Nine arms reach for the sky. Everyone's except mine. I wouldn't dare ask a question, let alone one about commuting from home. They'll think I'm a baby.

Mrs. Mauchly calls on one of the twins.

"What do we tell our families?"

"That you've been recruited for a civilian army program. That you must leave school—at least one of you is in high school, but I believe most of you are in college—and begin working immediately. If they ask what you're doing, make up something clerical."

Alyce leans over to me and whispers, "Are you in college?"

I shake my head. "Are you?"

Alyce shakes her head, too. Sweet relief. I'm not the only baby.

"I graduated from West Chester State last year," she says. "I'm a math teacher at Mifflin Elementary School."

Again, she surprises me. Those kids who wrote her the goodbye letter were her students, not her schoolmates. She must be twenty-two years old already. Which only makes me feel more inexperienced.

"This class is called Mathematics for Ballistic Computers," continues Mrs. Mauchly. "And by that, I don't mean the desktop machines you see in front of you. You ladies are the human computers!"

A girl with victory roll hair, swept up in two sections off her face, raises her hand. She's the one who'd been powdering her cheeks earlier. "Now that we've been selected, can someone tell us what ballistics are?"

"Ballistics is the science of projectiles and firearms. Our boys can't just fire willy-nilly. There's too much room for error. Errors that cost money and lives. So to improve target accuracy, we're going to calculate the ballistic trajectory ahead of time."

A hand is raised. It's the willowy girl. "You mean the soldiers are depending solely on *our* numbers?"

"Indeed."

Chair legs scrape the floor. She darts out of the class. From the retching sounds in the hallway, she doesn't make it to the bathroom.

"Will one of you please see to . . ." Mrs. Mauchly checks her clipboard. "Ruth, I believe that is?"

The girl with glasses and plump cheeks accepts the task.

"Now then, where were we?" asks Mrs. Mauchly.

"Ballistics tables," says one of the notebook carriers, not disturbed in the least about the enormous responsibility of all this.

Mrs. Mauchly rests her bottom on the corner of her desk, surveying her charges minus two. "Does anyone know how we achieve target accuracy?"

Crickets.

"The trajectory formula?" ventures one of the twins.

I know that formula. The equation of motion for a trajectory is $y = x \, tan(\theta) - \frac{gx^2}{2v^2 cos\theta}$ . But it's not that simple. There are other factors to consider here. That equation is mainly used to compute a projectile path from a stationary object, like someone throwing a stone, in a vacuum. But in real life, we don't live in a vacuum. We have things like gravity and drag that depend on the weight and shape of the projectile or the temperature and density of air. It's too complex to solve analytically. But I might be wrong. I stay silent.

"That's a starting point," says Mrs. Mauchly. "But what if a soldier is shooting from behind a hill and a windstorm comes up suddenly? We must continually refine the trajectory by repeating the cycle of adjustment."

So I *am* right. I suppress a smile.

Then she adds, "You must slice the path into small increments of time and space. It's like the Runge–Kutta method. In other words—" I whisper it at the same time she says it aloud. "Iterative approximations."

Next to me, Alyce hears what I murmur. She raises an eyebrow that's already naturally arched even when not impressed.

During a five-minute bathroom break, I wash my hands next to the twins. Their plaid jackets are both wrinkled in exactly the same place—the crease of their elbows. I smile shyly at them, and they smile back. In the mirror, I discover a way to tell them apart, subtle though it is. The twin on the left has longer eyelashes than the twin on the right.

"Why'd you have to tell Mom about Aberdeen?"

"She saw the telegram. It was on the table." Even their voices have the same timbre.

"Well, you should have hidden it better."

"I'll just say that was for a different math program that we didn't get chosen for. She probably won't even remember."

I guess not everyone was recruited from a MathMeet. But there's one thing we have in common: We're all keeping secrets from our parents. Though I'm fairly certain I'm the only one here who's got two secrets to keep. I can't even tell my own family I'm a mathematician at all.

# 5.

"**Before** we learn how to use these contraptions on our desks," begins Mrs. Mauchly after the break, "let's introduce ourselves. Tell us briefly what you're doing with your life, math-wise."

I loathe speaking in front of a group. Every time I'm asked to do it, I'm slammed back to that book report presentation in first grade when I was anointed Nervous Nellie.

"I'm Kay," says one of the girls who'd been holding a notebook. "I'm studying under Grace Hopper at Vassar."

I remember Grace Hopper from a journal on Dad's desk. She was rejected by the navy for being too old and too small. Then she did research for another famous mathematician who happens to currently be helping the British crack Enigma cryptograms. The navy's loss, definitely.

"I'm Louise from Ardmore," says the other notebook girl. She seems very put-together with her sleek blond pageboy haircut. "I'm a sophomore at Bryn Mawr College."

Two down, eight to go. I'm getting more nervous by the second.

Next come the twins. Donna is the one with the longer eyelashes;

Sharon's her sister. Recently, they've been working on math tables for the WPA in New York, Roosevelt's program to get the country back on its feet from the Depression.

I look around, checking the exits for an easy escape, just in case.

Alyce introduces herself, and then it's Joyce with the plump cheeks and glasses. She's twenty-one and teaches high school math at a school in Washington, DC. The willowy girl who threw up earlier, Ruth, goes to Cornell and studies matrices. Marjorie, the one with the victory roll hair and the powder compact at the ready, is eighteen. She never went to college but works for a hatmaker doing his accounting.

Only one more girl and me. I can't do this after all. Forgive me, E.R., for being weak. I'll never be able to come out of my shell like you did. I'm going home. Besides, I can't move out anyway. Dad needs me.

A daddy-longlegs type speaks. "I'm Frances, just turned eighteen, from Westminster, Maryland. I'm truly happy to be here. For the past two years, ever since I graduated school early, I've been working on our farm. I'll take solving equations over milking cows any day."

I stand up as quietly as possibly.

"Leaving so soon?" says Mrs. Mauchly.

Everyone looks at me. I'm trapped, unable to quit in front of the whole class and unable to introduce myself. Betwixt and between. Like the pushmi-pullyu from *Doctor Dolittle*, an animal with no tail and a head at each end. Every time he moves in one direction, the other part of him reverses course, so he never gets anywhere.

Mrs. Mauchly walks over to me, gently resting her hands on my shoulders. "Everyone, this is Eleanor."

Someone coughs. Someone else scrapes her chair on the floor. I lower my book bag. "Um, hi. I'm from Jenkintown." What do I say next? Mrs. Mauchly nods at me encouragingly. "I answered the toughest question at a MathMeet." I sit down with a thump, relieved to be out of the spotlight.

"Now, ladies," says Mrs. Mauchly. "Let's turn our attention to the machines in front of you."

Did she just make my decision for me? I may be in this chair, but I'm not sure I'm going to stay.

The machines look sort of like typewriters with a full keyboard and carriage, except there's a power cord sticking out the back. Mrs. Mauchly explains these are called the Marchant Silent Speed, newer variations on the old manually cranked Marchant calculators.

I've seen the manual ones at school, but never an electric one.

I suppose I could just wait a little bit longer before leaving, to see how they work.

We practice inputting numbers and learn how to use the addition and subtraction keys and the multiplier keys on the far right, then how to clear the machine after each problem. There's no paper. The numerical answers are visible inside tiny oval windows in the twenty-digit display register.

It sounds like a gentle churning, a steady hum of *ka-chung, ka-chung, ka-chung*. "This isn't so silent," I say to Alyce. I do a simple problem using the red auto division key. 355 ÷ 113. It takes just over nine seconds. 3.141592020, otherwise known as pi. If I didn't already know the answer, it would take me at least twice that long to calculate nine digits past the decimal point. Incredible!

"Don't think these machines are just here to give you a shortcut," Mrs. Mauchly informs us. "Computing a one-minute bomb trajectory will take forty hours of labor."

A bunch of the girls exchange worried looks.

Not me. I'm itching to work hard. I've been coasting my whole life, even choosing the easier math track at school so as not to risk anyone discovering my abilities. My eyes trace the shape of Mrs. Mauchly's cursive where she wrote *iterative approximations* on the board. If I became part of this team, I'd get to do real-world applied mathematics rather than just teach myself from a textbook. Am I a fool to walk away now? Maybe so, but at least I'd still be a devoted daughter.

And yet. Couldn't a nurse do the cognitive exercises with Dad? Learn his speech patterns and translate for him at the dinner table? A trained professional would be a bigger help than I ever could be. Mom might even find time to go back to volunteering for the Joint.

Who am I kidding? The whole idea is a fantasy. No matter how much my salary could improve their lives, the bottom line is that Mom and Dad must never find out. It would crush them. The math community is small. I risk everything if someone at U Penn recognizes me as the daughter of Professor Schiff from Penn State.

"Right, ladies?" says Mrs. Mauchly.

Everyone nods. I have no idea what she's been saying. I need to pay attention.

"Our men overseas are putting themselves in danger every day. The least we can do is use our skills to try to keep them safe. So let's remain focused, keep our heads down, and compute, compute, compute."

How ironic. Out of everyone here, I'm probably the best at keeping my head down. I've been lying low my entire life.

She hands out some practice figures for us to try inputting into the Marchants. While everyone click-clacks away, I think: What if I've been looking at this all wrong? What if my shyness can work to my advantage? As long as I don't call attention to myself, no one will pay me any mind and Mom and Dad will never get wind of it.

I can't believe I'm saying this, but being a Nervous Nellie could turn out to be something positive. And maybe, just maybe, end up helping Batja in the process.

# 6.

The fraternity house is on Locust Walk, the main artery of the University of Pennsylvania campus. We're led inside by the housemother, Mrs. Goldstine, a dustbin of a woman with brassy, unkempt hair and a dress twisted so far over her wide hips that the zipper lies off-center. She seems stunned to find herself back at work with a group of new charges, girls no less.

"It's a four-story brick mansion," she says without enthusiasm.

"Mansion" is used in the most generous sense. After we walk past the vibrant elms framing the front steps, inside there is nothing majestic whatsoever. The main room is a large, decrepit gathering space with one tattered beige couch and two armchairs, heavily stained with heaven knows what. A scratched-up end table stands forlornly off to the side. That's it. Not even a reading lamp. Above the couch, the Sigma Chi crest hangs crookedly. It features an eagle with a key in its beak resting atop a Norman shield with a large white cross. Underneath a layer of dust are some Latin words. If I remember correctly from school, it translates to: *In this sign, thou shalt conquer.* I wonder how my Jewish family would feel about me living beneath this symbol of Christendom?

The kitchen isn't any better. The Formica countertop is peeling at the corners. My shoe heels stick to the floor as I walk through something old and tacky. One of the twins opens the icebox and the smell is so rotten that poor Ruth, recovered from her earlier episode, nearly retches again.

"No food in there," Mrs. Goldstine informs us. "I threw all that rot away. It just needs a good scrubbing down."

"It's going to take more than that," says Bryn Mawr Louise, holding her nose.

In the bathrooms there's black goo growing on the shower floor and crusty things caked all over the sink tops.

One of the twins mimes washing her hands in a urinal. "That's about all it'll be good for from now on." Even the housemother cracks a smile.

At least the bedrooms are clean. Doubles, with twin beds or bunks, their empty white mattresses lying ghostly in the waning late-afternoon light.

"I insisted the army replace the mattresses," says Mrs. Goldstine.

That may be true, but the whole place gives me the creeps. Some rooms still have pinups on the walls. Veronica Lake, Hedy Lamarr, Betty Grable. In one room, there's an empty beer can on a windowsill and a pencil on the desk.

I turn to Alyce. "It's as if their lives got interrupted mid-sentence."

She's quiet, her mind elsewhere.

Mrs. Goldstine shuffles over to where the ten of us have gathered on the landing. "I suppose you should choose rooms now. That way, you can move in at your own pace this evening."

There's no turning back now. Alyce and I claim one of the third-floor rooms with two single beds. I smile my thanks at her, grateful I have a partner and that I'm not left until the end, like I used to be when we picked teams for sports in grade school.

"The view's nice," I tell Alyce, peering out the window over Locust Walk. She doesn't come over to look, but remains where she's standing, still pensive.

"That's because it's the best room in the house," says a disembodied voice. We both turn. It's confident Marjorie with the victory roll hair and farm girl Frances behind her, looking sheepish.

Marjorie purses her red made-up lips. "Why don't you girls run on up to the fourth floor. There's a nice bunk room up there that's perfect for the two of you."

I hate bunk beds. I'm a light sleeper and don't want to be woken up every time someone else moves. But I've lost my words and can't seem to muster a protest.

Alyce doesn't flinch. She looks directly at Marjorie, saying, "Sorry. Finders keepers."

A flicker of surprise registers on Marjorie's face, then she quickly recovers. "What's the big deal? The rooms are all the same. It shouldn't matter."

"Yet you just said this is the best room in the house," Alyce corrects her.

"Come on, Marjorie," says Frances. "We can find another room."

Marjorie hesitates, gives Alyce a final stare down, then spins on her heel and leaves.

"That was impressive!" I tell Alyce. "I'm such a wimp."

"People always think they can push the colored girl around."

How naive of me. I thought they were pulling rank because I was the baby of the group and they assumed I wouldn't protest.

"I'm sick of it." She kicks the baseboard for good measure.

This is her reality, yet her life experience is completely unknown to me. I have no Negro friends. I can call the boys who work at Trudie's tennis club by name, but of course we don't socialize with them. The few Negro kids at Jenkintown High always sit at their own table in the cafeteria. But seeing how Alyce was treated just now, I can imagine how out of place my Negro schoolmates might feel.

"I've been called Nervous Nellie my whole life." What a stupid thing to say. Of course, it's nowhere near the same thing. I'm still white. "Forget I said that."

"No, I appreciate your honesty. I couldn't tell, by the way. You cover up your nervousness well."

"Really? I thought it was totally obvious when I fumbled through my introduction in class earlier. I hate that kind of thing."

"Yeah, being the object of people's attention really stinks."

"Amen."

I want to ask her about what it was like in her own high school cafeteria. If there were other Negro girls at West Chester College or if she felt lonely. If the elementary school where she teaches has mixed races. School segregation legally ended here in Philadelphia in the late 1800s, but obviously it still goes on. Blame that FOR SALE sign currently across the street from my house. Negroes don't live in white districts and therefore don't go to white public schools.

I toss my notebook onto one of the mattresses, my name big and bold in cursive on the cover. I do the same with one of hers. "That way no one can steal the room out from under us."

She smiles.

"Do you feel okay to go downstairs now?" I venture.

"Sure. I'm fine."

She leads the way. But I suspect she's not fine.


All ten of us go our separate ways to make the break from our families. I think my situation is the most fraught, but I have no idea what anyone else's story is. When I walk home from the train, no one's in the house. Mom has left a note for me taped to the Frigidaire. *Gone with Dad to physical therapy. Sarah's next door. There's macaroni salad on the counter. Back at 6.*

Lucky break. I'll have a chance to pack and come up with my ruse, as Mrs. Mauchly called it.

Samsonite claims their suitcases hold enough clothes for a week. That's not very long. I suppose if I can solve for the limit of a function, I can learn to wash my blouses in a rotation. I take my freshly cleaned temple dress from the closet, then add four school-type outfits to my pile. I pack two nightgowns, a pair of slippers, and count out seven pieces of underwear, seven pairs of bobby socks. I sweep everything from my bathroom counter into a paisley zippered case: toothbrush and paste, hairbrush, cold cream, shampoo, creme rinse, a bar of Palmolive, a box of U hairpins, Kotex, shower cap, and a few lipstick cases. I pretend I'm Eleanor Roosevelt packing to move into the White House. She'd been married for twenty-eight years by that time, but I suppose she still had to choose her clothes and toiletries like the rest of us. Was she frightened? Probably not, as her uncle Teddy had been president when she got engaged to her fifth cousin, Franklin. I'm sure she'd visited before. But this was different. This would be *her* house with her own role in the country's story.

It's 5:55 now. I hear noises below. Everyone's home.

I sit on the suitcase to help it close. One last look in the mirror. I tissue-dab the perspiration from the sides of my nose, pinch my upper arm for good luck, and head downstairs.

"Are you having a slumber party at Trudie's?" asks Sarah, eyeing my bag.

Trudie. Again, I forgot about her.

"I would hope not," says Mom, unwrapping Polish sausage. "It's a school night."

I clear my throat. Here goes. "You know when I left Shabbos dinner early the other night?" My voice quavers just the tiniest bit.

But it's enough. Dad looks at me, concerned.

I quickly go into the dining room and grab his special chair so he can sit in the kitchen and be with all of us. "Well, I didn't go to Oswald's. I went to a meeting at school."

"At night?" says Mom. "How strange."

"I thought so, too. But the army is very busy these days. You see, it was a recruitment event. They're looking for civilians to help with the war effort."

"Which civilians?" Sarah wants to know. "Why'd they pick you?"

"I can type sixty-five words per minute. So they're putting me in the ROTC office at the University of Pennsylvania."

"You mean you're not going to school anymore? That's not fair!" says Sarah.

"I've finished all my finals. I'll really only be missing graduation."

"Actually, Principal Candioti's office called before we left for the clinic," says Mom. "Given the state of things, the school has decided *not* to have a commencement celebration. Those who'd like to get their diplomas early because they're helping with the war effort can do so."

I give the principal a silent thanks. Not that I think I'm the sole reason he canceled graduation, but it does make things easier for me. Mrs. Mauchly made good on her word.

I help myself to macaroni salad so I have something to do with my hands. "There's one more thing. They want us to board on the campus. The hours are really long, I guess. So I'll be living in an empty fraternity house with a housemother—Mrs. Goldstine is her name—and a bunch of other girls."

Dad nods up and down. I guess he likes the idea of me being on a college campus. It probably reminds him of his students and his old job, which makes my gut twist.

"You're moving out?" cries Sarah.

Mom turns off the stove, leaving the sausages cold. "Housing costs money. Campus food costs money. We can't afford this."

"They're paying me, Mom! A lot more than what I earn babysitting."

Her eyebrows rise.

"I can finally make a difference for you and—" I can't finish. I can't look at Dad's face.

"But that means . . ." sputters Sarah, her nose all snotty now, "that means I have to do everything now!" She runs out of the room sobbing.

"Sarah, wait!" I call. "My salary is enough to hire a nurse to free up time for everyone. And then some."

"Your sister's just being dramatic," says Mom, softening. "She'll come around. We're going to be fine. Don't worry about us, Eleanor. You've done so much for this family already. It's time for you to fly. My word! A secretary for the army."

I exhale, unaware I'd been holding my breath.

She walks to the linen closet and pulls out a pile of sheets, a set of towels, a blanket, and a pillow. "I'm proud of you, Eleanor."

A little part of me dies inside. She wouldn't be proud if she knew that I'll be working with the Philadelphia Computing Section and that my math abilities are what got me there. It feels strange, like I've taken one step forward and two steps back.

Dad stands up from his chair all on his own, takes his cane from where it's leaning against the counter, and hobbles over to me. I lean into him. He smells like he always does, earthy with a touch of spearmint gum. He tries to hug me with his good arm but he can't hold the cane simultaneously.

Mom joins us and our duo becomes a triangle, the most stable shape in geometry. We three stand there, holding Dad up, the Schiffs against the world.

# 7.

Uncle Herman drives me to the Sigma Chi House, which is a relief. Had Mom and Dad dropped me off themselves, the guilt would have overwhelmed me. As it is, I'm moving out without a full-time nurse yet in position. Mom promised me she would hire someone by Friday. In the time I waited for Uncle Herman to come pick me up, she had already lined up four interviews. But this week is going to be tough for her. I pray Sarah rises to the challenge.

I'm grateful for the thirty-minute car ride, the comfortable silence, the cherry tobacco smell lingering in the upholstery. It acts as a sort of transition, like taking pre-algebra to get you prepared for algebra.

Inside the frat house, the girls dart back and forth, yelling instructions, carrying cardboard boxes and suitcases up and down the stairs. I take a breath and step into the fray.

"Incoming," says one of the twins, hefting a suitcase up the stairs before I have a chance to ascend.

On the second floor, stuffed shopping bags, hatboxes, and pillows dot the hallway. A teddy bear wearing a two-corner infantry hat sits on a pile of records. Frank Sinatra croons from a turntable in the bathroom where Ruth scrubs a sink counter with surprising strength considering her willowy arms.

Inside our room, Alyce has already made up her side.

I point to her bedcover, a purple, flowered, shiny number. "I like the lavender."

"It was my grandma's. She died in it. Well, not in it, exactly. More like on it." She registers my stricken face. "It's been washed multiple times. My mom's a laundress, best in town."

"That's a relief. About your mom, not your grandma. Wait, that didn't come out right. I'm sorry about your grandma, but maybe you can teach me how to wash my blouses, so I don't ruin them by week two?"

She's laughing at me. "Sure, no problem."

Could I feel any more babyish at this moment? Why in the world would a twenty-two-year-old math teacher ever want to hang out with me?

I open the closet and see an empty rod. Another rookie mistake. "I forgot about hangers."

"Don't worry. I've got extras." Alyce pulls out a set of wooden hangers painted light blue with a white dog chasing a ball. They're cute.

I hang up my good temple dress, but it promptly slips off and pools onto the floor. The hangers are too short.

"Sorry," says Alyce. "Some rich client of my mom's gave them to us when her kids got too big for them."

"No matter. I'll make it work."

Joyce pokes her bespectacled head into our room. "Hey, you two. Have you decided on a name yet?"

Alyce and I exchange a look. Neither of us knows what she's talking about.

"For your door, sillies! We're making signs with everyone's names. Only you can't use your given one. You have to choose a famous female mathematician."

What a clever idea. Except I can't think of any. I know about the Babylonians and Pythagoras, but I don't know of any historical women.

"Hypatia," says Alyce.

"Taken," declares Joyce.

"Grace Hopper?" I offer.

"That's Louise's."

Of course it is. I rack my brain. Then something pops in, a gauzy memory taking shape. "There's that German woman . . . Emmy . . . what was her last name? Neither? Noether. That's it. Emmy Noether."

Joyce pushes up her eyeglasses and her cheeks pink in happiness. "Good one! She's yours."

"I can't believe I remembered her," I say, speaking more to Alyce than Joyce. "Albert Einstein called her the most significant creative mathematical genius since the higher education of women began, or something like that." Dad had her eulogy stuck into one of his books. He used to like reading about ordinary Jews who accomplished great things.

"You taught this teacher something new!" exclaims Alyce.

I grin back.

"Joyce!" someone calls from the down the hall. "We need you!"

"Alyce can be Ada Lovelace," Joyce says to us hastily. Before darting off, she points to the pile of blue hangers on the floor and giggles. "I used to have some just like those."

I don't have to look at Alyce to know how she must be feeling. In minutes, she's gone from older, wiser roommate to being cut down to size. I hadn't thought about income or class when we were all introducing ourselves at the lab earlier today. But of course, it makes sense that the white girls likely grew up privileged. It's also likely that most of us were given the option to study more advanced math, whereas Alyce's school probably didn't offer those classes. No doubt she had to work that much harder to make it here.

With Joyce's departure, it's a bit awkward. We fit the sheets onto my bed in silence, each taking two rounded corners.

Alyce starts speaking, haltingly at first. "Before, during the house tour, I mean, when I was upset . . . it wasn't about only Marjorie."

I tuck the top sheet into hospital corners the way Mom does, but mine don't look nearly as tidy.

"Seeing those boys' rooms, with their lives interrupted, as you put

51

it, made me melancholy. I started thinking about my dad, who had to flee Arkansas in the dead of night. And all he left behind."

"Both your parents migrated north?"

"Not my mom. She was born in Pennsylvania, not far from here, actually. But Daddy was a day shy of his tenth birthday when they came for his family."

I have a bad feeling. "What exactly do you mean by 'came for his family'?"

"His father, my grandfather, was a preacher. He officiated a marriage between a white man and a colored woman." Her voice is low, weighted down.

"That was against the law in Arkansas, right?"

"Still is. My grandfather believed in love under the eyes of God, but of course that didn't matter." She sits on her own bed, runs her hand over the purple flowers. "That night, a bunch of local men surrounded the house and lit it on fire. Everyone screamed, running outside, desperate for air. As my grandfather went around back for the bucket to fill with water, they grabbed him. Somehow my daddy and his mama managed to run off."

I don't dare ask what happened to her grandfather, trying not to picture his lifeless body hanging from a tree. "How did your dad manage? How did they survive?"

"A friend hid them in a storm cellar and helped them sneak onto a northbound train the next day." Abruptly, she stands, straightens up those small shoulders, an action that is now becoming familiar.

"Daddy told me I could be anything. He's the one who encouraged me to apply to West Chester. I think he wanted me to choose my own kind of escape, because he didn't have a choice."

I'm quiet, thinking about her father. Now would be the time to tell her about mine.

"My dad's a math professor at Penn State." It's partially true anyway.

"So you got to grow up with math in your house all the time," says Alyce.

"Sort of." I deflect the conversation back to her. "Is your grandma still alive? Wait, is she the one who died on that bedspread?"

Alyce nods solemnly. "It's haunted. Put your nose super close. Sometimes the smell of her lilac perfume comes wafting up."

I take a hesitant step toward the bed. "I . . . I thought you said it was washed thoroughly."

Alyce cracks up. "I'm pulling your leg."

I toss my blanket at her. "Not funny. Not funny at all!"

"You may not be Nervous Nellie around me, but you sure are Gullible Gertie."

"Probably true."

She picks up my blanket, folds it, and hands it back to me. "Truce."

"Truce," I reply.

It's nice having a roommate. And hopefully a new friend. Which reminds me. "I'll be back. I need to make a call."

The house phone is mounted on the wall outside the twins' room. It's not exactly private, but it's all we have.

"Where were you today?" says Trudie. "I almost stopped by your house after school, but Don trapped me, and, well, you know how he gets." She giggles.

"I called to let you know I'm not coming back to school."

"What's wrong? Are you sick?"

"Everything's fine. I'm just . . . starting a job at University of Pennsylvania."

"Well, now that graduation isn't happening, I suppose you're not missing anything. No matter. Just meet me at Wanamaker's tomorrow after work."

"I don't think I can."

"Don asked my mom for my ring size!" she continues, not hearing me. "I can't believe it's really happening! I need your opinion on wedding dresses. Then we can have tea. I'm thinking of a lace veil with pearls and . . ."

As she drones on, I realize something about our friendship. It's completely uneven. When I was in the sixth grade, our class put on the play *A Midsummer Night's Dream*. I was too shy to perform, so my teacher let me help the actors with their costumes and read them their cues from the wings at the side of the stage where I could watch the activity without being seen by the audience. She had me learn the understudy parts of Hermia, Helena, Titania, and Hippolyta—all the female roles—in case someone got sick. Thankfully, no one missed a performance. It feels like I've been waiting in the wings forever, watching Trudie, ready to jump into her life; available whenever she calls me, to be her second in her quest to get a boyfriend and ultimately land a husband. But what about my own life? Will I always be someone else's wingwoman?

"I'm so sorry, Trudie, but I can't."

"You don't want to go shopping with me?"

"I have too much work to do here. In fact, the hours are so long, I'm living on campus so I don't have to commute. It'll probably take me through the summer at least. Maybe longer."

Silence.

"When did all this get decided?"

"It's very recent. It wasn't a sure thing until—"

"Never mind," she interrupts tersely. "I guess old friendships don't count for much these days."

She has a right to be mad. I could have called her over the weekend, instead of being a no-show at school Monday. I could have skirted around the math part, let her in on my possible army clerical job before it was already decided. But the truth is, I was afraid she'd pooh-pooh any plan I had. And then I wouldn't have the guts to go through with it. She's a force of nature, that girl. And I've always bent to her wind.

"I'm sorry I didn't tell you sooner, Trudie. I'll be at the wedding for sure. I wouldn't miss it."

"I have to go. My mom's calling me." She hangs up.

I fit the receiver back onto the phone as I picture Trudie's peach cheeks and the way her left shinbone bows out slightly. I could probably draw her in my sleep.

There are all kinds of sacrifices people make during a war. I just didn't know a friendship would be one of them.

# 8.

In the morning, the bathroom is steamy and teeming with bodies. There's not a free sink nor a single space in front of the mirror. Alyce and I stand there, holding our toiletry bags, towels wrapped around our naked torsos, watching the circus.

"I guess we'll have to shower this evening," I tell her.

"The showers may be taken, but I'm still brushing my teeth and combing out my hair," declares Alyce, squeezing in between Joyce and Bryn Mawr Louise. "I didn't grow up with six siblings for nothing." She turns back to me. "You want in?"

Begrudgingly, Louise moves over to make space in front of the mirror. She smooths down her already coiffed pageboy. "I didn't realize you could even get a comb through that type of hair."

Alyce seems flustered, unlike the way she acted yesterday, staring Marjorie down when she tried to steal our room out from under us. "We use combs."

"I've seen all those products in the stores," says Louise. "Relaxers and irons and such. You people just want to style your hair like us."

"And who's us?" There's the Alyce I recognize.

"Why, us blonds, you silly little thing." Then she giggles as if she really wasn't talking about white people at all.

Alyce's jaw tightens.

Louise adjusts a hairpin. "You know, like the blond bombshell Jean Harlow."

"Harlow's dead," says Alyce. She turns around to me. "You want in or not?"

What moxie my new roommate has, I think, squeezing in next to her. Between Alyce, Louise, and Marjorie, the queen bee position is up for grabs.

Back in our room, Alyce puts on a sensible blue skirt and white blouse. I stand there staring at my choices.

"It's not calculus," says Alyce. "Come on."

"It's just . . . everyone was getting so dolled up in there . . ." Impulsively, I put on my temple dress, stiff with its starched doily collar and cinched waist.

The smell of breakfast wafts upstairs. "Hurry up, I'm starving," says Alyce.

We make our way into the dining room. I observe everyone else's tailored skirts with matching cardigans. They have that effortless look and I look like I'm trying too hard.

I turn to Alyce. "I forgot my notebook in the room. Be back in a jiff."

Upstairs, I strip off the temple dress and put on one of my school outfits, another gray jumper and white blouse, instead. It may not be glamorous, but it's me.

"Oatmeal's gone," snaps Mrs. Goldstine when I return to the kitchen. "If you're having toast, only one spoonful of jam per person." Does she ever smile?

While I wait for the bread to pop up, Alyce appears on my left, topping off her coffee with powdered creamer. "What's with the new outfit?"

"Oh, there was a stain I hadn't seen." I don't meet her eye.

"What are you so worried about, Eleanor?"

I sigh. "I guess I want to make a good impression?"

"I thought it was our math skills that make the good impression."

When Mrs. Goldstine turns her back to us to rinse a pot in the sink, Alyce slathers extra jam on my toast. I start to protest, but she puts her finger over her lips to shush me.

Once we're back in the dining room, out of earshot, Alyce says, "Eleanor, you're going to have to learn to seize opportunities when they present themselves. It's an equivalency thing."

"But two spoonfuls of black-market jam does not equal a bowl of readily available bulk oatmeal," I argue.

"You really are a Nervous Nellie."

I must look shocked because she quickly says, "Oops, I didn't mean that."

I reach over and help myself to her last bit of oatmeal.

"Hey!" she yells playfully.

"Don't mind me. I'm just seizing an opportunity."

# 9.

We definitely stand out, ten well-dressed young women walking down the campus path, at a school where the ratio of undergrad men to women is 7:1. A boy on a bicycle nearly crashes into a tree, staring at us for too long. A couple of whistles and catcalls come our way from across the quad.

Marjorie tips her felted hat, one of many in her extensive collection. "Thank you kindly, boys."

Being noticed by men must be an everyday occurrence for her. This is my first time. I'm grateful for the cover of the group, letting me enjoy the attention while still staying somewhat hidden.

Mrs. Mauchly is waiting for us in the basement classroom, arms crossed. Behind her, the chalkboard is filled from top to bottom with equations. She's been busy. "It's one minute after 0800."

We all hold our breaths. Is this how it's going to be? Will we have to do push-ups or something for every minute we're late?

She grins and claps once. "Still, nice job on being close to on time your first day. Let's make it 0800 sharp tomorrow."

A collective sigh of relief.

"Now then. We're looking to accurately predict the area where a missile will land or a shell will fall," Mrs. Mauchly explains.

At the word *missile*, I glance at poor Ruth to make sure she's okay. Her eyes are watching our teacher intently, but thankfully, she doesn't run out of the room again.

"But as we started to discuss yesterday, the flight of a ballistic varies with atmospheric conditions such as wind velocity and air density, in addition to its own features like weight and diameter. These types of computations can't be solved with known mathematical expressions. Since we need to know where the bullet is from the time it leaves the muzzle until it hits the ground, we measure its movement every tenth of a second. Sometimes in even smaller increments, once the bullet slows down to the speed of sound. Therefore, we must use a step-by-step method of successive approximations."

She passes out papers for us to share. Alyce and I scoot closer and lean over the desk toward Donna, the longer-lashed twin, so we can all see what looks like a kind of chart. "This is a firing table for the 105 mm howitzer using an MI shell with charge 4, giving a muzzle velocity of 875 fps."

The chart looks like a foreign language.

Donna is excited. "My sister and I did something similar to this when we were in New York working at the WPA. Fps is feet per second, in case you were wondering."

Correction: Apparently, it's only foreign to me.

"As you can see at the top of the chart," continues Mauchly, "we're approximating range, elevation, fork, etcetera, as well as various probable errors."

There are so many different symbols and abbreviations on there, it reminds me of hieroglyphics. But when I take a hard look at Mauchly's chart, my worry fades. Most of the symbols are fairly straight-forward, $a$ for azimuth, $PE$ for probable error, $W_t$ for tailwind, etcetera.

"What's fork?" I whisper to Donna.

"When you want to change the mean point of impact, you adjust the elevation of the firing point. Fork is used to express that change."

"Measured in thousandths of an inch?"

She nods.

"This is a multistep process," continues Mauchly. "After you girls compute the data, it will be sent to Aberdeen Proving Ground in Maryland. The mathematicians there will then convert the information into a printed range table similar to the one in front of you. Finally, those tables will be used directly by the gunner or incorporated into the firing mechanisms attached to the artillery equipment, antiaircraft gun, or bombsight."

I feel a bit queasy, like Ruth did yesterday. It's an awesome responsibility.

"But before we get into all those calculations, let's review the Gregory–Newton interpolation formula." She proceeds to give us a quick lesson on interpolation—in other words, filling in the gaps between given points. All familiar stuff. "So for our purposes, we're using the Gregory–Newton forward difference formula to estimate the value of an unknown function with some given data points and how that function evolves."

Ruth raises her hand, concerned. "But that could go forever."

"Don't worry. As I said, these are finite differences we're talking about. The series has a termination point. You'll be calculating five input values, or four orders of correction. In a perfect world, the artilleryman hits his target on the first round, but that seldom happens. Our tables allow him to adjust his fire and hit the target within the third or fourth round. After that, well, there's nothing more we can do."

This seems like a rather grim outlook, but I keep my mouth shut.

"Where's this given data coming from?" asks Marjorie. She has a permanent scowl on her face, like she's suspicious of everyone.

"That's classified," replies Mauchly. "But suffice it to say, it's based on thorough research." She divides us up according to where we're seated. The twins, Alyce, and I practice making corrections based on the ballistic coefficients. The other six get wind speeds to make wind-drift corrections.

Mauchly walks in between our chairs, looking over our shoulders, checking our work. "That would be gamma to the power of one, not two, Donna. Marjorie, don't round up. Keep the decimal place to the hundred thousandth. No, the deflection due to cant is automatically compensated for, Kay."

I bite the inside of my cheek, hoping she won't find anything wrong with my computations.

A handheld bell rings for our attention. I look up and the clock reads five minutes to twelve. My eyes are blurry and my right wrist aches. We all show signs of wear. Ruth rubs her lower back. Joyce's eyes are bloodshot behind her glasses. Louise's normally smooth pageboy hair is matted in back where she's been twisting strands of it for hours. Mrs. Mauchly, on the other hand, looks fresh as a newly ironed bedsheet.

"You have forty minutes for lunch," she announces.

I smile at her as I walk past, but either she doesn't see me or she's not playing favorites. It's just as well. I need to stay in the background anyway.

The cafeteria of the Moore School is on the main floor. Three men in suits and ties sit at a corner table, and some boys huddle in a center three-top, but other than that, the room is empty. It doesn't smell bad in here, but it doesn't smell as good as Mom's kitchen, either. A pang of homesickness comes over me. Did Sarah put the straw in Dad's juice glass this morning and move his cushion to the kitchen? I wonder what they had for breakfast, if they stared at my empty chair or were just fine without me.

After forty minutes, we're back at our desks. More charts. More scratching sounds of pencils on paper. More *ka-chung*s of the desk calculators. A mathematical symphony. No wonder our trigonometry teacher used to play classical music in class to help us see patterns and repetitions. I should have thanked him for that. I never even got to say goodbye.

At some point, a suited man walks into the classroom, causing us to look up. Mrs. Mauchly is clearly happy to see him. I recognize him from the cafeteria. He's tall, with a tufted beard on his chin, about ten years older than Mrs. Mauchly. She and the man confer quietly.

"Don't they look cozy?" says one of the twins.

"Yeah, even we don't talk that closely," admits her sister.

Mrs. Mauchly rings her little bell. "Ladies, may I present my husband, Dr. John Mauchly, an instructor here at the school of engineering. He's had an impressive academic career in physics, too long to list here today. But he wanted to meet you all."

Her husband? I can't believe it. I've never known a professional couple like this, let alone a mathematician married to a physicist, where the woman is on equal footing with the man.

He clears his throat and leans forward, nearly tottering, trying to balance his great height. "On behalf of Moore and the Ballistics Research Lab, we're so happy to have all you mathematicians here. This is time-consuming work, work that would normally be done by men. Your contribution to the war effort will no doubt be extraordinary and necessary. I don't know if Mary, er, Mrs. Mauchly has told you how fluid the situation is. Our artillery is changing daily, and we must keep adjusting accordingly. Whenever a new combination of weapon and ammunition goes into the field, a firing table must accompany the system. I've just been informed of a new cannon being deployed. I'm afraid we're going to have to throw out all your computations from before lunch."

Groans of protests ensue. I surprise myself by how loud I moan, too. All that hard work down the drain.

Mrs. Mauchly flashes her husband a pointed look. "Don't despair, girls. Every time you put pencil to paper, you're honing your skills, oiling those synapses in your brains. We mustn't look back, but redirect. Flexibility is the name of the game. Think of our men overseas. Think of how many different directives they must receive from the moment reveille is played to the moment they lay down their heads."

I sink lower in my chair.

She claps her hands once. "Back to work, everybody."

I may be chastened, but I'm still frustrated. There's got to be a more efficient way to compute these numbers. I think about how long a trajectory takes from the point of fire to impact—maybe two seconds? Unless it's a bomb; then I suppose it takes a few minutes from the time it drops until it lands. But for our new friend, the 105 mm howitzer, let's say, there are ten girls computing nonstop for an average of ten hours a day. That's at least one hundred hours of work for a two-second benefit. I look at the new chart Mrs. Mauchly's written on the board.

| $x$ | 1 | 3 | 5 | 7 | 9 |
|---|---|---|---|---|---|
| $f$ | 0 | 1.0986 | 1.6094 | 1.9459 | 2.1972 |

Under that, she's written:

Find $f$ for $x = 1.83$

Next to me, Donna is busy calculating. I know without looking that she and the other girls are creating the exact same tables where each column is linked to the next through consecutive differences. After five total rounds of this, their results will end up looking like a family tree turned sideways, only with numbers where the leaves of the names of cousins and aunts and uncles should be.

I'm picturing this when my left eye starts to twitch. I set down my pencil and close my eyes, just for a second. The twitching stops, but a shape takes hold from behind my eyelids. A simple line appears between the first two points. Next thing I know, the line lifts and transforms into a parabola that includes the first three points, extending majestically into the air like a rainbow. The arc continues to include all five data points.

I open my eyes. Did anyone else experience that? Nine heads are bent down in concentration. No one has shifted from where they were a few minutes ago. I'm always so surprised when the knowing occurs, as if maybe I'm not the only one who sees things differently. But it never happens to anyone else.

The first time was with the circles on the kindergarten carpet. I didn't quite understand the vision, but once my teacher recognized what I'd figured out, I knew to bury it. Otherwise, I'd be discovered. I didn't deserve to have the gift. I'd done a terrible thing. My father was suffering and my mother's life was destroyed. I vowed to stop any future twitch of the eye. But then it happened two years later. We were learning fractions. A whole chocolate cake appeared in my head, and I understood how to slice it for sixteen people, and that if only twelve people ate the cake, three-fourths would be gone. It was as though I wasn't doing math with numbers at all, but with images instead. I asked my tablemates, "Does anyone see a cake in their head?" The kids shook their heads. How silly Nervous Nellie is.

As much as I tried to control the knowing, I couldn't. In pre-algebra, there was an equation on my worksheet: $20 - 7x = 6x - 6$. I closed my eyes and saw a scale, like the one held up by Lady Justice. I knew this image because it was the symbol for Libra, Eleanor Roosevelt's zodiac sign. The equation had to be balanced the way the scale was, trays hanging evenly with equal weight. If I took away something on one side of the equation, I needed to do it to the other. Parts of the equation fell away like leaves on the maple tree in our front yard until all that was left was $x = 2$.

Eventually, I stopped trying to suppress it. I accepted that the knowing was a part of me. A part that I would never reveal to anyone.

So here I am in this basement at University of Pennsylvania, and I've just visualized a quartic fit function, something I've never seen before. Before I realize what I'm doing, I'm drawing the graph exactly as I saw it in my mind, and plotting the rest of the coordinates until $x = 9$, the end point of Mrs. Mauchly's chart. Next to that, I write:

*the approximate value of the function at* $x = 1.83$ *is 0.57*

Quickly, I move to erase it. But I'm too late. Mrs. Mauchly is peering so close over my shoulder that I can hear her breathing. "Well, I'll be damned."

# 10.

"Eleanor, phone call!" Mrs. Goldstine yells up the stairs.

"Coming," I say dully, getting up from my bed. I know it's just Mom. She's the only one who ever calls me.

On my way downstairs, I pass girls with curlers, wrapped in towels, carrying makeup bags in various stages of preparation. It's another Saturday night out that I'm not joining. The tenth one, but who's counting?

I grab the telephone receiver in the first-floor hallway as Goldstine waddles off.

"I'm afraid I have bad news," says Mom in a shaky voice.

"Did something happen to Dad?"

"He's fine, thank God. But Aunt Roza and Uncle Azriel . . . They're missing."

I sink to the floor, curling my knees against my chest. "How do people just go missing from a ghetto?"

"We think it happened months ago, but we're just now getting word. Letters take so long to get here. There was a raid. Apparently, Aunt Roza and Uncle Azriel were hiding. But the German police set a fire and they were forced to come out. They were marched to the train station and put on a wagon. We don't know where they were taken. All we know is that the head of the Jewish Council managed to escape to the forest and he got word to someone. Roza's and Azriel's names were on his list."

"That means Batja might be . . ." I couldn't say the word.

"We think she is still in the ghetto."

I allowed myself a smidgeon of hope. "But who's taking care of her? Who's she living with?"

Mom sniffles. "We just don't know, honey. I'm so sorry."

And here I am, safe in this ridiculous fraternity house. Are our computations even getting to Europe? It's the RAF that's fighting the Germans at the moment, not the Americans. I feel like I'm not making a direct impact on Batja's situation.

Two girls run by me, giggling and holding soda bottles on their way back from the kitchen. "Watch it, Eleanor!"

"Are those some of your new friends from ROTC?" asks Mom.

A beat. "Yes, we're all getting ready to go out tonight." I make my voice peppy.

"You have fun, Eleanor. Live your life. God knows it's much too short to waste even one moment."

I swallow the lump in my throat and slowly make my way back to my room. In the hallway, I pass one of the twins, avocado-colored cream covering her face like an alien. "Where are you all off to tonight?" I ask, knowing I'll have to come up with something to tell Mom if she wants details later.

"Actually, we're staying in. Ruth's got a nasty cold and Mrs. Goldstine's letting us use the kitchen. We're making chicken cacciatore. Joyce's mother's recipe. Join us!"

Through the open door to my room, I see the *Philadelphia Inquirer* resting on my nightstand. My Saturday night routine goes like this: I wait until all the girls are gone and Alyce heads home, which she does every weekend to help her mom with the little ones. Then I take out a hot pot from under my bed, make my mac and cheese, and read the paper. I always search for battle details, thinking I might find information about where our firing tables might be used. But of course I never do. It's all classified. But I linger on other war headlines, like this one: *First Negro Division Forms at Fort Huachuca.* Why do Negroes need their own division in the army? Aren't we all fighting for the same cause? And this one: *Los Angeles Japanese Americans Relocate to Santa Anita.* That's the stables where they race the horses Uncle Herman likes to bet on. It disgusts me the way they're ripping all those people from their homes and tossing them together in dirty, cramped quarters. Like the Germans are doing to the Jews.

I force my thoughts away from dark newspaper stories, from the room where I've spent every Saturday night for two and half months. Mom's right. Life is precarious and could be cut short at any moment. Dad's stroke taught me that. I don't have to be the life of the party tonight. I can just chop vegetables. I smile at the twin in front of me. "If I can convince Alyce to stay, then count us in."

"Hot dog!"

It's easy to talk Alyce into staying. She's dying for a break from playing hide-and-seek and tossing jacks. She calls home and her mother gives her the night off, as long as she goes to church with them tomorrow morning.

During dinner, I don't contribute to the conversation, but I feel closer to the group than I have before. Maybe it's the hour we spent working together doing food prep, or the fact that we're alone, without an audience, whether that be Mauchly or her husband coming to observe, or a group of boys eating nearby in the cafeteria. Tonight it's just us. No makeup. No fancy hats.

"Now what?" asks one of the twins a little forlornly, licking her fingers of the last of the red sauce.

Marjorie dabs her lips with a napkin. "Everyone meet down in the basement in half an hour. We have unfinished business!"

What unfinished business? Should I be worried?

We make quick work of the dishes and I use the remaining time to write a V-mail letter to Batja. It's hard to fit all my sentiments into the special stationery that's smaller in size and converts to its own envelope. I want to ask her about her parents, how she's surviving on her own. But I'm sure none of that will even make it through the censors. Instead, I write that I've been doing a lot of math in my spare time and living and working on a university campus. I describe the

Sigma Chi House and how disgusting it was when we first moved in. Then I graph a little parabola, opening upward, turning it into a funny smiling face.

I know the chances of a letter reaching the ghetto are slim, but this small act of writing keeps me connected to her. I manage to squeeze in her whole address on what little space is left on the outside of the V-mail stationery.

> Batja Sejdel
>
> 86 Ulica Podzamcze
>
> Stanislawów
>
> Distrikt Galizien

The words look unnatural, ominous even, *k*'s and *z*'s where they shouldn't be. I take care to get the accent over the *o* just right.

I must have spent too long with the letter, because when I go downstairs, there's no one on the main floor except Joyce, standing on the couch in her stocking feet underneath the Sigma Chi crest. She's holding a piece of paper and a roll of tape.

I hesitate, not sure what to say. She speaks first. "Why aren't you down in the basement with everyone?"

"I could ask you the same thing," I say, surprising myself.

"I'm trying to cover up this dumb motto, but I can barely reach it." She stretches one arm as high as she can. "Is there a ladder in this place?"

"I haven't seen one." I swat away a mosquito. "I take it *In this sign, thou shalt conquer* doesn't speak to you?"

Joyce laughs. "Definitely not. I just haven't found the right inspiring quote yet. I figure I'll come across it eventually."

"My go-to person for inspiration is Eleanor Roosevelt."

"Of course. A famous person with your name."

"Maybe when I was nine and she became First Lady I gravitated toward her because of that. But there are lots more reasons to admire her."

She tosses the paper and tape onto the couch. "I'm a big fan of E.R., too. Anything come to mind?"

" 'All human beings must hold some belief in a Power greater than themselves'?" I suggest.

She shakes her head. "Too religious."

"Um, let's see. 'Even from life's sorrows some good must come'?"

"Too depressing."

" 'A woman is like a tea bag. You can't tell how strong she is until you put her in hot water'?"

"Bingo!" Joyce pulls a fountain paintbrush from her pants pocket. "Have at it."

"Really? You want me to write that?"

"It was your idea."

I grin as I write down the quote in large capital letters.

After we tape it onto the crest, she grabs my hand. "C'mon. Everyone's waiting for us."

As Joyce and I descend the stairs, Tommy Dorsey's version of "Oh! Look at Me Now" gets louder.

*I never knew the technique of kissing*
*I never knew the thrill I could get from your touch*
*I never knew much*
*Oh, look at me now!*

Marjorie lies bent-legged, back flat on the floor. There's a pencil behind her ear and a notepad rests on her thighs. A few sit cross-legged around her on unused mattresses we dragged down here from the fourth floor, while others lean against the wall, their legs stretched out in front of them. I notice Alyce is the only one not sitting on a mattress, but on the floor instead.

Joyce plops down next to Marjorie and I find a spot next to Alyce.

"What do you have so far?" asks Joyce.

Marjorie reads. *"'I never knew a sine from a cosine, I never knew the things you could do with a log.'"*

"I love it!" exclaims Joyce.

They're making song parodies with math lyrics? What fun! I concentrate on Sinatra's voice, listening to his phrasing.

"How about *'till I took this job'*?" I venture.

There's a short pause, then everyone joins in together: "Oh, look at me now!"

We hammer out another verse in no time.

*I never knew synthetic division*
*I never knew about an inedible pie*
*Or the powers of "i"*
*Oh, look at me now!*

Then Louise says, "It's Kay's birthday next week."

"Let's go out to Kugler's next Saturday and celebrate!" suggests Marjorie.

"I'll make the reservation," says Louise.

I think my eleventh Saturday night at Sigma Chi will be the magic one. I'm finally ready to go out. I can wear my fancy dress, which has been trapped in the closet, unworn since my bout with clothing anxiety that first morning.

"Maybe we should pick another place," offers Joyce.

"What do you mean?" asks Marjorie.

Joyce's eyes dart to Alyce, then back at us. "Um, well, Kugler's doesn't serve . . . everybody."

Something tightens in my chest.

"Don't worry about it," Alyce says lightly. "My mom's expecting me home anyway. You know, since I didn't go back tonight. You all keep your plans."

"Aces," says Marjorie.

Just like that? They're going to exclude Alyce from the birthday party because of the color of her skin?

"Make the reservation for eight," I blurt out without thinking.

"Eight o'clock?"

"Eight people. If she can't go, I'm not going."

It feels like someone hoovered the air right out of the room.

"Don't make a big deal about this, Eleanor," whispers Alyce.

Marjorie and I stare at each other. Kay looks back and forth between us, waiting to see what's going to happen to her birthday dinner. It's a showdown.

"Kugler's it is," says Marjorie finally. "Why should one person ruin it for everyone else?"

I can't take any more of this I'm-better-than-you nonsense. It's plain racist. "So should we just make Alyce sit alone in a different classroom during ballistics lab? Because she might sully our computations? And while we're at it, let's make sure the Negro Army regiments get trained at a separate facility, where they learn to cook and dig ditches. If we arm them, they might endanger the Allied forces. In fact, why don't we put everyone who looks different than us all together in one place? Like those Japanese American families being sent to the camps. And the ghettos full of European Jews. They're ruining it for the rest of us by merely existing."

The only movement in the room is my chest heaving up and down. So much for staying in the background.

Marjorie is seething. "You're one to talk. It's your fault we're even in this war."

"*My* fault?"

"Everyone knows FDR is a Jew lover!"

The twins, who are also Jewish, gasp in unison.

Unfazed, Marjorie gets up off the mattress and takes Frances's arm, helping her stand. "I'm tired. Aren't you, Frances?" She yawns dramatically and they leave.

No one has an appetite for songwriting after that and we all head upstairs, too.

Alyce and I are silent as we change into nightgowns, too worn out to speak. We slip into our twin beds and I squirm around, trying to get comfortable. Then Alice says, "For a white girl, Marjorie sure showed her true colors."

We burst out laughing.

She turns her lamp back on. "Hey, how do you know so much about the Negro Army and the Japanese camps?"

"I've had a lot of time to read the paper."

She gives me a sideways look. "You haven't been going home for dinner, have you?" Without waiting for an answer, she reaches across the gap between our two beds and gives my hand a squeeze.

# II.

The air is heavy Monday morning, filled with humidity and the lingering tension of our argument in the fraternity basement Saturday
night. By the time we arrive at Moore, we're all irritated and sweaty.
Even Marjorie's powder can't save her face from melting. The lab door
is locked. There's a note taped on it, directing us down the hall to
room 33. Mrs. Mauchly is nowhere to be found.

A greasy, metallic smell hits me, then a blast of cool air, as we
head into the heavily air-conditioned room 33. The space is five times
the size of our usual classroom, with some sort of machine running
its entire center length, taking up most of the square footage. It makes
me think of that game we heard about from a London transfer student
to Jenkintown High. She called it *table football* and all her friends were
crazy for it. We didn't have it in the States, so she drew us a picture:
a table with metal poles that two players maneuver, controlling little
men trying to whack a ball into a goal. This machine looks like that,
only it's giant, long enough for forty people to play on either side.
Across the top are horizontal rods running lengthwise with vertical

rods crossing them every few feet. In between some of the rods are wheels and discs. I can't imagine what it could be used for.

"Ah, there are my ten geniuses," says Mrs. Mauchly, emerging through a door at the other end. She's accompanied by three men: her husband, Dr. Mauchly; an officer in full military dress who has the narrowest head I've ever seen; and another man, nondescript but for horn-rimmed glasses and a black suit matching his grim expression.

Mrs. Mauchly sweeps her hand out. "Welcome to the Differential Analyzer Room."

As in differential equations?

"There are only three of these in the country. One at MIT, one at Aberdeen in Maryland, and this beauty here." Her face is enraptured, as if she were in love. "I don't need to remind you that the very existence of this machine is top secret."

"Yet she just did," whispers Alyce, and we both try not to smile.

"There's a fourth machine in Norway," continues Mrs. Mauchly. "In order to prevent the Germans from getting their hands on it, Svein Rosseland, the astrophysicist in charge, removed the torque amplifiers."

"What the heck are torque amplifiers?" murmurs Frances.

Marjorie shushes her.

"He wrapped them carefully in cloth and buried them in the garden," continues Mrs. Mauchly. "One of the things we'll be teaching you girls is how to render this fine machine useless. Just in case it falls into the wrong hands."

I gasp. Is there actually a possibility of the enemy being on our soil? Could *they* be at the University of Pennsylvania right now? Despite the little bolt of fear that thought creates, it also brings a familiar sensation of doing something forbidden yet thrilling.

Turning to the men next to her, Mrs. Mauchly says, "General Gillon has come all the way from Washington, DC, to show us how the differential analyzer works."

The uniformed man salutes formally. Though there are no windows down here, the shiny gold badge on his hat, pins on his collar, and buttons on his epaulets are a light source unto themselves. Something about being in the presence of a military officer makes me feel safe, as if he alone can save us. In contrast, the dark-suited man isn't introduced, standing under his own cloud, inscrutable and silent.

"Good morning," begins the general. "On behalf of the Chief of Ordnance of the United States, I thank you for your service. Even though the work you're doing is secret and can't be acknowledged publicly, it's vitally important. In fact, I believe that those who don't seek fame or recognition from their good deeds possess character of the highest order. This war will be won because of the efforts of everyone: our men on the front lines and you, our silent Rosies."

He waits to let this sink in. I hear some sniffles behind me. All of us are moved by his words.

Striding to the middle of the room, he points to the machine. "The differential analyzer calculates rates of change, specifically differential equations up to the sixth order."

What? This giant table-football-game-like thing can actually do calculus?

Then a pinprick of worry. A tiny nagging at the back of my head.

"As Mary mentioned, it uses a torque amplifier mechanism. Basically, you have two friction drums that are rotated by belts attached to electrical motors. The input shaft is connected to the knife-edge wheel of an integrator here, which in turn gently nudges an input arm there."

I let my eyes roam over the machine, trying to match what he's saying with their actual parts. It seems important that I pay close attention, though I can't say why. Undoubtedly, they have engineers to repair it, oil it, keep it spinning. That's probably not going to be our concern. It just feels like there's something big at stake here.

The general goes on. "The slight movement of the input arm causes the string to momentarily tighten on the right-hand friction drum. It then gives a pull on the output arm, which causes the output shaft to rotate. With considerable force, I might add." He stops, gauging our reaction.

Crickets.

"I hope I'm not boring you all." He chuckles. "I tend to get too technical sometimes. Any questions so far?"

One of the girls scoffs lightheartedly. "That reminds me of a Tommy Dorsey song."

Gillon looks stiff and out of place at the mention of anything popular.

"'The Music Goes 'Round and Around,' I believe it's called," interjects Dr. Mauchly, coming to Gillon's rescue. "There's some truth to that. The way the differential analyzer works is not unlike the pathway air takes through a sax horn. Or the rear-axle mechanism of certain automobiles. Gear and disc systems are used in mathematical calculations as well. For our purposes—the need to improve weapon accuracy—it's now possible to calculate several integrating units at the same time, because of the amplified power."

Ah. That's where the torque amplifiers come in. And all at once I understand what's been eating at me: What we girls do with our quaint paper and pencils and chalkboards is simply too slow. With this machine, we will become obsolete.

The general, now fully recovered and back to his spick-and-span self, points to a desk behind him. "These are the input tables, one for each function being integrated."

I must admit, it's remarkable. It appears that this thing can turn a function into its antiderivative. But I refuse to give neither the Mauchlys nor the general and certainly not the evil-looking man even the slightest hint of how impressed I am. As if little ol' me and my non-reaction will slow or stall what's happening here. These adults who hold multiple Ivy League degrees already realize how wonderful this analyzer is and that they don't need Mrs. Mauchly's little geniuses any longer.

I should be happy for this invention. Its speed is a boon to the war effort. But where does that leave me? After all my indecisiveness and worry about taking this job, manually computing ballistic tables has become the most rewarding and important work I've ever done. Aside from having to live with the impossible Marjorie, I don't want to lose this chance.

The general paces up and down the length of the analyzer. "These mechanisms can add, subtract, multiply, and divide." He gives us a half smile, as if he doesn't want to seem too haughty. "The best part, though, is that it doesn't make mistakes."

And we girls do? So that's it? Humans are now dispensable? I raise my hand, anger overcoming my fear of drawing attention. I don't know who to address my question to, so I pick a point on the wall to the left of the general's bony cheek. "What will our role be in all this?"

Dr. Mauchly answers for the group. "Why, you'll be configuring the settings and inputting the empirical data."

But we won't be using our brains. Even twelve-year-old Sarah with her C in math can feed data.

Mrs. Mauchly clears her throat. "Ladies, what Dr. Mauchly is saying is that nothing's changed. You're still our silent Rosies."

No, everything has changed.

Her husband nods emphatically. "The great mathematician H. T. Davis was standing in his backyard in a small town in Colorado when he saw Halley's Comet cresting just above the western mountains, its head brilliant, its tail sweeping across the sky through an arc of one hundred and thirty degrees. He speculated that the comet's return seventy-five years later would mark the beginning of an epoch in science that has had no parallel in the history of the world." He pauses. "That was in 1910. And here we are in 1942, about to establish computing as a formal scientific field unto its own! How prescient Davis was! And even earlier than he predicted!"

Alyce aims those perfectly plucked arched eyebrows at me and speaks softly. "Don't you think he's getting a bit ahead of himself?"

"Maybe," I whisper. "But regardless, I won't be replaced by some machine."

"What are you talking about?"

There's no time to explain, to convince her that I'm right. Mrs. Mauchly claps her hands and we're off and running. Five girls on the input table, five on the output. I'm on input, which is just a piece of graphing paper mounted on a carriage.

"This first input function has already been plotted," explains Mrs. Mauchly. "You'll be doing the plotting yourself after this. But for now, let's watch the analyzer calculate the 1.9-second trajectory of an artillery shell."

She turns on a motor, and the machine comes to life. One of the two discs begins to revolve, causing a horizontal rod to spin and the gears attached to it to move forward, backward, and sideways, interlocking with other gears and shafts, causing a vertical rod to spin in response. It's a vast, interconnected grid, a masterful dance of moving parts. We're mesmerized.

"The horizontal rods, or buses as we like to call them, represent time, weight, and diameter of the projectile, the prevailing wind, altitude, atmospheric density, and the rotation of the earth," explains Mrs. Mauchly. "The vertical rods drive the rotation of the discs in two integrators. Two because this is a second-order differential equation."

At the input table, we watch as a little box with a magnifying glass follows along a curve, tracing over the function already plotted on the graph paper, down up, down up, in parabolic shapes.

After about ten minutes, Mrs. Mauchly runs over to the opposite side of the room. She's surprisingly fast, making me wonder if she chases after kids at home. I wouldn't be surprised. Mother, mathematician, multitalented member of a secret all-male ballistics team. She's Wonder Woman in sensible pumps. If Eleanor Roosevelt is my guardian angel, Mrs. Mauchly is who I want to be when I grow up.

The other half of our group at the output table moves aside as Mrs. Mauchly rips off the paper and holds it up. An ink pen has plotted a graph, charting both the position and velocity of our artillery shell over time.

"And voilà! The output team will then write down these plot points, converting them into numbered tables, just like you've been doing all along."

From the sounds of excitement and awe coming from all the girls, it's obvious they're as dazzled as the Mauchlys are by this machine. I stay quiet.

"Are you okay?" asks Alyce.

"Peachy."

Mrs. Mauchly hands the input team sheets of graph paper with functions written at the top and we get to work.

By noon, I'm still upset and famished as well. Clearly, I've burned too many calories worrying about the future of computing. In the cafeteria, I take the first plate I see, a mystery casserole with a few overcooked green beans on the side, instead of making one slow walk down the line like I usually do before deciding.

The rest of the girls seem chipper and gay. "Let's have a party in the living room tonight," suggests Kay, lining up her fork and knife in perfect parallel lines next to her plate. She always has to have everything just so. "I could hoof all night!"

"Me too," says Louise. "To think we've been spending forty hours entering numbers on those Marchants when it takes just fifteen minutes on the differential analyzer to do the same trajectory!"

I wipe casserole from the corner of my mouth, scowling behind my napkin. "Annie isn't all that special."

"Annie?" asks Kay.

"As in analyzer." The name came to me about an hour ago, while I watched the pointer trace a tiresome parabola. Okay, maybe calling her Annie is my way of bringing my enemy down to size. And also a way of expressing my frustration without risking an attention-getting outburst.

"What are we, in kindergarten?" says Marjorie, looking around, hoping others will follow suit. Only Frances laughs.

As we walk back to room 33, Sharon says, "Does Annie need her own room at the frat house?"

"Well, at least a sign on her door," says Joyce.

And with that, the name sticks.

After lunch, Mrs. Mauchly has us trade positions. The output table is a little less boring. At least I'm writing down actual numbers.

Next time I look up, the wall clock says 3:15. Mrs. Mauchly is gone, as well as the men. It's just us girls. I guess our leaders feel confident we won't screw anything up, though I don't see how we could. It's so darn easy. I decide to take advantage of being unsupervised and pour myself a cup of coffee from the big red thermos Mrs. Mauchly always leaves for us. It's too bitter for my taste. I usually take a heaping spoonful of sugar, but it's being rationed. Plain coffee it is. I rub my eyes, stretch my arms, and begin again.

After just a few minutes, a mathematical alarm bell goes off in my head. Something's not adding up between the graph Annie just drew and my numbers. "Isn't this supposed to be 2.2-second trajectory?" I ask my teammate, Donna.

She nods. "Why the concern?"

"Well, look at the velocity column: 1770.4 is for a 2-second trajectory, not a 2.2."

She stops what she's doing to read the figures. "There must be a reason. I can't imagine this thing is wrong."

I copy down Annie's last four plot points from the output graph and recheck the math by hand. It takes me over an hour. I get a velocity of 1721.2 feet per second. Again, I tap Donna on the shoulder. "Look."

Donna shrugs, unable to explain. "Go find Mauchly."

Except I don't. I squat down and crawl underneath Annie instead.

"Eleanor!" shouts Donna.

I pretend I can't hear her with all the churning, which is practically true. I've never been inside a factory, but this view from below is exactly how I picture it: the machines grinding away, carrying us toward the next century. Through the gaps between rods, I see my teammates in their sweater sets and oxfords, and the comparison comes to a halt. Workers in a real factory would be wearing denim jumpsuits and scarves around their heads like Rosie the Riveter. This is a fake factory, nothing like what Batja is experiencing. Are the machines dangerous where she is? Do her hands bleed? Is her dress slipping off her shoulders, which are thin from starvation? Stop it, Eleanor. That isn't helping at all. Concentrate on the task at hand.

Looking upward, I watch a few of the gears, starting and stopping, starting and stopping. Then my left eye starts to twitch. I'm gliding in between the gears like Charlie Chaplin does in the movie *Modern Times*. Over and under I swim, feeling the cogs churn under my stomach. Each time a gear stops, it rotates slightly in the opposite direction and my body goes backward for a split second. Then the gear starts up again and I move forward. When the vision stops, I know what the problem is.

All gears slip. It's like my bicycle chain. When I brake, it slides back a tiny bit. But that means with each input of $x$, Annie's not starting up again in the exact same spot. It's fine with a bike or even a car, because the minute you start pedaling or press the clutch and shift gears, you can move forward. But with the differential analyzer, where pinpoint accuracy means everything, that's a problem. Could this slippage be the reason for the inconsistencies I caught earlier? I think so. And as the trajectories become more complex, the errors will only become greater.

I crawl out from underneath Annie and bump into a pair of brown pumps attached to shapely calves.

"What in Euclid's name are you doing down there, Eleanor?" asks Mrs. Mauchly.

I quickly get to my feet and brush dust off my knees.

She crosses her arms, waiting.

"I was, um, wondering what it felt like to crawl around under there with no nylons on, now that we need to turn in all our silk for the war effort."

She levels her gaze at me, not buying it.

Just walk away. Don't create a scene. They'll realize the gear problem on their own eventually.

But what if they don't?

"Well, actually . . . I did notice something else, while I was, you know, testing out my stocking theory. The gears are slipping."

Mrs. Mauchly uncrosses her arms, apparently relieved I fessed up and that it's merely a minor concern. "We know about backlash.

We expected some of that. In fact, I'm about to dismiss you all a little early today so we can reprogram for the next trajectory. We need to dismantle and re-create the gearing anyway."

"But you don't understand!" I protest. "Besides the backlash, I fear that any slack in the system, even if the gears are slightly misaligned or loose and worn, will cause errors. This will only get worse as more trajectories are calculated. Annie, I mean the differential analyzer, may be fast, but she isn't reliable."

The other nine girls have stopped their work and are watching us. Mrs. Mauchly purses her lips in renewed displeasure.

"At least let us take the time to recheck the analyzer's math," I beg. "There's too much at stake. Lives are on the line." And then I say out loud what I've been thinking all along. "Machines will never be as accurate as human computers!"

Oh God, oh God. What have I done?

The room is hushed. Someone has turned off the motors. A sound comes from the corner—a throat being cleared. It's the evil-looking man in the dark suit. How long has he been standing there?

Mrs. Mauchly and I have switched roles. She's the quiet one and I'm at the center. But what's worse is the man in the corner. He's no longer inscrutable. The expression on his face reads loud and clear.

Keen interest.

And he's looking directly at me.

# 12.

Two hours earlier than our usual quitting time, and after conferring with her three male colleagues—heads down, whispers inaudible—Mrs. Mauchly makes an announcement. "You're free to go, girls. Everyone except Eleanor."

I've ruined everything. They're going to fire me for insubordination. Why can't I keep my mouth shut? Look what happened in the basement the other night. Once again, I've taken one step forward and two steps back.

As the nine girls file out of the differential analyzer room, Alyce steals a look at me. *What's going on?*

I blink back my tears and give a tiny shake of my head.

When the last of the girls leave, the door slams behind me and I jump. It's just me and the four adults. The inscrutable man returns to his place in the corner, watching. Dr. Mauchly and the general gather chairs from the input and output tables. Mrs. Mauchly finds two more, folded up in a supply closet. The digital analyzer is turned off, so the only noises are footsteps and the scraping of chair legs across the floor. *Step, step, drag. Step, step, drag.* And in between, my heart beating three times its normal rhythm. Finding the pattern isn't calming me down this time.

Dr. Mauchly strokes his beard. "Maybe you should take a seat, Eleanor."

The four of us settle into a tight circle at the end of the room, the inscrutable man's empty chair like the symbolic one we set out for Elijah the Prophet during our small Passover Seders. The only difference is that I'm hoping this man doesn't make an appearance in the seat.

General Gillon lights a cigarette and I suppress a cough. He blows smoke over his right shoulder. "I'm sorry, do you mind if I . . . ?"

"Go right ahead," I eke out.

Mrs. Mauchly moves to open the doors on either end since there are no windows. At least the visual of my escape route helps ease the choking sensation.

A secretary enters, click-clacking her heels efficiently. She carries a tray filled with a pitcher of water and five glasses. As there aren't any free tables other than those containing expensive equipment, she places the tray right on the ground. I watch beads of condensation drip down the side of the crystal pitcher, my throat in a silent cry of thirst. No one makes a move to pour.

Finally, General Gillon speaks. "What level math did you reach, Eleanor?"

"I'm in, I mean, I *was* in trigonometry."

"Hmm . . ." His eyes dart to the man in the corner, then back to me.

They're going to use my youth, my low-level high school math, as the reason to sack me. And I'm certainly not about to tell them how I taught myself advanced calculus from my dad's books in his study.

The burnt end of the general's Lucky Strike is seconds away from crumbling to the floor. He looks for an ashtray and when he doesn't find one, uses one of the water glasses instead. My mouth gets even drier watching this.

Mrs. Mauchly uncrosses and crosses her legs.

Dr. Mauchly pours himself a glass of water but doesn't offer one to anyone else.

Gillon takes another long, slow drag from his cigarette. "You're a math shark, Eleanor. We need someone like you out in California."

Math shark? I can't quite process what he's saying.

"That's why we're transferring you to the army air base at Muroc Lake," he adds.

I'm so relieved I could kiss him. They're not kicking me out!

But wait. California? That's on the other side of the world. How will Mom reach me? What if they get news from Poland?

Dr. Mauchly chimes in. "You should know that you won't be working on the analyzer."

"That's correct," says the general. "You'll be calculating ballistics tables for other . . . equipment." He shifts in his chair. "The desert ranges out there, dry lake beds—it's an ideal testing ground."

Other equipment? Testing ground? He's being awfully cagey. Could he be talking about real bombs? No. That's impossible. They wouldn't send a civilian into a dangerous situation. And yet, nothing about this day has gone the way I thought it would. I'm sitting next to a machine that does calculus. I'm having a conversation with a top-ranking US military officer and there's a man in the corner who looks like he wants to kill me. Anything goes.

The scary man is stepping forward. He doesn't take the empty chair, but stands behind it, his hands resting on the back. Now, in the light, I see the shadow of his beard, as if a permanent reminder of his dark persona.

"Eleanor, is it?" Shockingly, his voice belies his face. He sounds normal, friendly even. "I'm Deputy Director Hayden from MID." He pauses as if I'm supposed to either be impressed or know what this is.

I look at him blankly.

"Military Intelligence Division."

Still nothing.

"Among other things, we oversee the Ordnance Departments, specifically the Army Air Corps technical services, to make sure—"

"Eleanor, dear," interjects Mrs. Mauchly impatiently. "He's a spy."

Is she giving me a line?

The deputy director scoffs. "Mary, don't be crass. My people aren't lurking in dark alleys or forcing traitors to swallow poison pills. We're officers of the United States government with a mission to know our enemies. And right now, the military is testing a secret weapon that the Germans would very much like to get their hands on." He turns to me. "I can't say anything more at this time, but the numbers you deliver at Muroc will interface with this piece of equipment. We need your utmost secrecy."

"She already knows the drill, Bill," says Mrs. Mauchly. "She hasn't even told her parents what she's been doing at Moore. None of my girls have."

He nods, then removes his glasses and starts to clean the lenses with a hankie. I'm startled by how innocent he appears without them. "Any questions, Eleanor?"

I want to say, You're a real spy? Like Dan Dunn, Secret Operative 48? But instead, the cough that I've been holding in erupts into a real fit.

They sit patiently while I recover my voice. "Who else is going?" I ask hoarsely, praying it might be Alyce.

"Just you," he says.

A trolley car plows headlong into my gut. I'll be alone.

"This is quite an honor, Eleanor," begins Mrs. Mauchly. "We wouldn't be asking you to go clear across the country if we didn't think you could handle it. Since your first day in lab, you've shown an ability to see things with your mind, not your eyes. We need that kind of vision on this project. Your contribution could mean the difference between victory and defeat."

Even if I *were* sanguine about being so far away from my family, which I'm not, someone could recognize my last name at Muroc. I'm sure an army base is crawling with scientists and engineers. It will be harder to lie low considering I'm the only girl being sent from PCS.

I cough again, then manage to ask, "When would I start?"

"You'll board a train as soon as possible," answers Hayden. "There are some logistics, of course. You'll need to get fingerprinted and be given your military ID along with security clearance."

"We'll take care of that at the army offices downtown," adds the general.

Dr. Mauchly has a hint of a smile. "We hope this all sounds good to you."

Four pairs of eyes stare at me. Are they asking me or telling me to do this?

What would Eleanor Roosevelt do? She'd be on the first train west, of course. Her country has already called and she's answered. "Can I have a day to think about it?"

"You can have the evening." The deputy director hands me a piece of paper. "Be at this address at 0800 tomorrow morning. Wear a dark blouse for your ID photo." Then he stands, puts his glasses back on, returning to his inscrutable self, and exits the room.

Something tells me the guy has never heard the word *no*.

Mrs. Mauchly waits until the door has closed after Hayden. Then she turns to me. "What do you think, Eleanor?"

"May I have a drink of water?"

# 13.

When I walk into the fraternity house, the girls are talking softly in the living room. We don't usually gather right here, so it seems like they've been waiting for me, maybe out of concern? Not Marjorie, of course, who's busy with a small mirror, penciling her eyebrows.

Alyce runs over, putting her hands on both my shoulders. "Are you all right?"

I pause, not sure what I am.

"Are you done for?" asks Joyce, getting right to the heart of the matter.

"Not exactly. They're sending me out to California . . . to an army base in the desert."

"Like Napoleon, exiled to Elba," moans Ruth.

Donna waves Ruth away with her hand in the air. "No. Then they'd just send her home. This is something more."

Marjorie snaps her makeup case closed. "Don't you people know anything? It's a promotion. I think congratulations are in order."

I have to hand it to her. She knows how to turn enemies into allies.

And she clearly figures she'll be better set with her competition gone. You don't get to be a queen bee by being stupid.

"When would you leave?" asks Alyce, faking being nonchalant. I know her well enough by now to tell.

"Soon." I hesitate. "There's a night train tomorrow, I think." I pretend it's conjecture, but it's fact. Dr. and Mrs. Mauchly showed me the schedule.

"Then let's hit the town tonight!" says Joyce.

"Count me out," I say. "I'm completely discombobulated . . . I have to call home and—"

Joyce interrupts with a playful pout. "You're going to miss your own goodbye party?"

I'm confused. "Aren't you talking about Kay's birthday dinner? I figured you were moving it up since I might be gone by Saturday."

She puts her arm around me. "It's for you, silly. So you don't forget us."

My eyes sting.

"And I know just the place. Somewhere we can *all* have fun," says Joyce, smiling only at Alyce.

Everyone runs off excitedly to get changed. Alyce lingers in the living room. She turns one of the potted plants so its leaves face the window. "Your mind's already made up about this job, isn't it?"

"I . . . I don't know. I guess. It's just . . . everything's happening so fast."

"It's war, Eleanor. I think this is how it's supposed to happen."

I take a seat on the arm of the sofa and let out a huge sigh of air. "I'm scared, Alyce. I was afraid to come here and now I'm afraid to leave."

"You're not the same girl you were two months ago, Eleanor. You've grown."

I let this sink in, wanting to believe it. "I wish you could come with me."

The twittering sounds of girls getting ready reaches us in the living room. The other night, I thought I was ready to finally go out with the gang, but now that it's here, I'm not sure I can go through with it. I'd prefer to stay home and hear more stories about Alyce's family. I still have questions. What does the inside of their church look like? What does her mom cook on Sundays? How many teeth has her little brother lost?

Can you measure a friendship? Like a finite number? Alyce and I have only known each other for ten weeks, as opposed to the six years Trudie and I were friends. But ten weeks feels like a lifetime.

"Hey, Eleanor, do you want to borrow this?" It's Donna, holding up a pink sequined sweater.

"Sure!" I say with forced enthusiasm. "That's so pretty." And with that, the night is written.

Twenty minutes later, I'm pushed into a taxi. Joyce tells the driver to drop us at Eleventh and Market. Once we get downtown, the ten of us gather on the sidewalk, careful to avoid a crowd spilling out the doorway of a brick building.

"Alyce, Eleanor, come with me." We follow Joyce as she squeezes her way through the throng and into a vestibule. Cigarette smoke lingers in the stairwell and I try not to cough. Horns blow musical riffs from somewhere beyond the top of the stairs. Somehow, Joyce elbows her way up, snaking a path through the waiting club-goers. At the top of the stairs, a beefy doorman guards a rope tied across the entrance to a club.

"Howdy, Ray," Joyce says, giving him a peck on the cheek. "You got room for me and my gals? We're ten."

"Anything for Christopher's little sis."

Joyce throws Alyce and me the biggest grin I've ever seen. "You girls grab a table. Look for one between the bandstand and the window. I'll go get the rest of the gang. Welcome to the Downbeat. Guaranteed to make a hepcat out of you yet."

She's so confident. All the girls are. But the Mauchlys, General Gillon, and the deputy director chose me. They think *I* can do this. Not the others. If I'm not brave enough to even walk into a jazz club, then how am I supposed to hold my own at an army base?

Alyce turns to me. "Ready?"

"Ready as I'll ever be."

Inside the club, everything is shrouded in a gray, smoky haze. People sit at tables or dance. Negroes. Whites. All mixed together like a salad. Four musicians play onstage. A fifth guy on vocals, a bar apron around his waist, is holding the microphone so close to his lips he looks like he could swallow the darn thing.

We find a spot right by the window, like Joyce wanted. The water-ringed wood surface is still sticky from the people who sat there before us. I fiddle with a tented table sign. Alyce bobs her head to the music. "I don't understand what he's saying," I say.

"He's scatting." She lifts those eyebrows higher. "It's bebop. You know, like Louis Armstrong?"

I draw a blank. I know he's a trumpeter, but I'm not familiar with his music. In fact, I don't know much about jazz at all.

"Instead of soloing on the trumpet, Armstrong started singing nonsense words to try and imitate the sounds of his instrument. Now everyone's doing it."

It's infectious. I drum my hands on the top of the table, not caring about the stickiness. Like in swing, this music is syncopated, only quicker, as if the off notes, the nonmelodic ones, are being played in double time. When the singer stops, the band gets back into it, louder, attacking, releasing, then embellishing. I can't find the pattern—it's random, unpredictable—but I don't care. I lose myself waiting for the next surprising note to come.

The rest of our group arrives and the girls squeeze around Alyce and me, some two to a chair, because there aren't enough seats.

The trumpet player introduces the rest of the band. The names float by me like birds. Red on piano. Chick on drums. Percy on bass. "And let's give a hand for bartender Mac, who unfortunately has to get back to work."

The room applauds and whoops.

Then the trumpeter says, "And I'm Dizzy." He goes back to blow-ing. His cheeks seem impossible, puffed out like bellows.

Most of our group gets up to dance. Joyce motions for me to come. I shake my head. I'll just look ridiculous.

"*No* is not in the vocabulary tonight," she insists.

Everyone out there does look like they're having fun . . . I turn to see if Alyce will come, too, but she has her back to me. She's talking to a handsome, lanky boy, brown like she is, with a polka-dotted bow tie. He's leaning into her ear and she's laughing at something he says. Lucky her. They head to the dance floor and I join the others.

We girls form a line. Joyce leads us in some crazy steps. Right foot over left, left foot back, right foot returns to original position to form a square. Raise your hands up in the air, shake them out, shout *Hey!* I try to follow, but I mess up. I move right when I'm supposed to go left.

But I keep at it. Soon, I'm in sync with Joyce, moving my arms and legs, picturing colors—reds, hot pinks, yellows, and oranges—as each note erupts out of Dizzy's horn. I'm wild and free.

Alyce and the bow tie boy are dancing near us. Things are heat-ing up between them. He's got her in a tight wrap, pressing himself to her as he leads. I can't see her face. Meanwhile, Joyce adds a fancy twirl after shouting "Hey!" and I do it perfectly. Alyce moves right into my sight line. She and her partner have some space between them now, their hands held together as they swivel on the balls of their feet. Wait. Now he's pulling her back in, his hands on her waist. She wrig-gles away, clearly not wanting to dance like that. She catches my eye, peeved. *Help*, she mouths. I move toward her just as he reaches around and forcefully pulls her to his chest.

His face goes slack. Now he's hopping on one leg and holding his crotch in pain.

I think she just kneed him!

There's a loud crashing sound. Chick on his drum cymbals? No. The stanchions on either side of the rope at the front entrance have fallen to the floor. Six cops storm in.

"It's a raid!" yells a woman behind me.

People scatter to the winds. Panicked screams blast in my ears. A heel digs into the top of my foot. It smarts like the dickens.

Someone grabs my hand. Joyce.

"This way!" She heads toward the bar.

"Alyce! Where's Alyce?" I call.

"I can't hear you!" shouts Joyce.

I'm jostled on both sides. Cold beer spills on my sweater. Donna's borrowed sweater.

I lose Joyce. I scream her name, but I can't spot the back of her head.

There's a narrow pathway between two tables. If I can just squeeze through there, I'll be able to get to the bar area. But I don't get far before someone shoves the table on my right, trapping me. I try to push one of the tables out of the way, but there are too many people and too much furniture hemming me in.

Directly in front of me, a mustached cop grabs a Negro woman.

She looks young like me. "Show me something with your name and birthday on it. A library card. Anything."

Her hand trembles, rummaging in her purse.

Mercy! Are they detaining minors? This can't happen. I'm supposed to leave tomorrow! I push the table again, but it won't budge.

One of the musicians, Percy maybe, sticks his arm through the crook of the girl's elbow. "Come on, Ida. These coppers aren't even legit."

The so-called cop raises his billy club. "Where do you think you're going?"

Percy stops. "Pardon me, sir. No one's done anything wrong here. What division did you say you were from?"

"Detective, Crime Prevention," the man says curtly.

The frightened girl produces a piece of paper, which seems to pass muster. The detective nods and moves on, his handcuffs at the ready. "No underage drinking allowed!"

Now I'm really scared. If I'm arrested, not only will I be detained, I'll be in major trouble with the WAAC. They'll kick me out. Then I'll never get to go to California. Bending my knees, I use my entire weight, thrusting my shoulder against the edge of the table. Grunting and groaning, I manage to create a little space, enough to duck under. I remember my line to Mrs. Mauchly about wondering what it feels like to crawl around without stockings. It hurts.

"Whoa, whoa, whoa," says a voice. Is that directed at me? No. When I stand, a white gentleman has approached the detective.

Everything about him is loose: his mop-topped hair, pants, and untucked shirt. "What seems to be the problem?"

"Nat Segall, you're under arrest for serving minors." The detective grabs his wrists.

"Bullshit!" yells Nat. "Why aren't you up at the Warwick? That's full of teenagers." He squirms, trying to make it harder to cuff him.

"Oh, my mistake. I get it. Those customers are all white."

Is that the real reason for this raid? The Downbeat is integrated?

It takes three detectives to get the handcuffs on him, but he's still yelling. "This is my establishment, and I can serve who the hell I want! Mac! Call my lawyer."

The bartender barrels through. "Where are you taking him?"

No answer as they lead Nat out the front. Around me, the chaos continues. Chairs topple. I almost fall on my face when I step on a wooden drumstick spinning on the floor.

Then a warm breath hisses into my ear. "Joyce sent me." It's Ray, her brother's friend who was working the rope. "The rest of your group is out back."

He pushes people aside, leading me behind the bar, through the kitchen, past crates of liquor bottles, an open meat locker, and a sink full of dirty glasses where the water is still running. No one has bothered to turn off the faucet. Finally, I emerge into a dead-end alley where eight PCS girls are huddled together, shivering despite the hot summer night. Marjorie stands alone, off to the side. Her dress is torn at the hem and there's a trail of black eyeliner down her cheek. I almost feel sorry for her. Almost.

"You'll be fine here." Ray points down the alley. "The only way in or out is that locked gate. I'll come get you girls when the club is cleared." He darts back into the service door.

"Eleanor, thank goodness!" exclaims Joyce. "I thought they were going to take all the minors away!"

"Me too!" I'm a bit breathless. "There was a girl . . . right in front of me . . . who almost got caught, but I think this whole thing is just a pretext for—"

Alyce interrupts me with a fierce hug. We're both shaking. "I've never been so scared," she says.

Does she suspect, like I do, that the Downbeat was targeted because they serve Negroes? I pull away and try to read her face. There's no light in the alley save for the slice coming out the open kitchen door.

"I thought all us colored folks would get rounded up for sure."

I'm grateful for her frankness and sad for every Negro here tonight. "This town is full of bigots. They hate any place that caters to a mixed clientele. The owner said as much when they were dragging him off."

She shakes her head in disgust. "You sure you're still too scared to leave Philadelphia?"

"I guess it doesn't matter. There's probably intolerance in the California desert, too. The war is everywhere, isn't it?"

We're both quiet, listening to the approaching sirens, trying not to smell the garbage cans nearby.

"It's even on the dance floor," says Alyce.

She's not talking about the raid now. "What happened with that boy in the bow tie?"

"He got too fresh, so I gave him the heave-ho."

"All four feet eleven of you."

She grins at me. "It's basic physics. Force equals mass times acceleration."

"Of course." I slap my forehead in jest. "A kick increases in speed as it gets closer to the target."

"Yep. A direct hit."

Our laughter is a welcome sound, echoing into the dark night.

# 14.

At 0730, the girls head off to lab as always. To see them stroll down
Locust Walk, knowing I'll never be part of that group again, makes
my throat ache. I won't miss sparring with Marjorie, though. I watch
until the back of Alyce's sweater turns a corner, then walk the opposite direction to the bus stop. I can't stop reliving the raid—the fear on
that girl's face as she searched for identification, the grip of Ray's hand
on my arm leading me to safety. I'm so lost in the memories, I nearly
miss my stop.

When I do get off at Chestnut and Fifth, I straighten the front of
my blouse, dark like Deputy Director Hayden requested. The downtown branch of the US Army Recruitment Office is easy to spot.
Though the building is dwarfed by the taller buildings surrounding it,
there are round emblems of each branch of the military mounted on the
stucco: Army and Air Corps, Navy, Marines, Coast Guard. I expect to
see lines of young men around the block, but there aren't. Last
December, when Mom, Dad, and I drove into town to see one of his
doctors, enlistees heading out to basic training snaked from the street

all the way to the train tracks. How eager and naive they all looked in their regular haircuts and civvies, overnight bags in hand.

I steady my breath and push the glass door open.

Two pimply-faced boys filling out their applications look up when I walk in, then go back to their paperwork.

"Sign-ups for WAAC and WAVES is at our West Philly location," says a mustached gentleman in a uniform, sitting behind a desk. His badge reads STAFF SERGEANT KELLY.

"Oh. I'm not here for . . . I mean, that's . . ." I stop. Then start again, speaking loudly and clearly. "Deputy Director Hayden sent me."

He stands. "Of course. The security clearance ID. Follow me."

As he leads me to a door behind his desk, one of the boys calls out, "Don't get P-W-O-P." Pregnant without permission. The two descend into hysterics.

Ever since FDR signed the bill into law establishing an army women's corps, the newspapers have been full of stories by male reporters worried that females in the military will wreak all kinds of sexual havoc on poor unsuspecting servicemen. Petticoat army, they call us. Wackies, too.

Staff Sergeant Kelly doesn't acknowledge the slight, but doesn't say anything in my defense, either. Which only reinforces my resolve. I feel like telling him: You men need our help in this war. Better get used to it.

We enter a hallway where a few other uniformed men are sitting at desks. One's on the telephone. Another is hunched over a desk, peering through a loupe. I follow Kelly into a tiny adjacent room with a file cabinet, standing scale, and a bright red poster taped to the wall. The poster shows a hand wearing a ring with a swastika. Fingers hold a ribbon and a dangling medal, like the kind awarded to those recognized for their military service. This medal has a Normandy cross with a swastika in the center. In black letters, the top of the poster reads AWARD. At the bottom, it says FOR CARELESS TALK. And underneath in smaller letters, it says DON'T DISCUSS TROOP MOVEMENTS, SHIP SAILINGS, WAR EQUIPMENT.

The sergeant notices me staring at the poster. "Can't be too careful. What with spies landing on the beaches of Long Island."

I read about that. Eight Germans, all of whom spoke perfect English, arrived by submarine, coming ashore on a dinghy—four in New York, four in Florida—burying enough boxes of explosives in the sand to sabotage American factories for the next two years. Turns out they were more stupid than dangerous, and they ended up blabbing to enough people that they were caught right away.

"Mark my words. They'll all get the chair," he said.

I shiver at the idea. Who ever thought words could be so dangerous? Spoken accidentally or on purpose. It makes me think about name-calling. That man on the train yelling "alien" at the woman from Germantown. The Nazis printing posters saying Jews are "lice." Marjorie calling FDR a "Jew lover." It's like fighting words are becoming acceptable. Normalized, even.

"I'll need your weight and height."

The red poster is directly above the scale. Unable to look at the frightening Nazi symbol any longer, I close my eyes and step on.

I hear him sliding the little silver weight across the top. I smell his coffee breath. Then a metallic clanking as he raises the height bar and rests it over my head.

I don't open my eyes until I step off the scale and turn to face him.

"Back against the wall, please." He holds up a 35 mm Kodak and takes my picture.

"Right hand, please," he continues, all business.

Using the top of the cabinet as a desk, he rests a wooden box on it, about the size of a checkers game. Inside are papers, a variety of inkwells, and a roller brush. He rubs the roller brush back and forth through a dollop of ink, then paints the soft part of my fingertips black. One by one, he roughly pushes each of my fingers onto a piece of paper, making five little oval prints. "You'll find some water and tissue to wipe your hands out front. Wait there."

There are no chairs. This is a place without women in mind, with our skirts and heels. I have to stand near the two boys as they snicker and stare at my chest. Crossing my arms to cover myself, I smell the sickly-sweet pomade in their hair. Also their sweat. They're nervous like me. The staff sergeant comes out a few minutes later but doesn't acknowledge me. He looks over the boys' applications, asks them to make a few corrections, then tells them which induction center they'll be assigned to. He musters up the same amount of enthusiasm he gave to me. At least he's not playing favorites.

They leave to spend their last few nights as civilians. It seems they're properly sober about the prospect because they don't give me any hassle on the way out.

After nearly an hour of watching Kelly process three more boys, when I'm just about to give in and sit on the floor, another officer comes out.

"Eleanor Schiff?"

Across the front of the card is stamped CLEARANCE LEVEL 2. Underneath is my photo and my name.

The staff sergeant rests his pencil and looks up. "Good luck to you, miss."

"Good luck to us all," I say.

Where to now? Reading Terminal is close by. I could go home to Jenkintown to say goodbye to Mom and Dad in person, but I think seeing them will just make me lose my nerve. No, I'll call them from the phone in the frat house.

I know I have to pack, but it's not even 10:00 a.m. There are hours to go before my 8:00 p.m. train. Instead of taking the trolley back to Sigma Chi, I decide to walk. I want to touch the sidewalks of Philly one last time. Meandering up Chestnut Street, I soon leave the suit-and-tie bustle of downtown office life and enter the residential section. The red-brick row houses all have white shutters and remind me of revolutionary soldiers standing proudly at attention. A man walks his dog on a leash. A young mother pushes a baby carriage. I drink it all in, these little signs of domesticity. I don't know when I'll see my hometown again.

A large lemon tree shades a victory garden in someone's front garden. I pause a moment to roll up my sleeves and cool down. At eleven o'clock in the morning, it's already steamy, as if someone just took a giant shower over the entire Rittenhouse Square area. Staring up at the tree bursting with ripe lemons gives me an idea. What's the rule Mom always said? If a tree branch is hanging over a public walkway, you can take the fruit? I pick as many low-hanging lemons as I can, untucking my blouse and scooping it upward to make the shape of a bowl. I fit a few more into my pocketbook.

By the time I reach campus, I'm dripping with sweat. Inside the frat house, Mrs. Goldstine's private door is ajar, her bed tightly made. She must be out. I've never wondered what she does during the day when we're at lab. Cleans and shops, I suppose. It's funny. Now that I'm leaving, I wonder if she'll mourn my departure like she did her boys.

I dump the lemons into a bowl, then carry the fan from the dining room into the kitchen. Now I'm ready to bake.

After that awful day when Dad collapsed in my room, I couldn't look at my play oven, nor could I eat a brownie. When I was big enough to use the main kitchen, I taught myself how to make a treat that was the total opposite of brownies in color, taste, and smell. Lemon bars.

I break two margarine capsules and mix the white fat with the liquid yellow coloring that comes with it. Some people say not having butter is the worst part of this war, but the fake stuff doesn't taste that bad. I combine this with flour, sugar, and salt to make a nice dough. I press it flat onto the bottom of a pan and set the oven timer for twenty minutes. While the crust is baking, I cut and squeeze the lemons until I have a cup's worth of juice. There are three left over, which I leave on the counter in exchange for taking Mrs. Goldstine's sugar rations. Who doesn't appreciate a spot of sun on dull Formica? Then I sift more sugar and flour together, whisk in six eggs and the lemon juice. The timer dings. I remove the hot pan and pour in the gooey yellow filling. Back into the oven for another twenty-five minutes.

I wash the bowls and wipe the counter. Then I go upstairs and strip my bed, carrying my sheets and bath towel back down to the kitchen. I throw everything into the Automagic washer.

I dial my parents from the phone in the hallway.

"Dad's napping," Mom tells me. This is a blessing. I'd probably cry just hearing his slurry voice.

"Any news on Uncle Azriel and Aunt Roza?" I ask.

"Sadly, I have nothing to report. Honey, hold on a sec. You can put that in the study, Mabel."

Mabel is the nurse Mom hired to help Dad. "How's it going with her?"

"She drives me crazy, telling me what to do. Lift him up from a chair this way. Make sure his arm can rest on the pillow that way. Don't speak too fast around him." She pauses. "But Dad likes her."

"You'll always be the woman of the house, Mom."

"Oh, stop." I hear the smile in her voice again. "Anything new on your end?"

"Yes, actually. The army is sending me out west to recruit students at UCLA." I thought long and hard about this, knowing I couldn't very well say they were sending me to the Mojave Desert. At least the California part is true. Also, I figured a move between universities made sense. But all these lies are weighing on me. Spies must experience this when it comes to their own families. They're working for the greater good, but by not talking about their job, they're betraying the trust of the ones they love the most.

Then of course there's the big lie, how I caused Dad's stroke and have been secretly pursuing math all my life. I wonder if after the war is over, I'll ever be able to come clean.

"That sounds exciting! I'm sure you and the girls will love seeing the country through the window of a train."

"It's just me going."

"Without a chaperone?"

I hesitate. Mrs. Mauchly must have forgotten I was the lone high schooler in the group when she handed me my train ticket because she didn't mention someone accompanying me. I didn't think to ask, either. I was too stunned by their offer and the idea of leaving Philadelphia.

"I don't like it, Eleanor."

"This war is forcing us all to do things differently. We have to throw the old rules out the window." I laugh, trying to make light of my traveling alone.

I hear her banging pots in the kitchen. "I suppose they have faith in you, or they wouldn't be giving you this transfer."

"Exactly! They aren't worried at all."

"They're not your mother." She sighs. "Call us when you change trains in Chicago and again when you get to UCLA. Do you have any spending money left?"

"I still have most of what Uncle Herman gave me when he dropped me off." Thanks to all those Saturday nights staying home. "And I'll be sure to take some more out of my paycheck if I need it."

"Be careful, Eleanor."

"Thanks, Mom." My voice catches. "Everything's going to be fine." The words are for my benefit as much as hers.

The timer dings and the lemon bars are done. Boy, do they smell divine. My spirits lift as I carry them with oven mitts into my room to cool.

Now, for the packing. It takes all of fifteen minutes. Most of the clothes I brought here aren't army base attire. I need more pants! Hopefully, they'll issue me a few uniform sets when I arrive. I leave my one nice dress in the closet. Maybe it'll fit another girl. I'm sure Mauchly's already putting out the all-call to math teachers. She said something about expanding the ballistics lab to get more shifts in, now that we have the differential analyzer.

I open the little desk Alyce and I share and pull out a sheet of paper and a pen.

*Alyce, no one needs to know these lemon bars exist if you don't feel like sharing, hee hee. Little-known fact: They won first prize at the Jenkintown Library bake sale. Stay strong (you already are, but as we said last night, the war is everywhere). Always remember: No one messes with the Newton Computin' Crew.*

*I'll write as soon as I get there.*

*Eleanor*

The late-afternoon sun dips below the window in our room. I won't wait for everyone to return from the lab. A long, drawn-out goodbye will be too painful.

Before I cover the lemon bars with one of my scarves, I use a kitchen knife to cut squares. Then I remove one piece and wrap it in a hankie and leave it in front of Mrs. Goldstine's door.

So this is it, then. Goodbye, Sigma Chi House. In the living room, I touch the Eleanor Roosevelt quote from the hanging fraternity crest, then kiss my hand.

Aunt Jona would laugh at me. "It's not a mezuzah!" she'd say. But I do it anyway, connecting my mind and heart to E.R., this place, and the people in it.

I carry my suitcase down Locust Walk to Thirty-Eighth Street and hail a taxi.

"Where to, miss?" asks the driver in a heavy Irish brogue.

I glance out the window for one last look at the trees. "The great unknown."

# 15.

I always get a tiny thrill when I approach the Greek-columned facade of the train station. But all my visits up until now have been with family for short trips to Atlantic City or Boston to see a specialist for Dad. Being here on my own is a whole different experience. Inside, I'm dwarfed by the nearly hundred-foot-high coffered ceilings. The marble flooring, decorative moldings, and dangling art deco light fixtures all make me feel like I'm not dressed for the occasion. In my khakis, loafers, and plain white shirt, I suppose I'm not.

Everywhere I look are men in uniform. Hundreds of them. Asleep on the floor with duffels as pillows, stretched out on benches, playing cards at tables. No business folks or families with squawking babies, like you usually see at 30th Street Station. I'm the only female for miles! Trudie and Marjorie would take this as a flirting opportunity. I see it as unbearable. I need to count something. Ten columns on either side of the atrium. Twenty-eight squares of marble flooring from end to end. If each square is 24″ by 24″, then the floor is 56 feet long, and the horizontal columns are placed every 5.6 feet.

When I feel calm, I head to the food counter. I order a cup of soup, two sandwiches, an apple, and an orange.

"You want a brownie with that, miss?" The man seems eager to get rid of the basketful of treats individually wrapped in wax paper next to the cash register.

I avert my eyes from the brownies and all the bad feelings they represent. "No dessert, thanks."

While I'm waiting for the food, I take out an old issue of *Ladies' Home Journal* from my bag. The first thing I see is an ad for Pullman trains. The headline reads: *Stay Home.* The copy explains that summer vacationers might have to wait weeks for railroad reservations. That first priority is being given to the military. They regret to say so, but pleasure travel will be something to look forward to, rather than to enjoy right now.

So that's the reason for this sea of servicemen.

When my meal finally comes out on a tray, I feel eyes on me from the tables in the eating area. A broad-shouldered soldier stands up, goaded on by his buddies. "Come rest your weary gams over here." He offers me his seat, extending his arm in a flourish. His tablemates laugh. No chance I'm sitting over there.

I scan the packed atrium. My instinct is to find a quiet, out-of-the-way spot to eat, but that probably wouldn't be ideal. What if I get hassled by a soldier and no one can see? No, I need to be in the midst of things. That's the safest bet. There's an empty corner of the floor near a bench occupied by eight soldiers playing cards.

They're deep into the game when I sit cross-legged on the marble. Only one jug-eared boy clocks me, then goes back to his hand. So far so good. I take a bite of my sandwich and open up my magazine again. I always go right to the If You Ask Me page, Eleanor Roosevelt's guest column. Sometimes the questions are dumb, such as why has there never been a cat as a White House pet, to which E.R. replied, it seems to me that cats aren't quite as companionable as dogs and have a rather reserved disposition. But there's a doozy of a question in there today. Someone asked Eleanor Roosevelt if she has colored blood in her family because she seems to derive so much pleasure from associating with colored folks. I'm nervous to read her response. What if she says something negative about Negroes? How would that make me feel about E.R.? Her answer is that she doesn't know of any colored blood in her family, but she feels that if we go back far enough, we will find that we all stem from the same beginnings. Then she says something even more amazing. She would have no objection if a child of hers chose a friend of another race or creed. If only everyone in the world felt like E.R. does.

The card-playing boys start whooping it up. They're playing pinochle. It's my parents' and aunt and uncle's favorite thing to do on Shabbos. Despite their colorful language, the boys seem harmless enough. I put down my magazine and steal a look. The jug-eared one sees me watching and the tips of his ears turn pink. In tenth grade, I had a painful crush on Eugene Miller. I wrote his name in the margins of my scratch paper for months. The guy never gave me so much as a glance. But Jug Ears here doesn't seem like the others. It gives me hope. Maybe I *can* be someone's girl one day.

One of the soldiers collects the cards, and they all get up, wrestling and walking at the same time, like puppies. Jug Ears turns back for one last glance. I give him a tiny smile and get back to my reading.

More men come and take their place, but I concentrate on the magazine's latest installment of *Frenchman's Creek* by Daphne du Maurier. By the time I look up, it's 7:40 on the giant wall clock. My train! I seize my bag and dash downstairs to the platform.

It's even more busy below. Soldiers shout and scurry every which way. If they're not in civvies, they're either starting furlough or returning for duty. I'm checking my ticket, trying to find the car number, and crash into someone.

"I'm so sorry. I didn't see—" I shut my mouth. Two crutches are in front of my eyes. And one leg. Mortification rains down on me.

The soldier gives a wan smile. "You didn't bump me too hard. I'm still standing."

"Dusty!"

An older couple and young girl, about ten years old, are making their way toward him. He hobbles in their direction to meet them halfway. I watch the soldier from behind, staring at where his leg should be. How many more men will return home like that?

The soldier reaches his parents, and they grip him hard. The little girl waves a cardboard sign, hoping her brother will notice, but his eyes are closed over his father's shoulder. The sign has a crude drawing of an airplane and says WELCOME HOME, DUSTY. OUR MIDWAY BATTLE HERO!

I used to skip over the names of Pearl Harbor casualties in the newspaper, thinking that would shield me from feeling sad. Those days are gone. This is a real, injured boy. America borrowed him and returned him, but the war stole something for itself. What a price to pay for freedom. And yet. This war has allowed me to start another chapter in my life. It's an uncomfortable mix of a sense of adventure and guilt.

The train itself has seen better days. Its normally shiny, tawny-colored exterior looks dull and rusted, nothing like the photo in the Pullman ad. The conductor punches my ticket and helps me onto the step. At least the interior is maintained nicely. I head left, to the second-class coaches. A soldier is putting his bag on a shelf above his upholstered seat, which I see is already reclined. Jeepers. This isn't some quick commuter jaunt from Jenkintown to Reading Terminal. It's two days until I make my connection in Chicago and then another three to the West Coast. How am I going to sleep at a 120-degree obtuse angle for five nights? I'll arrive in California exhausted and stiff as a starched shirt.

"May I help you, miss?" says a porter, his cap neatly framing a well-lined face.

"I'm just trying to find my seat." I show him my ticket.

"This is for a roomette. Car twelve."

"It is? I mean, yes, of course." I start to head down the train, then realize I have no idea where to go. "Um, excuse me, could you show me there?"

The porter nods and even carries my bag all the way through until we reach the sleeper cars. I peek into mine. One small sofa seat on the right, a sink and toilet on the left, and over the window, a curved compartment where the bed is stored. Mrs. Mauchly sprang for a private berth! Bless her soul.

After he puts my bag on a low shelf, he waits by the door. "Will that be all, miss?"

"Yes, thank you."

Why isn't he leaving? Doesn't he have more passengers to help?

Then I remember. Whenever we went to Atlantic City, Dad always gave the porters a coin or two. I place a quarter in his hand, feeling like a real adult for the first time.

"Have a nice trip," he says, touching the gold cord on the brim of his cap.

Minutes later, the train pulls out of the station. I nearly fall over but manage to grip the window curtain. The compartment jerks left and right, but finally the noise beneath my feet settles into a gentle rocking and I feel steady. I settle in, hanging up a few shirts and taking out my cosmetic bag. When my teeth are brushed, my pajamas on, I try to figure out how to lower the bed. There's a handle at the top of the curved cover, but I can't reach it. The sofa seat is bolted down and won't budge, otherwise I could move it closer and stand on top. I search in the corners. There must be a tool or something around here. Or maybe the porter is supposed to make up my bed?

I pop my head out the door to see if I can spot my wrinkled friend.

No porter in sight, but two enlisted men are making their way down the corridor, swaying. From this distance, I can't tell if the movement of the train is to blame or if they're drunk. They get closer and I recognize one of them. The broad-shouldered soldier who offered me his seat when I was ordering food. "Well, isn't thisss a coincidence?"

Definitely drunk. I pull my robe tighter and step back.

His pal licks his lips. "Hey, cookie."

"Thisss one's mine," the broad-shouldered one tells his friend. "I'll meet you later in the dining car." The next thing I know, he's stumbled into my berth and shut the door.

I back up until I can't back up any farther. "Get out of here!" But the train wheels are loud and my shouting voice isn't.

He just laughs. "You probably think I followed you here."

Did he?

I try to dart around him. But he blocks the exit. "Don't be scared. I just want to get to know you. Where you headin'? Chicago? Another coincidence. 'Cuz that'sss where I live."

He comes closer. He reeks of alcohol. "What kind of a guy would let a dainty little number like you travel alone?" His hands reach for me.

He must weigh 200 pounds. I'm 104. Basic physics, according to Alyce. I bring my knee up hard in between his legs. His eyes go wide. He falters, grabbing his crotch. I push by him, open the door, and run.

Six cars down I find the porter, setting up someone else's bed. "Help . . . there's a man . . . my roomette." My voice breaks. "Please hurry."

Quickly, the porter makes his way through the vestibules and back to my compartment. I'm too scared to look. What if the soldier comes charging out like an angry bull?

The porter goes in first. "No sign of anyone, miss."

Cautiously, I step in. Nothing.

He hands me a key. "Lock it from the inside. No one will be able to get in unless you let them." I smile weakly, feeling a bit better. "Let's get you set up for the night." He then turns toward the curved cupboard. He pulls out a short stick from his belt, which opens three more lengths like a telescope. It has a small brass piece at the end that fits perfectly under the handle of the bed compartment. The bed lowers easily, transforming into a hanging platform about three feet from the floor. As he fits the bottom sheet over the mattress, he says, "I'm sorry about the delay in getting to you this evening, miss. I'll come sooner tomorrow"

I grip the key so hard it makes dents in my palm. "I can't thank you enough . . ." I pause, glancing at his name tag. "Lester. Um, can you wait a minute?" I dig into my purse and tip him double. I need him to keep watch, this real-life version of a guardian angel.

I lock the door. With shaky legs, I use the fold-up stool Lester left me and maneuver myself onto the platform. Once I crawl under the sheets, I keep replaying what happened. I see Broad Shoulders coming toward me. Smell his foul breath. Then I have a more terrible thought. I could be going from the frying pan into the fire, heading to an army base where I'll be trapped among more soldiers. At least with a train, you can step off.

I'll never get to sleep. I try counting the folds of the curtain but it's not folded evenly. Instead, I mentally recite the formula for Newton's second law of motion. Force equals mass times acceleration, force equals mass times acceleration. Only when I hear Alyce's voice reciting it alongside me, in stereophonic sound, do I finally drift off.

# 16.

For the rest of the trip, when they ring the chime for meals, I fill out my menu and Lester brings me food inside the compartment. Dinner is quite pricey at $1.24, so I skip lunch and eat voraciously. Bread rolls, chicken and mushroom patties, crab salad, Dover sole, julienned vegetables.

I only go out of my berth to take some fresh air, but don't linger. It's not bad, because I can watch the world go by out my window. Small towns with the requisite church spires, rolling hills, and telephone poles. Big cities where smokestacks exhale their white plumes. West across Pennsylvania to Pittsburgh, then on to Ohio. In Orrville, three boys race alongside us on their bicycles for as long as their little legs can keep up. At the Cleveland station, a long line of railroad cars glides past filled with armored tanks. It's hard to fathom all the moving parts of this war, the industry of it all, until you see it for yourself. From my sister collecting scraps on the streets of Philadelphia to a factory in the Northeast to an army base in the desert. I'm part of this great big machine, too.

In Indiana, we stop at Fort Wayne and the train lets out so many soldiers I think we must be plumb empty. Until an hour later when a bunch of new ones embark and we're back to capacity. I watch a father wave bravely to his son, then as we pull out of the station, the father's head falls into his hands, his shoulders shaking with sorrow. So many goodbyes. The ones remaining aren't going into combat, but not knowing what's happening with your child has its own set of hardships.

After breakfast on the second morning, when the conductor calls, "Dearborn Station, Chicago," I don't want to get off. But I have to make my connection. Didn't Broad Shoulders say he was traveling to Chicago? I peek out my door at the men swarming the passageway. I don't see his distinctive shape anywhere, but everyone is packed in like cans of beans in a bomb shelter so it's hard to tell. What if he's lying in wait for me to disembark? I wait another twenty minutes, until the conductor yells last call and I have no choice but to exit.

I find Lester cleaning an empty roomette. Suitcase in hand, I humbly ask him one last favor. "Can you please walk me to the train bound for Los Angeles?"

"I'm not supposed to leave my post, miss." He looks around. "But I suppose I can point you in the right direction."

That'll have to do. As the two of us step onto the platform, we see a line of GIs at a newsstand. I freeze. Broad Shoulders is seventh from the front.

"Something wrong, miss?"

I point. "That's him. The man who accosted me."

Lester nods. He shows me where the north stairway is. "Take that to the street level and follow signs for the Santa Fe Line. Then you'll come back down some stairs to a different platform. It's about a six-minute walk from here."

I tip him one final time and head north. But after about two hundred feet I stop and turn around to watch. Lester speaks to the conductor and goes back inside the train. The conductor finds a guard. And the two of them, conductor and guard, sandwich Broad Shoulders as he's paying for a newspaper. He shakes his head, waves his arms. More words are exchanged. They each take one of his elbows and escort him out of the line. No need to see any more. Whether he talks his way out of the predicament or not, it doesn't matter. He's been confronted, and that's satisfaction enough.

That took a lot of guts for Lester, a Negro, to tell a white conductor that a white soldier did something wrong.

Once I locate my platform, I find a phone booth and call Mom as promised.

I leave out the part about the soldier. But I tell her all about Lester.


The Super Chief train is fancier than the one I took from Philadelphia. Also, it's only about a quarter full, which thankfully means fewer soldiers. After I unpack my clothes, I notice a bump in the inside zipper of my Samsonite. What in the world?

There's a pamphlet entitled "Traveling the American West." Did Lester slip it in when I wasn't looking? A note falls out.

*I "borrowed" this from the library at U Penn. You*
*can return it when you come back. Thought it might be*
*fun for you to follow along with the sights.*

*Miss you already,*

*Alyce*

She's too much. How she managed to get from lab to the library to Sigma Chi before I returned from the recruitment office is a mystery. I'm grinning from ear to ear with newfound confidence. Alyce is with me! Pamphlet in hand, I venture out to the observation car. I figure I can always knee someone in broad daylight if I have to.

All the chairs are upholstered in a turquoise-and-copper zigzag pattern. One wall has a painted mural of an Indian village while another is lined with books, held in place by a thick, taut rope across the middle of each shelf. But mostly the room is all windows for enjoying the view. Two GIs smoke and play checkers and there's one civilian couple sitting together, a man and a woman, their hats touching as they speak softly back and forth. A third soldier writes a letter at a desk. That gives me an idea to take notes on what I see on this trip so I can write Alyce all about it.

The booklet she gave me says there are many types of geological formations in the western United States. The names are strange yet fun: mesas, buttes, spires, sandstone fins, hoodoos. I'd like to match the photographs to what I see outside the train windows. But it's just fields and fields of wheat at the moment. I don't know what

I was thinking—that once we left Chicago, we'd be in the West? It seems most of Illinois is a vast expanse of crops. Though the landscape doesn't change much when we roll through Kansas, either, I appreciate the great emptiness. This is where our bread is buttered (or oleo'd) figuratively and literally. As the sun sets, the fields turn golden. Even the green cornstalks shimmer. A carpet of sustenance for the nation.

That evening, I ask my new porter for a key (definitely not as friendly as Lester), and though I lock my berth from the inside, it's not necessary. No one bothers me. I even eat in the dining car, feeling like a real lady, despite no dress and hat. With each passing hour, Broad Shoulders and Nervous Nellie begin to fade from view.

On the second day, I contemplate taking a shower. When I discover it's inside the barber compartment where two men are getting shaved, I nix the idea. I can hear Alyce now. "Come on, Eleanor. Walk right in and use that shower. The men don't own it." And my reply: "How about an anonymous letter instead: Dear Atchison, Topeka and Santa Fe Railway, have you thought about creating a women's hairdresser compartment?"

Late that afternoon, we hit Colorado, my first official western state. Still no interesting rock shapes yet. But oh, the mountains! *For purple mountain majesties.* I never understood what that described until now. It's the way the light hits the slopes and valleys. I vaguely remember something about the songwriter visiting Pikes Peak and writing a poem. I look up Pikes Peak in my pamphlet. Yes, it's part of the Rockies in Colorado. I put this in my notes for Alyce and add: *America the Beautiful. It truly is something worth fighting for.*

After long stretches of wooden ranch fencing and red barns, we cross into New Mexico. The terrain changes precipitously. All the way through Arizona, I spend every moment in the observation car finding the strange, earthly shapes in the pamphlet. Hoodoos are my favorite, pinnacles of reddish sandstone with a harder rock sitting on top like a hat. Hundreds of years of erosion formed them. I even spot a toadstool hoodoo, which looks like its hat could topple off any minute.

By the time we pull into Los Angeles, my excitement at reaching the end of the line is palpable. A quick ride to Muroc, then we'll arrive! I straighten my shoulders just like Alyce does and leap off the train. After locating a mailbox to send back the pamphlet and my letter to Alyce, I find a pay phone and call Mom. It takes a few minutes for the operator to call me back with the connection.

Now that I'm really at the other end of the country, I feel farther away from home than ever. I don't have time to be sad, though, because after Mom thanks God for delivering me safely, she peppers me with questions. "No, UCLA is not the same size as U Penn," I answer. It's bigger. I did my homework, knowing she'd want to know. "Yes, my dorm room is within walking distance to the class I'll be working in." I have no idea about this, but it reassures her. "Yes, it's less humid here in California." In fact, it's drier than I could have imagined. And I suspect it's about to get worse. I add another nickel, giving me enough time to tell her one true statement: "I miss you and

Dad and Sarah so much." I hang up before she can hear the announcement for the next train and discover I'm not at UCLA at all.

I have a whole car to myself on the two-hour train ride to Muroc. Drifting in and out of sleep, I imagine the sprawling complex that awaits me on the other end. Muroc Army Air Base, a place of innovation and learning. Lecture halls, classrooms, enormous hangars, radio towers. Military officers and their staff darting purposefully to and fro. I'll be greeted with a comfortable jeep to transport me. Waiting inside the jeep will sit the desert version of Mrs. Mauchly, a crisply uniformed woman, eager to tell me the lay of the land. Then when we arrive, the welcoming committee will whisk me off to my commanding officer, a gentle giant of a man, who'll greet me with a firm handshake and explain my duties. I'll salute him and get down to work.

At one point, my eyes flutter open and I see only one color passing by the window. Beige. Hunh. I thought the California desert was like the Sahara, with soft pink sand dunes, sparkling like face powder. This landscape is nothing but low, brittle, beige plants dotting depressing beige dirt.

In the dusk of early evening, we pull to a stop. I'm the only one disembarking. The heat slaps me in the face. The closest I can compare the feeling to is standing in front of our barbecue when the coals are white hot. I'm thirsty immediately.

I take in the view before me. A closed café and a desolate post office and general store, with one dusty truck parked in front. A plaque on the train station wall explains that this spot was originally homesteaded by the Corum brothers, but since there was another town in California named Corum, they reversed the spelling so as not to confuse the postmaster.

This is it? Where's my welcome jeep? My desert Mrs. Mauchly? Determined not to let my disappointment deter me, I walk into the store as a bell jangles over the door.

A middle-aged man smoking a cigar looks up from his newspaper. Canned vegetables crowd the shelves behind him.

"Excuse me, when's the next bus to the army base?"

"Ain't no bus. Sometimes they send a jeep for soldiers coming back from leave, but there's been nothing this afternoon." He picks up the phone mounted on the wall by the register and presses the disconnect lever. "Still dead." He squints at me. "If that's your destination, looks like you'll have to walk."

I gaze at that dusty truck outside, likely his. Even if he could leave his store and drive me there, I know better than to accept a ride with him. "How far is it?"

"Two miles."

That's eight laps around the track at school. With proper sneakers in decent weather, I can walk a mile in 22 minutes. Or about 2.7 mph. But in this heat, I'll need to slow down my pace. I do some mental math. With a 50 percent reduction in speed, walking at 1.35 mph, I'll add another 22 minutes to my time, making the total journey 66 minutes. If I don't collapse first. "Can I buy a Coca-Cola, please?"

He opens a refrigerated case, pops the top, and hands it to me. "You're in luck. The sun's heading down. Any earlier and you'd need about five of those." He points behind him. "It's a straight shot that way. Follow the airstrip lights."

As I open the door to leave, he says, "Stay on the road and don't get too close to the lake beds, mind you. You'll sink right in."

This sounds so obvious that I blurt out an uncharacteristic bit of sass. "I'm sure I'll be able to tell where the water is."

He chuckles. "Suit yourself."

Why don't these ridiculous Samsonites have shoulder straps? After a few minutes, the palm of my hand is so slippery from perspiration that I can hardly grip the suitcase handle. I'm tempted to just leave it on the side of the road. At least my purse can go over the shoulder. It's not long before my heels are raw with chafing and my Coke has been gulped down. That's when I see a large body of water in the distance. Is it blue? I run a few painful steps toward it, but it's no closer. So that's what the man from the liquor store meant! I've never seen a real mirage. I can understand how it might make a person go mad, though.

The sun goes down, but the temperature doesn't. It's as if the ground has been baking all day and even though the oven is turned off, the heat is trapped inside. The only sound is my shoes crunching on the dirt road. It's not pitch-black out so I'm not terrified quite yet. Until I hear the yelping. Like a pack of dogs barking, only higher-pitched and scarier. Wolves? Coyotes? They could be right next to me or miles away, hard to tell. I pray it's the latter. In between the yelping are the chirps of crickets and the screeches of bats. Please let there be no snakes on this road. Don't stop. Keep it at 1.35 mph. Finally, I see the twinkling lights of the landing strip. And nearby, some long, rectangular shapes that must be army buildings. Thank goodness I arrived safely.

"Halt!"

I drop my suitcase. A barrel of a gun points at me. Maybe I spoke too soon.

# 17.

"ID!"

I can't make out the soldier's face in the creeping darkness, but it sounds as if he's trying to make his voice deeper than it is. I fumble in my pocketbook until I find the newly issued ID card.

He shines a flashlight onto it. "You're in building J. Straight on down, then half a klick to the right." He turns away, continuing his patrol.

I don't know what klicks are and it's pitch-black out. "By any chance do you have an extra flashlight?"

"We're only issued one per. But building J is in between the mess and Admin. You can't miss it."

"Is there a lit sign or something so I'll recognize it?"

"You want the enemy to know where we are?" He sounds peeved.

I'm an idiot. "Of course. Nature's blackout curtains."

Maybe he feels guilty because he aims his flashlight beam to show me the way. The light lasts for a hundred feet or so, then goes out like a firefly, and I'm left in utter darkness. Right away, I trip, landing hard on my hands and knees. I cry out, but he doesn't come to my aid.

I suppose that's a good thing. This Rosie needs to toughen up. But it doesn't stop me from feeling sorry for myself and my throbbing knee. I tread more lightly, feeling for bushes with the toe of my loafers, making the short walk much longer than it would have been had I arrived in the daytime.

The sound of a radio playing "Don't Sit Under the Apple Tree" comes from one of the barracks. Could this be "J"? Indeed, it's between two other buildings, but I have no idea if they're the mess and Admin, whatever those are. I could cross another dirt path to check, but I'm hallucinating pillows and sheets by this point.

I open the door. Men's hooting and whistles greet me. "Hi, sugar, you rationed?"

Wrong barrack.

"Of course, she's got a steady. A looker like that."

I actually laugh. The fact that they think I look good after a five-day train ride, a desert trek, hair that a comb wouldn't even pass through, and a bloody knee is the funniest thing I've heard in a long time. I'm still laughing when a sweet-faced recruit who seems as out of place as I do volunteers to walk me over to "J" barrack.

All the women are asleep. I find an empty cot and join them in slumber faster than you can spell Corum backward.

Harsh trumpeting shocks me awake. I shoot up in bed, panting.

"Reveille's jarring the first time." Two cots down, a woman folds a pair of pajamas into a tight square and sticks it into a metal chest at the end of her bed. "It's coming from over there." She points to a corner of the ceiling, where a speaker is mounted, its cobweb-covered cord dangling down and disappearing into a plug.

As my breathing slows, I study her in the light seeping through the wood slats of the barrack walls. She wears a khaki all-in-one jumpsuit, zippered up the front with patches on the arms, black boots to the middle of her calves, hair in a short ponytail, and lipstick. She's pretty—Trudie-level pretty.

She sticks out her hand, giving me a calloused but strong shake. "I'm Helen. From the WAFS."

The Women's Auxiliary Ferrying Squadron. It's a fairly new program and there aren't that many members, something like two dozen or so. "You're . . . a . . ." I'm tripping over my tongue to be talking to a female pilot in the flesh.

"Pilot, yes. Just ferried a B-17 over from Delaware."

"So you're not stationed here?"

"No, but I'll be staying at Muroc for a bit. They've asked me to do . . . some research."

I pretend not to notice her hesitation and swing my legs out of bed instead.

"Are you the new public relations hire?" she asks.

My first question out the gate and I have no answer. What do I say? Numbers girl? Junior computer for some secret hardware that the Germans want to steal? Am I allowed to talk about my job even if I don't know what it is? Mrs. Mauchly gave me the name of the commanding officer I'm supposed to see when I arrive. Until I get briefed, best to remain vague. "My name's Eleanor. I'm doing ... research, too."

She winks. "Gotcha."

It's fairly clear we're both carrying secrets and don't know how much to reveal. I change the subject. "Where is everyone? I swear I saw more sleeping shapes in the dark last night."

"Trying to nab the hot water before it disappears. You'll meet the rest of the girls at breakfast. There's only four of us at the moment. Well, five now with you."

I cover a yawn.

"Come on. A cold shower will wake you up."

Right. Hot water's probably already gone. Which may not be a bad thing. It's already stifling in here.

Stepping out into the brightness from the barrack is like emerging from a movie theater in the daytime. Harsh and blinding. My eyes are still watering when we reach the women's bath quarters, which is merely a shed with an outdoor shower attached. The shower has four walls that reach up to my chin. Mathematically speaking, I know my chest isn't exposed at this angle. But it's a strange sensation showering naked outside. A group of men walks by and I duck instinctively.

"Sure wish we were in a plane right now!" yells one of them as they pass.

"With that target in our sights!" laughs another.

Oh dear God.

Only when their laughter fades do I stand up. The cold water is bracing, but I let it cleanse me from my journey, scrubbing the best I can with barely a sliver of bar soap. I call out to Helen, who's standing on the other side. "What am I supposed to use to wash my hair?"

"You'll have to make do without shampoo for now. I'll take you to the BX later."

"What's the BX?" I call, but she doesn't hear me. I find a stack of towels, unworn standard-issue women's jumpsuits, and a cubby full of lace boots and clean socks.

"A brand-new woman," says Helen approvingly when I finally come out.

August in the desert. The thermometer on the side of the shed reads 92 degrees Fahrenheit and it's only seven in the morning. I'm grateful for my momentarily wet hair.

As we walk along the dusty pathway, Helen shows me the library, then points her thumb at another building. "Best to stay clear of this one."

"Are there dangerous chemicals or something?"

"Worse. The bachelor officers' barracks, aka the Desert Rat Hotel."

My cheeks burn. "I think I already paid them an accidental visit last night."

"You poor thing. Bachelor officers are wolves."

A guttural *kerr* sound over my head makes me look up into the glare. It's a hawk sweeping across the cobalt sky. I shade my watering eyes and turn to Helen. "So tell me about these dry lake beds I keep hearing so much about."

"There are two of them. But Rogers is the biggest. Two and a half million years old. Forty-four square miles of clay and silt, flat as a board. It only rains five days a year out here. Aside from the rare storm, what little water we get is swept back and forth by desert winds smoothing it out until it's like glass. The first time I landed on it, I had to suspend my disbelief and have faith it could hold the weight of the plane. Rosamond is the other lake. It's farther north, where the secrets are kept."

She stops at a large building and pushes open the door. "Voilà. The mess."

Mess = food area. The space is about half as long as the 30th Street Station atrium, but just as loud. The smell of coffee and meat makes my stomach growl. Fifty or so soldiers eat around long tables. The noise quiets down for a moment as they inspect the newcomer. Me. A few guys yell out *hubba hubba* and *boing!* and some other obnoxious words. I want to disappear.

"All right. Show's over," Helen yells, leading us to a table of three women. I follow happily. Heck, I'd follow her anywhere. Introductions are made. There's Ann, also a pilot who's working at Muroc as a flight instructor. Carolyn, secretary to the chief of administration (= Admin!), who wears a khaki skirt and matching blouse with a two-cornered cap tilted on top of her auburn waves. And Ruby, a civilian, fiancée of the chief of base services, in dark capris and a white blouse.

"Ruby's wedding got postponed because the chaplain came down with the flu," explains Helen.

"Should happen later this week, though," adds Ruby. "Then I'll move into the married officers' quarters." Her voice is high and squeaky like a cartoon character.

"Let's grab some delicious powdered eggs," says Helen, dragging me toward the cafeteria-style food area.

"The meat is real, though, right?"

"Yeah, dogfood is real."

I feel nauseous. "Seriously?"

She laughs. "It's corned beef hash. We call it dogfood."

When we return to the table, the ladies are dishing on someone.

"He makes me quake every time he walks by."

Are they talking about some handsome officer, maybe?

"I'm so afraid he'll yell at me for something random."

Okay, definitely not a handsome officer.

"I heard his aide has asked for a transfer, the poor guy. But they won't give it to him."

"He uses more swear words than regular ones. I swear."

Everyone laughs, including me.

As I eat my powdered eggs, which aren't horrible, I think: I can do this, sit with a group of women and make chitchat. "Who are you all talking about?"

"Colonel Arbocast, of course," answers Ann.

I put down my fork. "The commanding officer of Muroc?"

"The one and only," says Ruby.

That's who Mrs. Mauchly told me to see. Don't worry, I reassure myself. You left Nervous Nellie on the train. You kneed a man in the crotch! You can do this.

After breakfast, Carolyn walks me over to the colonel's office since Admin is right next to it. The nonresidential part of Muroc consists of fourteen white-roofed one-room buildings, each with a flap that props open for ventilation. Compared to the barracks, they're tiny houses. All they need is a picket fence to complete the picture.

Carolyn waves goodbye. "Don't let the old man turn you into a Nervous Nellie."

I stop short. She couldn't know my old nickname. It's impossible, I know. But boy does it throw me.

With a trembling hand, I open the colonel's door.

A husky man in a beige uniform with three colorful ribbon bars lying horizontally on his lapel studies some papers on his desk. He has close-cropped black hair and graying temples. "Morgan, I already told you—"

"Sorry, I can come back later." Relieved, I back out. I've bought myself some time.

"You're not my aide," he bellows, raising his head. "Who the hell are you?"

"Eleanor. Eleanor Schiff."

Silence.

"Mary and John Mauchly sent me?"

His mouth hangs open, then his lips tighten. "I asked them to send me the best man for the job."

"I guess the best man is a woman." I chortle awkwardly.

He opens a desk drawer and removes a bottle of pills, emptying one onto his palm and downing it without water.

"So you're my goddamn expert civilian contractor, huh?"

I swallow and nod.

"They're getting younger every day." He slams the desk drawer, making the room rattle. And me as well.

"If the Mauchlys, Gillon, and Hayden all believe in you, then I suppose I may as well give you a shot. Hell, I've got no other options."

I clear my throat, which has become drier than the lake beds.

"I'm not sure how much they told you," begins Colonel Arbocast, "but we've got a secret weapon, the Norden bombsight. Developing this thing has cost the US Army over a billion dollars. We used to bomb only at night using celestial navigation. But with the Norden, we can now do high-altitude precision bombing in the shit-kicking light of day. This thing guarantees accuracy, see, because the bombardier feeds in information like altitude, drift, trail, etcetera, and the sight does the rest. Fairly straightforward, right?"

"Well, I—"

"Wrong! It's FUBAR. Something is going haywire up there. The Norden is supposed to be able to locate a target as small as a pickle barrel and drop a bomb into it from thirty thousand feet high. It can no sooner hit a pickle barrel than my fat ass." He's up and pacing now.

"We're going to put you into the Norden training class. Your cover is that you're an employee of Carl Norden himself, the inventor of this thing. You're overseeing the Norden instructors on bases all over the country, making sure they're teaching it correctly. That way you'll learn about how this device works. Bombardiers train for six months on this. You need to do it in six weeks."

"Yes. I mean, yes, sir." Do I salute? I start to raise my hand to my brow.

Wait, he's unrolling a map of the base.

I lower my arm. Too soon.

The map is so big it covers his entire desk. "You'll also be reading the output from machines we've got buried in North Base, here and here, near Rogers." His hairy index finger lands hard on two map points. "Maybe the computations from the test bomb drops will offer some clues." He continues to rant about how confounding the Norden is, how the Imperial Japanese Army is whipping the Allies' asses in the Philippines, and how the ground forces aren't hacking it. That the only way to win this thing is through the fucking air. Which means it's on him. The whole goddamn Pacific theater rests on his shoulders. And never mind what's going on with those Nazi SOBs.

On the map there's a compass rose with the four cardinal directions. I remember Dad teaching me the trick that west is always on the left because the compass spelled out WE. That way you'll never get lost, he told me.

My eye twitches and then the compass rose, along with mile

markers and intersecting road lines that form trapezoids, lift off the paper in front of me. The knowing is a welcome relief from this screaming man. I'll be able to get a perspective of the whole army base, which will help me know where to collect data. I see latitude and longitude degrees and scale proportions. But then something weird happens. The vision just vanishes. I blink, trying to get it back. But there's nothing in the air in front of me. The colonel continues talking, but I've tuned him out. I wait for my eye to twitch so I can try again. But when I look down, there's nothing on the paper. The map is completely blank. What in the world?

He stops his diatribe, squinting down at me. "Any questions?"

"I'm sorry, can you repeat that?"

"I don't repeat myself. EVER!"

I begin to quake again.

"Norden training class starts at 0900. That's one hour from now. You're dismissed, Schiff. Or should I call you our secret secret weapon?" Now he finally laughs. But it sounds hollow: laughter at a funeral.

Once outside, I lean against the side of his office building and sink down to the dusty ground.

What happened to my brain just now? Why did it go blank? Then a dreadful thought creeps in. I haven't lost my gift, have I?

No. I'm sure everything's fine. That was a momentary glitch. Anyone would cower beneath a superior officer yelling and cursing like that. Especially when you add the enormous responsibility of what's being asked of me. Back at PCS, the soldiers using our ballistics calculations were imaginary beings. Faceless men in the RAF and US Army. We did the math and sent it off to Aberdeen Proving Ground. We never knew where in the world our calculations were ending up. But here at Muroc? I'm going to meet the bombardiers and pilots who will be using the Norden and depending on my numbers. I'm going to know their names and see if they need a shave. No more imagining. This is real life and real death. On top of it all, Arbocast said I only have six weeks. Six weeks to diagnose a problem that experts with years of training haven't been able to figure out. The odds are against me. And even if I manage to solve it, something could still go wrong up in the air. Or even worse, down on the ground. If the numbers I give the bombardier are off, I'm not only putting the crewmen's lives in danger by making them take enemy fire for nothing, but innocent people might also die if a misaligned weapon hits an orphanage instead of an enemy trench.

Of course my mind would clam up. It makes perfect sense. Seems I didn't leave Nervous Nellie on the train after all.

# 18.

I have an hour before my first day of training class. I can't very well walk in there representing Carl Norden feeling unsure of myself. Helen mentioned the base library. That sounds like the perfect place to calm myself and gather my wits.

Except it's not quiet inside. There's a radio playing loudly. An older, gray-haired man is pinning military patches on a bulletin board in neat rows. It's a small space, just an anteroom with two wooden armchairs for reading, and then beyond that, the stacks. If you could call five bookshelves that amount to one-eighth the size of the Jenkintown Public Library actual stacks.

The man gives me a nod. "Help yourself to any of the books. If you need something just holler. The name's Anderson."

The books are arranged in categories, not by the Dewey decimal system. There's a whole wall of nonfiction: biographies, American history, world history, science, and sports. The fiction section, however, is slim pickings. It's mostly pulp novels with illustrations of women in the throes of passion or danger on the cover.

I choose an old *Reader's Digest* instead and take a seat. One article stands out, reprinted from a science newsletter, about children reared by wild animals. It claims that there's scientific evidence of two wolf children in Midnapore and someone called Lucas, the baboon boy of South Africa. I start to laugh, excited to escape into the ridiculousness and not think about math for a short while.

It's hard to concentrate with the voices on the radio, but I don't have the heart to tell Anderson to turn it down. Something tells me the radio is his only companion in here.

"This is my favorite show," says Anderson. *"Soldiers of the Press."*

I put down my magazine. It's clear I'm not going to get much reading done. "What kind of program is it?"

"War correspondents on the front lines interview someone new every week."

Two men are talking on the show. One has a heavy Eastern European accent. He sounds like Aunt Roza. Szmul Zygielbojm is his name. I know just how it's spelled, with *z*'s and *j*'s in strange places. He's probably Polish. The other man, with a British accent, can't pronounce the Pole's name correctly. Szmul doesn't try to correct him. The message is important, not the messenger.

*How did you get to London?*

*I used to work for Polish government. How you say, now I'm exile? Left in '39 when we still could.*

*How did you come by this information?*

*I gather eyewitness accounts. From secret network across Poland.*

*Tell us what you know.*

*They use mobile gas chambers.*

*What are those?*

*Death machines with wheels. To slaughter innocent Jews. One thousand gassed every day. And not only gas. Bullets. Entire villages massacred. My wife, Manya, my son, Tuvia, are prisoners in Warsaw ghetto. It is horror.*

*How many Jews have been killed thus far?*

*Seven hundred thousand.*

I look at Anderson. "Did you hear that?"

"Unfortunately, yes."

"That can't be right. The number's too big. He doesn't know how to say it in English. It must be seven hundred. Which is bad enough."

Anderson sighs. "War is my hobby. Ask me anything you want about the Great War." He tilts his head at the bulletin board. "Those patches are just a tiny part of my collection. But I'm telling you, I haven't seen the likes of this war. I don't want any memorabilia from those Nazis, that's for sure."

"This is the first I've heard about the organized killing of Jews."

"That's because hardly anyone is reporting it. And when they do, it's just too unbelievable to talk about." He sighs. "Either that, or people don't care."

An American disc jockey's voice comes on the radio. "'Jersey Bounce,' number six on Your Hit Parade."

"Wait! Is the show over? I need more information!"

"Have to wait until next week."

153

I'm forced to listen to Benny Goodman's clarinet. Too happy. Too out of place after that interview.

Seven hundred thousand. How is it possible? By itself the number is an abstraction. But when you apply to it the thing that's being counted, 700,000 murdered Jews, it becomes concrete. Tangible and real. Then, when you think of all those 700,000 as individuals with thoughts and dreams and beating hearts, that number becomes something else entirely. It has a value, not a place value where the 7 stands for hundred thousandths, and the 0 next to it ten thousandths, and so on. I'm talking about the worth of one human life.

One human life. One person. The number isn't 699,999. It's 700,000. That 700,000th person might have found the cure for polio. We'll never know. The man on the radio, Szmul? He's just one person. Now others have heard what he had to say. That multiplies. I'm one person, too. Back in Arbocast's office, my mind blacked out because I felt overwhelmed by the task ahead. But now I see what the power of the individual can accomplish. I can look at the Norden in a similar way. It's made of individual parts. All machines are. What if I examined one part at a time? Took it step by step. Then I could put the parts together and fix the whole.

There's no time for Nervous Nellie anymore when time has run out for so many.

I check the clock on the library wall: 8:55. I mutter a quick thank-you to Anderson and hurry to class. I can't be late on my first day!

# 19.

I'm back in school, only this time instead of thirty trigonometry students at Jenkintown High, or ten girls in Mrs. Mauchly's lab, there are twelve men: five pilots, five bombardiers, and two bombsight mechanics. Other than that, and the fan in the corner woefully trying to cool us down, it's like any classroom I've ever sat in. In other words, it's home.

Our instructor, Corporal Hemming, is a short, nasal-voiced man whose monotone delivery might be more effective than counting sheep. He stops lecturing when he sees me. "I was beginning to think you weren't coming. Gentlemen, this is Miss Schiff, a consultant from the Carl Norden factory. She's here to observe, well, me, I suppose. So let's continue. We have a lot of material to cover."

I weave my way through the desks.

"You can sit right here, baby doll," calls one of the GIs, pointing to his lap.

The men think this is extremely amusing. I think all this commentary on my womanhood is getting old.

I ignore him and look for a seat in the back. Not impossibly, one trainee is actually asleep. As I pass, I step on his foot to bring him back to the room. After all, it's my "job" to make sure these boys know what they're doing.

The actual Norden device isn't even here. Hemming has mounted a paper diagram of the sight on the chalkboard behind him. There are lines coming out in every direction. The lines are numbered and he's going over the names of each part.

I'm right. It *is* made up of parts. Twenty-four, actually. Hemming assures us that we will become familiar with all the knobs, plates,

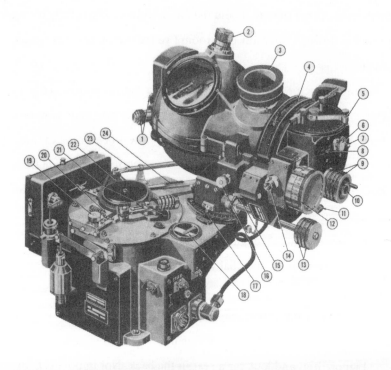

switches, and rods, but for now he wants us to think of it in two main sections: the sighthead and the stabilizer. The stabilizer is the base and the sighthead is mounted on top.

"The stabilizer holds the Norden bombsight's electronics and the AFCE," he says.

I'm lost. These army acronyms are driving me crazy.

"The stabilizer keeps the line-of-sight direction fixed, or controlled," continues Hemming. "It's paired to the airplane's autopilot so the Norden can actually fly the aircraft during the bombing run."

Autopilot. That could be the *A* in AFCE.

"The Norden is also connected to the bomb racks so it can automatically release the bombs at the right time."

Hemming pulls down another chart with a drawing of a B-17 bomber. "The stabilizer lives in the nose of the plane, maintaining horizontal stability. But the sighthead is removed after each mission and securely stored. We call it the football."

This I understand. So do the guys. They get distracted, tossing a pretend football and crashing their desks into one another, fake tackling. Hemming doesn't break from his monotone.

"It's your job to input the bomb ballistics from your Aberdeen tables."

"You're talking about our ballistics tables from PCS!" I call out.

"What was that, Miss Schiff?" asks Hemming.

"Oh, I was, um, just making sure you mention size, shape, and density of weapons, among other figures."

A GI pulls his desk into line again from the "football game" and asks, "What else do we need to know for input?"

"Altitude, true air speed, ground speed, drift, and trail," says Hemming.

I know what *drift* is, from my previous ballistics work. It has to do with direction and velocity of wind and affects the distance the ordnance will travel downwind. But I'm not familiar with *trail*. I thumb through the manual on my desk. *Trail* is the appearance of the bomb trailing behind the aircraft as it falls. In other words, the horizontal distance of the bomb between the forward moving plane and the point of impact. So the main objective of the Norden is to solve a three-dimensional space plus time problem. Fascinating.

Hemming drones on. "The name of the game here is deflection. This machine compensates for all ways the plane can go off course. It's up to you to tell it what to do."

It appears the Norden is essentially an analog calculator just like Annie! Maybe I'll catch on quicker than I thought.

Hemming covers up the names on the sight diagram and quizzes the group on the first four parts.

It reminds me of the MathMeet, only this isn't a game.

A GI in front of me says to the trainee next to him, "I can't wait to hit that pickle barrel!"

A heaviness comes over me. These men believe everything they've heard about the Norden. They think it's as accurate as advertised. I can't disabuse them of it. It will demoralize them. If I ever wondered why my presence here is classified, this is as good a reason as any.

After class lets out, I catch a ride with some GIs heading out to the flats of North Base, six miles away.

"I need to see your ID," demands the driver.

Is he putting me on? I'm already here, on base, in uniform. I have to show it again? The guy is wearing dark aviator sunglasses so I can't read his expression.

"The bombing and gunnery range is clearance level two and above," he adds.

Right. Helen mentioned something about where the secrets were kept.

I feel inside my pockets and realize the ID card is sitting inside the chest at the end of my cot. "Crap. I mean, dang."

The driver smiles. "You're already one of us with that mouth. Pretty though it is. I'll hold the jeep for two minutes."

I tear out of there, picturing the track at my high school, hoping I don't cramp like usual. I slip on some gravel and nearly do a face-plant, but I recover, running like the wind. Inside the barrack, my ID is right where I left it. How much time do I have? Don't look at the clock, Eleanor. Just get back to that jeep.

"Where's the fire?" yells a GI when I whiz past.

I arrive to the loading area only to find it's empty. The car has gone, leaving just its tracks leading north and a cloud of dust one thousand yards away. What a jerk. That couldn't have been much over two minutes. I double over, hands on my knees, gasping for air.

Water. It's all I can think about.

I stumble back to the mess and fill up a canteen, downing it without taking a breath, then fill it up again and hook it to my belt.

A man sweeps the floor in a never-ending battle to get control of the dust.

"Do you happen to know when the next jeep leaves for North Base?" I ask him.

"Every fifteen minutes, miss, on the quarter hour."

A jerk to the power of ten! I could have retrieved my ID at a leisurely pace and taken the next jeep. Fool me once, shame on you. I won't be fooled twice.

Another jeep comes along shortly and I hop into the open back area. As we bump along the dusty road, I run my fingers through my hair, shocked to find there's absolutely no curl left. When I think of all that time I spent fighting for a spot in front of the mirror at the fraternity house . . . it seems silly now.

Thankfully, the soldiers ignore me. They seem to be enthralled with one man in particular sitting in the front passenger seat. The guys all lean forward to catch his every word. He must be a pilot because he's the only one with a headset. The large ear cushions rest against his neck like a case of the mumps.

As we approach North Base, I see the area is made up of dozens of tents, at least triple the size of the pup tents Sarah and I used to pitch in our backyard when we wanted to "camp out." Four large, rudimentary airplane hangars abut Rogers Dry Lake, built hastily out of wood. Beyond that, way in the distance, must be the silt runway Helen told me about. It seems like everything here is still new, waiting for more troops, more funds to improve the facilities. I suppose if the war drags on, those hangars will be replaced by some fancy metal ones.

We all pile out and I catch the passenger's name tag. ROBERT STANLEY, BELL AIRCRAFT. What's so special about him?

A group of guys play horseshoes in the dust. Most of them have no shirts. Rather than blush, I find myself getting mad. It's not fair that they can take off their tops and cool down and we girls can't.

Did I really just think that? The heat must be getting to me.

Arbocast said there were instruments buried somewhere out here. I ask the jeep driver where they might be. He says they're out on the lake bed. Look for the little orange flags sticking up and you'll find them. So I can actually walk onto the lake bed without sinking in? Gingerly, I place my boot down on the silty surface. It crackles a little with the pressure of my foot, but it's solid. I guess there hasn't been rain in a while.

"You there!"

I turn, startled.

A different GI is striding toward me. The patch on his uniform says RANGE MAINTENANCE DETACHMENT. "You can't just walk onto the bed! This is a live bombing range!"

"I'm sorry, I didn't realize."

"You need someone to drive you. Someone who knows when the flight tests are scheduled."

The jeep driver could have told me that. I'm done with this campaign against me, one that delights in watching me flail. I straighten my shoulders and show the maintenance guy my ID card. "Arbocast sent me. I'm supposed to read the output from those machines. I'll need to do this every day around this time."

He shrugs. "Let's get going, then."

His jeep is smaller than the one I rode down in. It's just a two-seater with a canvas cover. The GI is quiet, his eyes focused on the emptiness in front of us. How in the world he can find these machines with no natural marker, not even a sagebrush, is a mystery. Presently, he slows down and brings the jeep to a stop.

Three small orange flags, about 500 feet from one another, poke out of the ground. I approach one flag and see that it's marking a shallow hole. Inside is a seismometer of some kind that likely measures vibrations and shaking after an explosion. I kneel down and tear off the paper readout. Using the signals from the other two seismometers, I should be able to calculate the epicenter of the point of impact. I squint at the GI, who's cleaning his fingernails, clearly bored. I'm envious of his large, brimmed hat.

"Will there be more test runs today or is that it?" I ask him when he drops me back off at the starting point.

He checks his watch. "Three more at 1700."

That's three hours from now. I find a spot in the shade of a nearby

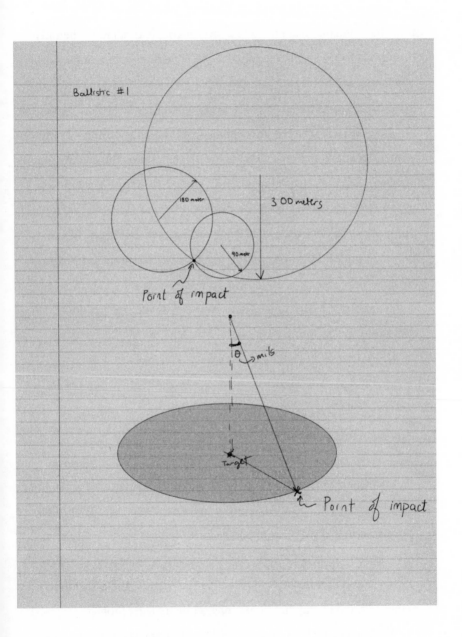

Ballistic #1

180 meter

90 meter

300 meters

Point of impact

θ mils

Target

Point of impact

tarp that someone has pulled taut over a couple of chairs. The only problem is that it's right near the latrine and stinks something awful. Shaded stench or blazing sun. It's an easy choice. Breathing through my mouth, I open my notebook and get to work.

I need to take the readout signals from the seismometers as well as their location, and do a triangulation to determine the coordinates of where the bomb struck the ground. Arbocast's aide gave me the test pilot's notes so I know both the elevation he was flying at when he dropped the ballistic as well as the coordinates of the target. My next step is to put all that information together to determine the ranging error.

It takes me a few hours, but I come up with this for the three explosions this morning:

35 mils 7:00

32 mils 8:30

41 mils 3:00

At the lab in Philly, we used a milliradian standard, or mils, to measure range and distance to target. With a 1,000 to 1 ratio, at 1,000 feet distance, 1 mil = 1 foot. So the first bomb landed 35 feet away from the target, at a location of 7:00 on the geometric clock. That doesn't sound that far off, but if the pilot needs to ascend 10,000 feet higher to avoid enemy fire, it becomes a much bigger problem.

Yet something rubs at me. The Norden bombsight doesn't have

mechanical gears that slip like Annie does. So is it human error that's causing the bad landings?

I rest my notebook on my knees and roll back my aching shoulders. My feet feel hotter than usual. I was concentrating so hard I didn't notice that the sun had arced farther west. My boots are no longer in the shade.

"Watch it!" yells a voice.

I topple off my chair, landing on my hip and rear end. I spit dirt from my mouth and look up. "Did you just push me?"

It's the pilot everyone was listening to in the jeep. Stanley, was it? He points to a rattlesnake, slithering past the leg of the chair.

I scramble to my feet, getting farther away from the thing, even though it's moving in the other direction now. "Oh my gosh, thank you!"

But he doesn't hear me. His headset is now over his ears and he's already walking toward one of the hangars.

I check the ground around the chair once more. All clear. Nervous Nellie would call it a day and head back to the barrack, having had a near encounter with a poisonous bite. But I'm not budging. I don't want to miss the afternoon explosions. I tuck my legs up underneath me just in case, and get back to work.

# 20.

My days are full: Norden training class in the mornings, lunch at the mess, then out to North Base when the sun's not so high in the sky. I copy down figures from the seismometers and do my subsequent calculations. And always, there's the ticking clock. We're halfway through six weeks and I haven't yet diagnosed what's wrong with the bombsight. I have, however, become an expert at avoiding Colonel Arbocast. Kids would love this new version of hide-and-seek. Quick, there he is. Dip behind a pair of Joshua trees. Here he comes walking toward the mess. Duck into the latrine. The other day I saw him get off a jeep at North Base. I slid into a saguaro cactus. It took Helen an hour to pull all the tiny spines from my arm, which is still red, by the way.

At the end of my first week here, I stuck an Eleanor Roosevelt quote over my bed: *No one can make you feel inferior without your consent.* Then Helen started getting curious about my past. "What does a smart cookie like you have to feel inferior about? Did someone bother you in grade school?"

How about every year from first grade up until now? I thought.

Maybe up until now isn't such a fair assessment. I wouldn't say Arbocast is teasing me, per se. Not like the kids who called me Nervous Nellie. I think it's just his way of interacting with people and I'm reacting the way I always do: cowering in fear. I ended up taking the quote off the wall. I don't need my guardian angel to remind me that I'm my own worst enemy. I'm trying to hang on to my growing confidence, but the doubts creep in at night. Can I really do what's being asked of me?

The women's barrack has seen a steady stream of arrivals and departures. Ruby finally got married and moved out to couples' housing. Helen is still here, as are Carolyn and Ann. I don't go out of my way to chat with the newbies. You make friends in the evening and they're gone the next morning. Every few days I write a V-mail to Alyce, but I don't write home, I call instead. Obviously, Mom can't see a government postmark from Muroc. I scribble notes on our conversations so I can have a record of what I've told her. That way the stories I concoct about UCLA will have continuity. I also make sure I call her from a quiet place like the library or Admin so she won't hear the planes flying overhead. With Alyce, at least I can write about real life here on base. I keep the math to a minimum, but I did tell her how thrilling it is to see how our work is used in the field.

Today before I head out to North Base, I stop by the BX (= base exchange). I want to pick up a deck of cards to replace the deck of Ann's that I ruined. We were playing rummy and someone mentioned

Arbocast, which made me dog-ear the corners of the two of diamonds so severely, it's a dead giveaway now for anyone who collects twos.

I chat with the woman behind the BX counter as she rings me up, a sweet older lady who was married to one of the original Corum homesteaders. "I'm surprised you're not buying some of that new Chantilly perfume for the dance tonight."

"Dance?"

She points out the window. A bus has pulled into the depot, depositing a bevy of women. They're all gussied up, seams drawn down the backs of their calves and everything.

"Looks like they used a whole beauty parlor's supply of hairspray," I joke.

"Probably right. They're from Bakersfield. Red Cross bused all fifty of 'em in."

They brought in girls from outside the base? I feel slighted. We may be just a few women playing cards in a barrack, but still. We're female. And even if I am a terrible dancer and tongue-tied in a social situation, I'd like the chance to meet a nice soldier like that one with the jug ears at the train station.

I'm a little gloomy as I walk toward the jeep dispatch. Once I get into my calculations I know I'll forget all about the pretty girls and dashing soldiers and budding romances that are sure to bloom. Math has always been my favorite companion. I've been working on some new differentials to try to solve the mystery of the Norden's inaccuracies. At PCS, we computed incremental numbers for bullets and cannons, but never bombs. This is a whole different situation. Unlike bullets and cannons, the bombs are launched from a moving airplane, where the parameters of the motion make the physics problem even more dynamic. This looks fine on paper, but in the real world, the drag (the force that opposes the motion of an object in a fluid) calculations are much more complex. In the case of our B-17s, air acts as the fluid, or the resistor. I just haven't figured out exactly how.

"Well, well. If it isn't my secret secret weapon."

Arbocast is smack-dab in front of me. I've lost the hiding game. Serves me right for letting my emotions about some silly dance fill my head instead of remaining vigilant.

"Have you solved it yet?" he asks.

"Er, I'm working my way closer, sir." I stare at my boots.

"Look at me when I'm speaking to you, Schiff!"

I squint up at him, fumbling in my many pockets for my new sunglasses, which aren't where they're supposed to be. Water pours out from the corners of my eyes. "It's only been three weeks, sir. I believe you gave me six?"

"I say a lot of things. I need this yesterday. Make that the fucking day before yesterday."

"Sorry, sir." Quit apologizing, I tell myself. Remember when you crawled underneath Annie and told Mrs. Mauchly what you saw going wrong with the gears? You were rewarded. Ask him for what you need.

"Progress might move a lot faster if I were able to test my skills on an actual Norden, sir. I noticed another classroom had a flight simulator for pilot training. Is there no simulator for a bombsight?"

"We can't risk removing the football from its bunker just for training purposes. It's the only one we have and it's too valuable."

"You're just going to throw our airmen into the fire without hands-on experience? How sensitive is the search knob? The disc speed drum? What if it takes someone one hundred tries to get those crosshairs right? How can I figure out which of the twenty-four parts is the issue if I can't touch it?"

I cover my mouth with my hand. I can't speak to my superior officer this way. I brace myself for the tirade.

"That'll be all, Schiff." He makes an about-face and leaves.

That was odd. I'm sure he was screaming at me in his head. I can hear it in *my* head, at any rate. But I'm not quaking. Maybe I really am growing as Alyce said. Emboldened, I think of what she told me that first morning at breakfast in the frat house. It's time you learned to seize an opportunity.

If they won't bring the Norden to me, I'll have to go to the Norden.

Hemming told the class it's stored in an air-conditioned bunker with a twenty-four-hour-a-day security detail. At North Base, there are only four buildings that aren't tents. I had assumed they were all airplane hangars, but now that I think about it, one of them always has guards out front. That must be where they keep the Norden.

I get out of the jeep and march right up to the guard, who promptly laughs at me. "Clearance level four only." He's a pasty fellow who looks, impossibly, like he's never seen the sun. "Go join a conga line."

"Look, Colonel Arbocast has given me orders and if you don't let me in, I'll never be able to complete them. You really want to make him come all the way down here? I can hear him screaming already."

The guard tightens his jaw. He isn't budging. Someone comes out of the bunker. A pilot I recognize from training class. He's tall and dreamy-looking, with red hair. I confess I've often caught myself staring at the back of his head. Now, facing him, I can see light freckles over his nose.

"What's the problem, Murphy?" asks the pilot.

"This dolly is trying to gain access without proper clearance."

He flicks his eyes at me ever so briefly. "She's legit. I saw the requisition papers myself."

The vampirish guard, Murphy, puts up his hands, palms out. "It's your funeral, Captain."

Then the pilot winks at me. Typical. He's just like all the rest. Too full of himself. I hope he doesn't assume I owe him something. I enter the hangar without so much as a glance in his direction, but he follows me in, shutting the door behind us. The air-conditioning hits me first. I want to drink it up and let it penetrate all my pores. Once I'm good and cool, I turn around and face him, trying to ignore how handsome he is. "Why'd you lie for me?"

"Thank you, Sky," he says in a pretend female voice. "I really appreciate you going to bat for me just now." He spins to the opposite angle in his own voice. "My pleasure." His normal voice is rather deep and delicious. "I've seen you in class and out by the latrine, writing furiously in that notebook of yours. I respect hard work. I thought it was high time you got to see a Norden up close."

I suppress a smile. "Well then, I guess a thank-you *is* in order."

"See. That wasn't so hard." He sticks his hands in his pockets, as if he's going to stay awhile. "How many notebooks do you have anyway?"

"I'm on my seventh."

"Impressive."

"Not really. Filling notebooks with rows of neatly printed numbers and not yet figuring out—" I stop. I shouldn't be talking about my job. "Sky, huh? Did your parents know you were going to be a pilot?"

"Where I come from, everyone's named John, James, or Samuel. They're big on the Bible in Provo. My given name is Samuel. It was my squadron who came up with the nickname Sky."

"I'm Eleanor."

"You want to see the Norden, Eleanor?"

"Do fish swim?"

His answer is a hearty laugh.

The Norden is stored in a small annex room toward the back of the hangar. On our way, we pass by an airplane in the midst of repair. A rolling staircase is pulled up alongside one of the propellers where a man in a greasy work suit is standing and peering inside. Sky waves to him. There's a white tarp covering half the plane, but the part that's exposed is unmissable. Painted on the side is a woman posing like Betty Grable. Two bombs are drawn next to her. The name of the plane is *Flamin' Mamie.*

"Why do they call these planes by women's names?" I feel like I'm back in the Sigma Chi House, seeing those posters of pinup girls. Everywhere I turn I'm either being jeered at for being a girl or forced to look at drawings of other half-naked women.

"Nose art is supposed to bring good luck to the crew," answers Sky. "A pretty lady is better than Donald Duck, I reckon. They also tell stories. This plane made two hits at the battle of Midway. Each time a plane returns from a successful run, someone paints another bomb on the nose. The B-17s that fly in the Pacific use much racier girl models than the ones on aircraft we've sent to the RAF. Maybe because it's hot as blazes on those islands and no one wears much clothing, who knows." He shrugs. "But I think my mama would agree with you. She disapproves of the pinups on aircraft. I sent her a photo of me in front of a plane called *Hail Mary* with a bathing beauty behind me and boy, did she let me have it. She hates this war. She wanted me to object on account of our religion, but I couldn't live with myself if I didn't fight."

His words move me, making me think of Mom. How would she feel if I were a boy about to turn eighteen in a few days instead of a girl? Her only worry was me taking the train across the country on my own. I'm not enlisting.

Sky jingles some keys on a ring, finds the right one, and opens a lock. Then he does this twice more with two different keys, until all three locks of the vault are opened. And there it is, resting on the floor in a glass case. The bombsight.

"That's it?" I ask. It looks too small to wreak havoc on a factory. The illustration on Hemming's poster was so much bigger. I guess I was so caught up in learning the parts that I didn't stop to think about scale.

"Shhh. You'll hurt its feelings."

I giggle, remembering that this is just the football part. "I don't suppose you can show me how it fits on the stabilizer?"

He looks around. "I guess we could take it out for a bit." He removes the glass covering and lifts up the football with two hands. I walk ahead of him to hold open the door.

"Thanks," he says. "At eight bucks an ounce I can't exactly afford to let go even for a second."

"So each Norden costs thirteen thousand dollars?"

"Quit showing off, smarty-pants."

The repairman helps Sky carry the football up the scaffold stairs to *Flamin' Mamie*. I wait at the bottom. It's happening! I'm finally going to see the Norden the way it's supposed to be experienced.

"This will be my first time stepping into a military plane," I confess. "Actually, any plane."

"Fair warning: The army's not known for their meal service," he quips.

"You're funny." And I'm not nervous. Hunh.

After the repairman backs down the stairs, I climb up, duck my head, and step in. It's much more crowded than I imagined, filled with a myriad of controls and equipment mounted on curved metallic walls.

"Behold, the Flying Fortress," says Sky, resting the football for a bit. He obviously loves this aircraft and is an enthusiastic teacher. I learn that the B-17s were originally a coastal anti-sub and anti-naval plane. But recently, they've been discovered to be excellent at high altitudes. No longer does the squadron navigator need to use a combination of dead reckoning (using airspeed and time elapsed between checkpoints to compute position), pilotage (using visible landmarks such as rivers or mountains), radio, and celestial navigation. Now they have the Norden and can go on precision bombing missions during the day.

"I could tell you about Carl Norden, but you already know all that, being his employee and all."

"Actually, I'd like to hear your thoughts. He keeps to himself mostly."

"Well, you know he's a very talented Dutch engineer who invented not just the Norden but robot-flying bombs, catapults, and lots more."

I nod. But no, I didn't know that at all.

"His devout belief in Christianity informs everything he does. Carl's goal is to have the least number of war casualties. With high-altitude precision bombing, whoever doesn't need to be killed, won't be. Now it's just GI Jap or Kraut at risk."

It's impressive and disturbing. I'm not sure I want to know who the people are on the receiving end of my computations.

I notice open spaces where the windowpanes are supposed to be. "Are they repairing the windows, too?"

"They're supposed to be like that. Without glass. The crew has to be able stick out their guns and fire."

"But how do you survive in the cold, thin air?"

"We wear oxygen masks. And really big coats."

Sky points out where the ten-man crew sits. The top turret is for the flight engineer, and just below him is the cockpit for the pilot and copilot. Behind the cockpit is the main area of the plane, where the radio operator and two waist gunners work. There are two more gunners, one at the tail and one in the ball turret. The bombs are stored in the belly of the plane, though there are none in here now. I'm relieved. Seeing one would just give me the heebie-jeebies. It's bad enough having these guns in front of me, with rows of bullets twisting out and down like Medusa's hair.

There's even a photograph of someone's girlfriend under the glass of a pull-down desk. Could she be Sky's?

He spots me looking at the picture. "That's Abe Cohen's wife."

Relief floods through me, which catches me by surprise.

Below the cockpit is the nose for the navigator and bombardier. Sky makes his way to a large bubble window with a green office-type swivel chair in front of it. "Here's where the Norden lives." I watch as he attaches the football onto the gyroscope of the base.

Just like when I impulsively crawled under Annie to check her gears, I'm like a kid with a bowlful of Dots gumdrops in front of me. I want to touch every knob on the bombsight. I reach for the clutch to push it in. Sky leans in for the clutch at the same time. Our fingers brush. I yank my hand back. But I still feel his touch all the way up my arm.

"I'll be right back," he says, his cheeks the color of his hair. "I forgot we need a target."

He leaves the plane, finds a small 2″ by 2″ box of rivets, and places it about twenty feet from the nose, right on the hangar floor. When he returns, his pink cheeks are back to normal and my insides, which had been aflutter, are quiet.

"You need to line up your crosshairs right in the center of that box," he explains.

We wait for the gyro to warm up. Then I place my face onto the rubber telescope eyepiece and move the turn and drift knobs forward a couple of turns. The crosshairs speed up, aligning the vertical direction. Then I turn the displacement knob and the rate knob, aligning the horizontal crosshairs. I go through the steps, hearing Hemming's instructions in my head. Check the rate index. Turn off the rate motor and clutch in the stabilizer. Uncage the vertical gyro. Set the sighting angle for 70 degrees with the search knob. When the crosshairs are on the target, clutch in. Turn the rate motor switch back on. It's a constant battle to find the balance between the displacement and rate knob. Those two are so reactive that the smallest movement can prevent the crosshairs from lining up.

The little box of rivets remains elusive. "My range angle is too narrow," I say, frustrated.

"You're flying too fast and too low. Uncage the vertical gyro and try it again."

I start over. Set my sight angle at 70 degrees. Clutch in.

"Easy does it," he says. "The Norden is tuned like a fine Swiss watch. Its parts are tiny in there and supersensitive."

I'm too far off the target. Again. I lift my head. "I can't imagine how hard this would be in a freezing airplane!"

"That there's the understatement of the year."

Sky is endlessly patient. After dozens of tries, I still don't get the crosshairs to line up and never get to "bombs away."

In spite of that, sitting next to Sky has made this the most enjoyable afternoon I've had since I arrived.

That night, after a barely edible meal of beans and franks (= army chicken) for the third time this week, I stay longer in the mess to fill up with two helpings of peach melba. When I get back to the barrack, Helen is out of her usual flight suit. Instead, she's wearing a cap-sleeved flowered dress with a sash. The other girls, also in dresses, are squeezing in front of the one small mirror, putting on makeup.

"No gin rummy tonight?" I ask.

Helen smiles demurely. "I'm going to the dance."

"I didn't think we were invited." I sound prickly, but I know I'm just feeling sorry for myself.

"Of course we are, you goof. Anyone can go. Robert just happened to invite me personally as his date."

"Robert?"

"Robert Stanley." Then she whispers, "Bell Aircraft sent him here under the cloak of secrecy."

"Ah. The chatty pilot who saved me from death by snakebite."

"You should come!"

"I look a fright. I have dust in my ears, under my nails, in my nostrils." I spread out my hands. My fingers are full of pencil calluses from doing so many computations. Then I remember the way it felt when I brushed those fingers against Sky's and the way his eyes crinkled when he told a joke.

I did dance at the Downbeat and eventually got the hang of it. Maybe I won't be so clumsy this time around.

I make an announcement to the room. "Anyone have a dress I could borrow?"

# 21.

The gym is festooned with streamers, which it desperately needs. Like the inside of the B-17, the space isn't exactly fancy. It's tall and airy, but nothing is finished. Scaffolding and open beams cover the ceiling and walls. There *is* a hardwood floor, however, along with two baskets on either side of the court. Above one of the baskets is a big white banner with the Red Cross symbol.

Helen runs off to find Robert, leaving me, Ann, and Carolyn to fend for ourselves.

A soldier manning a portable Victrola flips through a stack of records. I don't know what I was expecting. A jazz band like they had at the Downbeat? It seems forever ago that we were there all together. Alyce's last letter mentioned a dinner at Bookbinder's, so maybe things are easing up between her and Marjorie and Louise. Which makes me notice that as crowded as it is in here, there aren't any Negroes. Of course the nighttime social scene in the army would be segregated the way the jobs on base are. When will things change?

"Jingle, Jangle, Jingle" plays from the phonograph. Immediately,

Ann and Carolyn get swept onto the dance floor by two boisterous soldiers.

Looking for something to do, I wander over to the refreshment table. Sodas, pretzels, and beers are arranged neatly over a red tablecloth.

"One should never line up crosshairs and drink at the same time."

To my left, Sky grins at me, handing me a beer. My heart somersaults.

"I'll make a note of that," I say.

He sips from his own can. "Is your head spinning?"

I go pale. Is my crush on him that obvious?

"You know, from seeing the Norden for the first time," he adds.

"Oh, right. Definitely. I can't wait to see it again tomorrow."

Now it's his turn to look uncomfortable.

"Never mind," I say quickly. "I didn't mean to presume I could just waltz into the hangar—"

"It's just I have test flight duty at 0630. So I won't be on base tomorrow."

I'm reading all the signals wrong. I need to relax. He's just a person. Albeit a very handsome person. "I'm curious about something."

"Ask me anything."

"What part of the Norden has given your bombardiers the most problems?" I figure that's a neutral enough question for a "consultant" to ask.

"That's your big pressing question?" He laughs at me, then reaches for my hand and leads me to the center of the room. "No more shop talk. Let's dance."

The next thing I know, Sky has one hand around my waist and his other clasps my hand close to his chest. I have no idea what to do here. I can swing, but it's not that kind of a song. It's a very slow song, as a matter of fact. I copy the other girls around me, with their left hand draped over their dance partner's shoulders, and try to follow Sky's lead without stepping on him.

*Although some people say he's just a crazy guy*
*To me he means a million other things*
*For he's the one who taught this happy heart of mine to fly*
*He wears a pair of silver wings*

It's as if the song were made for me and Sky. It's too embarrassing. Don't listen to the lyrics. Ask him something.

"So does red hair run in your family or did your mother eat a lot of carrots when she was pregnant with you?"

He smiles and shakes his head. "You know that's an old wives' tale, right? But carrots did do something else to me." He brings his face closer to mine. "I was set on being a fighter pilot, see? Since I was a kid. All those stories about the Great War. I wanted to be in the clouds. I decided that I would get the highest score on my vision test so they'd have to take me. A week before the test, I ate more carrots than you can grow in a victory garden. I ate them day and night. My skin turned briefly but brightly orange. You couldn't tell where my hair ended and my forehead began."

I pull back, astonished. "Are you putting me on?"

He makes an *X* over his uniform. "Cross my heart." Then he pulls me close again.

> *And though it's pretty tough, the job he does above*
> *I wouldn't have him change it for a king*
> *An ordinary fellow in a uniform I love*
> *He wears a pair of silver wings*

Oh heck. Everything feels so good. This dance. His arms. The gentle vibration of his voice against my temple. I don't even care if his carrot story is true or not.

"Where are you from, Schiff?"

"Philly. The city of brotherly love."

"Why do they call it that?"

"*Phileo* means 'love' in Greek. *Adelphos* means 'brother.' William Penn named it."

Sky whistles. "You know so many things! How'd you get so good at math anyway?"

I stop moving my feet. "What makes you think I'm good at math?"

"You figured out how much the Norden costs quicker than a roadrunner crossing the highway."

That's true, but all this math talk is making me uncomfortable. And not because my job at Muroc is supposed to be a secret. The subject is just too close to home.

"Did I say something wrong?" he asks.

"It's just, guys don't usually want to talk about my math skills." I start swaying on my feet again.

"Are your parents smart like you?"

Everything leads to Dad. I'm so tired of being on guard all the time. I want to tell this man the truth. I doubt he would say anything to anybody. I'm sure it's safe. I open my mouth to confess everything, but this comes out instead. "My cousin Batja is really good at math."

I couldn't confide in Alyce and now I can't do it with Sky. Will I ever be close enough to someone to be able to unload my burden?

"Tell me about Batja."

"She's my age, and honestly I'm really worried about her. Right now she's probably at work, toiling away in a factory in German-occupied Poland."

"You're Jewish?"

I bristle. "Don't act so surprised."

"You misunderstand. I hate what's happening in Europe. The Bible is the Bible. Old Testament, New Testament, the Book of Mormon. I don't care. In fact, the Jews are God's chosen people. What's Hitler's problem?"

"Exactly!" I tell him about the radio interview I heard. The 700,000 and the heinous mobile gas chambers.

"I can't wait to get over there and bomb the crap out of those Nazis."

I love his fury, but immediately I worry for his safety.

We fall quiet, listening to the words of the song, our feet moving softly around in a circle.

> *He wears a pair of silver wings*
> *Why, I'm so full of pride when we go walking*
> *Every time he's home on leave*
> *He with those wings on his tunic*
> *And me with my heart on my sleeve*
> *But when I'm left alone and we are far apart*
> *I sometimes wonder what tomorrow brings*
> *For I adore that crazy guy who taught my happy heart*
> *To wear a pair of silver wings*

Sky moves his cheek away from me and I feel the coolness of its absence. But it seems he only pulled away to look into my eyes. "Now I have a burning question," he says. "What's it like to kiss a pretty mathematician?"

I'm about to tell him let's find out when a piercing siren blasts into our ears.

# 22.

The gym is in chaos. People scatter from the dance floor, head to the exits. The Bakersfield girls are screaming, trying to strap on gas masks, unaccustomed to something like this. I can relate.

I plug my ears and yell to Sky. "What's happening?"

"Steady tone. Been going on for at least two minutes. It's not an attack. A disaster warning, probably."

"What sort of disaster could it be if it's not an enemy attack?"

"A natural one."

Mercifully, the siren stops. That's when we hear the thunder.

"Likely a flash flood," says Sky. "We have to get back to the barracks. The water can come fast without warning." I don't see Helen, Carolyn, or Ann anywhere. Sky takes my hand and guides me out of the cacophony.

Lightning zigzags across the sky, illuminating the desert in a dazzling display. If it weren't so frightening I'd stay and marvel at it. By the time we get to the women's barrack, the rain is pouring down in sheets and we're both soaked.

Sky, seemingly unconcerned about the storm, turns his face

upward and opens his mouth to let the water fall in. I do the same. The rain tastes warm and sweet.

"My test flight will be canceled tomorrow," he says.

"I'm sorry."

He's smiling like a watermelon. "That's good news, silly. It means we can take out the Norden again."

We linger at my door. Is he going to try again with that kiss? No, he takes a step back, waves goodbye, and says, "See ya later, gator."

I'd be lying if I said I wasn't disappointed. But I can tell he's sweet on me. I fall into bed thinking about what his lips might feel like. Does it matter that he's not Jewish? Not to me, but Mom and Dad are a different story. I push them out of my head and let Sky back in. A bit later, I hear my roommates come in, but I pretend I'm sleeping. I want to stay in this half-dream, half-awake state as long as I can.

"Pssst." Helen touches my shoulder. "You awake?"

"Now I am," I say, rolling to face her.

The other girls are busy getting undressed and brushing their teeth in the tiny barrack sink.

She slides my legs over to make room for herself on the cot. "So who was that guy you were dancing so close with? Give me the skinny."

I prop myself up on my elbows. "His name is Sky. He's a pilot from Utah."

"And . . ."

"And what?"

"Did he kiss you?"

"Did Robert kiss *you*?"

"Multiple times."

I giggle. "Don't you worry about him, though? I mean, he's a pilot. I don't know the stats, but I can't imagine the odds are good."

She doesn't answer me right away, just exhales slowly. "Never did I believe I'd be flying for the WAFS. When I'm up in the air, it's a rush. It feels like I can do anything. Every time I land, I feel guilty. How can I be living my dream while so many people are dying overseas in this war? Then I think, well, I'm also risking my own life every time I take off. So when it comes to Robert or your Sky or any of these boys, I say: Give them their moment of joy. If we're a part of that, then all the better. Live for today. Because who knows what's going to happen tomorrow."

I smile at Helen, though I don't know if she can see my teeth in the darkness. "My mother would love you."

The next morning, the Norden training classroom smells like sweat and wet wool. Doesn't anyone use umbrellas here? I'm shaking mine out when I notice something large in the back of the room. I can't believe it. It's a simple scaffolding setup about fifteen feet high. At the top is a platform with two chairs. And resting right in front of the chairs is a Norden bombsight.

Arbocast. He heard me. He's more bluster than bite after all.

Murphy, the same pale cadet who was guarding the hangar the

other day, stands next to the trainer setup, arms crossed, legs spread. He's not going to budge while this thing is out in the world. But if he's here and not down at North Base, that means this is the same Norden that Sky showed me in *Flamin' Mamie*. So there's no reason for me to have my own private lesson with him this afternoon. Darn it. I'll just have to settle for being near him in our very public classroom.

Hemming uses chalk to draw a cross target on the floor and all the guys elbow one another, vying to be first in line. I keep one eye on the men and another on the door. But Sky doesn't show. He does occasionally miss class to do inspections down at North Base, so I'm not worried. It's just as well. This way I won't be distracted by his presence and can concentrate on seeing where the challenges lie on the Norden. I take notes as each pilot and bombardier goes through the steps, turning the rate knob, moving the sight, checking the trail arm.

"Remember, more than two thousand moving parts perform these calculations," explains Hemming. "Ground speed times disc speed equals whole range. Whole range minus trail equals actual range. Actual range will determine your drop angle. When the sight angle of your telescope equals the drop angle, that's bombs away."

After lunch, we return for more simulator time. Murphy hasn't moved from his sentry position. Eight hours later, not one person has been able to hit the target.

This is going to be harder than I thought.

I finally see Sky in line for dinner at the mess. He looks as cute as ever despite a smudge of grease on his cheek. I give him my handkerchief, which he promptly sniffs dramatically and sticks into his front pocket. "I'm not dirtying this. I'm saving it forever." Then he kisses me on the cheek, right there in front of everyone, which causes a lot of whistles and hoots.

I feel my whole face heat up. Does this mean I'm his girl? I watch him shyly, thrilled he kept my hankie.

He and Robert join us at the gals' table and we all try to understand how a turbo jet might eventually become a rocket plane. It sounds like science fiction and he can't tell us any details anyway, so it's both amazing and frustrating at the same time.

Over dessert, I let it slip that today is my eighteenth birthday. September fourteenth. I figure I better tell someone before midnight comes and it passes for another year. Obviously I didn't get a call from home because Mom doesn't have the phone number at Muroc. She thinks I'm at UCLA. I tried reaching them myself after class this afternoon but no one answered. Alyce doesn't even know when my birthday is. I felt so young compared to the other PCS girls that I never mentioned it. The lack of birthday wishes had me feeling sorry for myself.

"Well, in that case, I'm going to take you somewhere to celebrate," says Sky.

I'm so flustered by this second public declaration of affection that I say something sarcastic. "Muroc isn't exactly a bustling metropolis." I remember all too well the sorry general store and post office when I first arrived.

"There's a place about twenty miles northeast of here that you didn't see when you stepped off the train." He winks. "Something only us pilots know about."

"Ooh," squeal the girls.

Sky stands. "I need to clean up. Meet me at the jeep depot at 2000 hours."

Wow. A real date, off the base. If I could talk to the girls back home at Sigma Chi, I'd say, Oh! Look at me now!

When Sky leaves, everyone turns to Robert, the only pilot left and therefore resident expert. "Do tell," says someone.

But Robert just turns his mouth into a Cheshire Cat smile, making me wonder what in the world is in store for me.

# 23.

Sky commandeers a two-seater jeep and we drive out the gate. The rain has stopped and for once there's no dust kicking up into my nose. Being alone with him is so much easier than when other people are around. Remnants of Nervous Nellie. Trudie always knew just how to act with Don and his friends. I doubt I'll ever be that relaxed in public.

He glides right through a stop sign.

"Don't you have to stop for the roadrunners at least?"

"Not when we have somewhere to be." He sticks his head out the window and gazes up, all while his foot is still on the gas pedal. I poke my head out my side. The sky is black with pinpricks of glitter. The wind whips my hair. And I think about what Helen said. How can I feel such a rush when there's a war going on?

"Is this where you wanted to take me?" I yell into the night. "Because I love it!"

"This is just the means to an end."

After about fifteen more minutes of bumping along a muddy road, we pull into the driveway of a large ranch. Our headlights illuminate a sign, RANCHO ORO VERDE, DRIVE-IN OR FLY-IN. Horses graze in a corral and there's a pen with dozens of pigs honking and lolling about. Lights are on inside the main house. I hear the faint tinkle of jazz.

"Who lives here?"

"The famous Pancho Barnes."

I picture a mustachioed cowboy with spurs on his heels. But when we open the door, we're greeted by a double-chinned man with a mischievous grin. His brown hair falls just below the ears and he wears blue jeans and a white button-down shirt. He hugs Sky as if he hasn't seen him in ages.

"Eleanor, this is Pancho: stunt pilot, hog farmer, rodeo impresario, flight school proprietor, hostess with the mostest."

Pancho is a she.

"Come in, come in. We're just about to toss Wilkins in the pool," she says.

"You do know the lightning storm can kick back up at any moment and that pool water conducts electricity?" asks Sky.

She shrugs. "It's tradition, what can I say?" Pancho leans into me conspiratorially. "We have more fun here in a night than most of the weenies in the world have in a lifetime!"

She's the most original woman I've ever seen.

A piano player hammers out a ragtime. In the salon, pretty girls in green sashes mill among the crowd of about two dozen male pilots. Sky seems to know everyone as he shakes hands and makes his way to the front of the bar. Green is for verde, Sky explains, which is named for the alfalfa that Pancho grows on her natural aquifer. A woman who Sky calls Dazzling Dallas Morely circulates and keeps all the pilots happy by making sure there's at least one green-sashed girl for every two men.

Sky buys us drinks, a Tom Collins for me and a whiskey for him. The first sip tickles my throat but then it's easier the second taste.

We all traipse outside to watch the group throw Wilkins into the pool, uniform and all.

"A dodo no more!" shouts one of the men.

Sky explains that a dodo is a cadet who hasn't flown yet, and since Wilkins finished his first solo flight a few days ago, he needs to get baptized. Wilkins takes it all in good humor and then pulls two more pilots into the pool and a green-sashed girl to join them. Soon it's a splash fest.

Sky gently places his hand on the small of my back and moves us to a private spot away from the water. He clinks his glass against mine. "Happy birthday, Eleanor."

We sip from our glasses, watching each other. Then he lowers his head, putting his cheek against my hair. "You smell like primrose and a little like BX shampoo. But mostly primrose."

"Is that a native flower to Utah? I've never smelled one."

"It's sweet and just like spring, with a hint of orange lollipop." He moves his head so we're facing each other. "I wonder if your lips taste like primrose, too."

With his free hand, he tilts up my chin and we kiss. Finally. I can see what all the fuss is about. I don't want to stop.

"You're sure you want to drive all that way back to base?" asks Pancho, seeming to appear out of nowhere.

We pull apart quickly.

She's eyeing us with a grin. "We're a hotel now. I've got so many people flying in for civilian pilot training, I thought it made sense to offer rooms."

"We're good," says Sky. "But thanks." I'm too embarrassed to meet his eye. I wonder if his cheeks are the color of his hair. I know mine are.

After another drink and a round of pinochle and some rowdy sing-alongs with the pianist, we drive home. It's past 2:00 a.m. Sky holds my hand across the center gap between the jeep seats and doesn't let go until we're back at the depot.

At the door to my barrack, I stand on my tiptoes and kiss him. Multiple times.

# 24.

The following day is still cloudy with a small chance of rain. But it's just as hot as ever. I'm about to order powdered eggs when a shy cadet brings a scrawled message to me in the mess.

> *Norden class before Norden class? S.*

Breakfast forgotten, I hop into a jeep shuttle for North Base. Once I arrive, I spot Sky drinking coffee and laughing with a few guys in the canteen. He pops out from the crowd like a color bar on a dull khaki shirt. No one holds a candle to him. Or else I'm just smitten.

I wave shyly.

"Duty calls, brothers!" Sky jogs over to me and plants a quick kiss on my cheek.

"It's awfully early, Captain," I tell him.

"The early bird catches the worm."

He's already installed the football onto the stabilizer. Inside the hangar it's starting to get warm, but *Flamin' Mamie* is still nice and cool.

"We don't have much time before Murphy the Stickler comes to pick this puppy up for Hemming's class. Let's get a move on."

"Yessir."

It takes all my willpower to focus on the little box of rivets with Sky standing right behind me. I can smell his soap and picture the soft red hair on his forearms.

"What's the delay, Schiff?"

I wipe the smile off my face and turn the drift knob.

Unfortunately, after seven attempts, I don't get to bombs away.

"One more try," I beg him.

"No can do. Murphy will be here at 0845."

I watch him carry the Norden back into its vault. What a special person. This morning, Sky left his buddies and went out of his way just for me. Just so I could have more practice time. After he locks the door, I take his hand. "I feel like the luckiest girl on the planet."

He kisses one side of my mouth. "Luck has nothing to do with it." He kisses the other side. "It's your brain."

"Not my lips?"

"Well, maybe those, too."

"I suppose we should head on up to Main Base for actual class?" I say reluctantly.

"I need to take advantage of this rare desert storm or not-quite-rainstorm, whatever this is, to catch up on my reading. A Super Marauder arrives next week, which means a different manual, different instrumentation."

"Got it. I will definitely not maraud you any more today. Is that even a verb?"

"I don't think so, but you can maraud me tonight."


Some AAF brass are visiting Muroc and class is canceled for the afternoon. Like Sky, Helen is grounded due to weather. She and I linger in the empty mess after lunch, not quite ready to get up and face the heat.

"Gin rummy in the shade somewhere?" I ask.

She clicks her tongue. "I'm bored of that game."

"I know! Let's while away the hours in the library."

"Perfect!"

When we walk in, Anderson is hanging various newspapers over wooden dowels. It looks like the drying rack Mom uses at home. What a clever idea.

The librarian beams when he sees us. "Welcome back, Miss Eleanor." Anderson is the only one on base, besides the women and Sky, who doesn't call me by my last name. It's nice.

"My friend Helen and I are looking for something interesting to read."

"You can check out these newspapers. They're a few weeks out of date, but we have a *New York Times*, a *Kansas City Star*, and the *Daily Express* from the UK."

"More bad news?" I ask.

"Things are looking up in Stalingrad," he answers. "I still can't believe Germany attacked the Soviet Union. We fought the Bolsheviks in the Great War and now we're all on the same side."

Before I left home, that was all the talk of our Shabbos dinners. How the Russians and Germans split up Poland and what that meant for the Jews, but I've lost track of what's happening between the two powers now, being so wrapped up in my numbers. "So things aren't as dire as Arbocast says they are?"

Helen scoffs. "I wouldn't bet against Arbocast."

Anderson nods. "She's right. The government office of censorship controls all the news. Let's just say they want us to have hope. During the Great War, the military took over all the radio content and censored photographs. I actually have a few never-before-seen pictures in my collection. But believe me, they're rare."

"That doesn't seem right," I say. "We should know the truth."

"If a reporter wants access to what's really happening, they have to have credentials. Only the gatekeepers from the military can grant that." Anderson frowns, rubs his age-spotted hands. "Arthritis is acting up again."

"My grandma used to place a warm compress of black cohosh tea on her knuckles," offers Helen. "They probably don't have that in the mess, but maybe some dried ginger?" She grabs the *Daily Express* and pushes the armchairs closer so we can read it together.

"Thanks for being so nice to the old guy," I whisper.

"He reminds me of my grandpa."

The headlines leap from the front page.

*Allied Victory at the Battle of El Alamein*

*Japs Open New Guinea Offensive*

*Russians Cross the Volga*

Helen flips past the front page. "I find it best not to think about who's winning or losing. It can drive a person crazy. Just give me my flight instructions and let me do my work. That's what I say."

That's probably sound advice. Reading Philadelphia's *Jewish Exponent* certainly felt like a roller coaster of emotions for my family.

Helen and I laugh at the Marmite ad. We agree it probably tastes disgusting.

"But it promises to fill you up in times of rationing!" I say.

"Ovaltine guarantees a sound sleep even through the Blitz!" chimes Helen.

"Can't smoke on duty? Chew Robinson's Gums!"

We spend the afternoon reading an installment of one of Agatha Christie's Poirot novels, which immediately hooks us both.

"How's Robert?" I ask her as we walk back to our barrack. It's dusty as usual, the heat oppressive and still. A flock of small birds, unbothered by the weather, zip by us as if late for a party.

"He's leaving at the end of the week for Caltech near Los Angeles."

"Oh no! Well, at least he'll still be in California."

"Yes, but I could end up in Europe at some point, who knows." Helen's expression is stoic. "It's like with those newspaper headlines. Best not to let your emotions rule you or you'll drive yourself crazy."

"I suppose . . ." I stop to admire a lone pink wildflower. I'd like to pick it, but it's defied all the odds just growing here like this.

"What? You don't agree?"

I get the part about not being too involved in the daily war battles. But love is a different thing. I keep silent.

Now Helen stops walking. "Don't tell me you've fallen for Sky."

"Okay, I won't."

And I do just that. I stay quiet and don't tell her.

# 25.

Last night, while we were watching the sun descend, making the Sierra Nevada Mountains look purple, Sky told me to come even earlier to North Base the next morning. "In case the weather clears and I have to go up on a test run, I want to make sure we have enough time for you to practice on the Norden," he said.

Now it's 0600. I had to track down a driver to take me down here. No one is at the canteen. There's no one around at all. Sky takes my hand and leads me to an open-air jeep. I wish I'd brought my new hat.

"Where are we going?" I ask, trying to gather my hair in a ponytail as we bounce down the road. "*Flamin' Mamie* is south of us."

"And you don't even have a compass. Impressive."

"Are you taking me to another brothel like Rancho Oro Verde?" I tease.

He lets out a booming laugh. "Pancho would be appalled. Those green-sashed ladies are on the up-and-up. But I do want to be away from prying eyes." He places his hand on my leg, which feels warm on top, tingly underneath.

In just a few minutes, Sky turns off the motor. *Flamin' Mamie* is in front of us, in all her glory, sitting on a lake bed.

"This isn't Lake Rogers, is it?"

"It's Rosamond. I had her towed."

I notice the tow tractor still attached to the plane. "We're not . . . going up, are we?"

He snorts. "They'd have my neck. Heck, they'd probably chop it all the way down to the stripes on my shirt. No. We're staying right here. I just thought it might be helpful for you to practice on something other than a box of rivets."

I grin at him as we get out of the jeep. "You're incredible, you know that?"

"So they say." He kicks the ground, looking kind of sheepish. "Okay, no one has actually said that. Except you."

"Well, you are."

We get out of the jeep and walk to the rolling ladder in front of the plane.

"Usually, this area is full of cocky turbo-jet pilots from Bell or Lockheed trying to break a record," says Sky.

I elbow him. "Are you saying Helen's boyfriend is cocky?"

"I said nothing of the sort," he says in mock denial.

"Can you imagine flying with jet propulsion?"

"I'm probably just jealous."

I remember the other cadets hanging on Robert's every word that day in the jeep. He really seemed like a superhero out of the comic books.

"Anyway, since it's not flying weather today, we have the place to ourselves." He points downwind about two hundred yards. "See that Joshua tree? I've taped off a red circle around the base. That's your target."

"What about the presets?"

"We're going to input them ourselves."

"Hot dog!"

Sky has ballistics tables already spread out on the radio operator's desk. The math isn't from PCS specifically, since we didn't work on bombs, but seeing all those familiar columns with tiny numbers is like running into an old friend. Of course I can't let on to Sky about any of it.

He flips one of the pages. "So you know the Norden solves for the point of release by computing the dropping angle. For that, it needs three factors. Disc speed, trail, and ground speed. We get disc speed and trail values from these bombing tables."

"And who writes these fabulous bombing tables?" I ask, playing with him a little.

He shrugs. "Some chrome dome holed up in a tiny room somewhere at Aberdeen, I guess."

"What makes you think the person is bald?"

"Okay, someone with a lot of hair, then."

That's more like it.

"The third factor, ground speed, is solved when you synchronize for rate, which we've been doing in class," he continues.

I nod. "All those darn knobs."

"We'll get altitude and true air speed from our instrument panel. For today, let's pretend we're flying at 25,000 feet at an airspeed of 260 miles per hour. To calculate true air speed, or TAS, we—"

I interrupt him. "Take the indicated airspeed, and for each thousand feet above sea level, add two percent."

He bumps my shoulder. "Sheesh. Just humor me, will ya? Or else I'll feel like a hired hand."

I shut up. After we do all the calculations and presets, we're ready to go. He ducks his head out the door and starts to back down the stairs.

"Hey, where are you going?" I call.

"I'm driving."

"What do you mean?"

"I'm going to tow *Flamin' Mamie* to make it seem like we're actually flying. That way your sighting angle will actually decrease."

"Genius!"

"I guess we both are." At the bottom of the stairs, he pauses. "When you think you have the crosshairs lined up, stop and signal to me. I'll come back in and check to see if you hit the target."

I look through the telescope and make an imaginary line to the target. This is my line of sight.

I feel the plane slowly move forward. I begin to adjust the course knobs. While I'm doing this, I know that the two thousand tiny parts of the Norden are working like ants, multiplying, dividing, and calculating for actual time of fall and ground speed. As we approach the target, my line of sight sweeps toward the vertical and the sight angle decreases to 0 degrees. When the crosshairs are lined up, I signal Sky.

He shakes his head. "Your lateral bubble was too far to the left."

The next time, he says, "Your fore and aft bubble was too far front of center."

The third time, he just says, "Nope."

This goes on for hours. My neck is aching. My eyes are burning. But I won't quit. Finally, on the twenty-third try, Sky lets out a whoop.

"Yes?" I peer up at him, my vision blurry from all that focusing.

"Yes!" And he bends down to kiss me.

"I can't believe it!" I say. "Now I know how mountain climbers feel." It's strange that accomplishing this feat has become so important to me. It's not like I'll ever have to actually use the Norden. Maybe mastering hitting the target is the last stage in mastering what's actually going wrong.

"I wish I could take you up in one of these for real," says Sky.

"To practice with the Norden?"

"Just to show you how beautiful it is from ten thousand feet." He looks out the window of the nose. "Maybe when this damn war is over." His eyes drift to the clock on *Flamin' Mamie*'s instrument panel. "Shoot. It's 0850."

Quickly, we both carry the football back to the jeep with Sky walking backward down the stairs. Sky unlatches the tow and we speed back to the hangar.

It's 0900. Class starts right now.

"Shoot, shoot, and triple shoot," moans Sky.

"Maybe we should just drive it up to Main Base?" I suggest. "We can just say we decided to help out with the delivery."

He parks the jeep, running around to the back. "It's against protocol. Best to just store it and pretend that we know nothing about a missing Norden."

Again, Sky and I carry the football toward the hangar. I'm facing him as he walks backward and see his expression change.

"What's wrong?" I ask.

"What the hell do you think you're doing?" yells an angry voice.

It's Murphy, that's what's wrong.

"I've been looking everywhere for this thing!" he screams. "Hemming has radioed me three times already. I had to lie, saying it was in maintenance. Jesus H. Christ."

My arms are about to die from carrying so much weight. "Can we just set the Norden down and then talk about it?"

The cadet shifts left, then right, like he wants to run, but can't because he's glued to the ground. "Arbocast is going to blow a gasket."

"Go right ahead and tell him," says Sky. "But she's the only one on this whole damn base who's gotten to bombs away."

Murphy makes a disgruntled sound. Then he elbows me aside and hefts the other end of the football. "I'll take it from here." He and Sky carry it into Murphy's waiting truck.

"You coming?" Murphy asks me. He's peeved, all right, but it's clear he's not going to say anything to anyone.

I may as well hitch a ride with him. I blow Sky a secret kiss so Murphy can't see. Sky pretend-catches it, then gets into his jeep and makes a U-turn back to Rogers to pick up *Flamin' Mamie*.

A few hours later, my stomach growls. I realize I forgot to eat today. Lunch can't come soon enough. But there's still thirty minutes to go in class. I'm looking over the shoulder of one of the bombardiers, trying to help him reduce his range angle, when I hear the explosion followed by the siren.

It's not on Main Base. It's coming from farther north.

# 26.

There are injured coming in. No one knows how many. I rush to the base hospital. Please don't let one of them be him. Please don't let one be him.

I throw open the door, scanning the beds. They're all empty.

Someone calls my name. Helen is standing in front of a desk, speaking to an administrator. I must have run right past her.

"What are you doing here?" I gasp.

Her eyes fill with tears.

No. No. No.

She opens her arms and I collapse into them.

"I came as fast as I could," she says. "I was actually airborne as well."

I step back from her. "Is he . . ." I can't bring myself to say the word.

"Sky's in surgery. I'm trying to find out more details, but that's all anybody knows."

"Where are the medics?"

"In the operating room. This isn't like a regular hospital. It's a skeleton staff."

We find some chairs to wait it out. I squeeze her hand tightly like it's my lifeline, but she doesn't let go. And she doesn't say anything about my darn emotions.

The ammonia smell is overpowering. They probably have to clean this place every day to keep it sanitary. Dust in a wound would be deadly. After a while, I muster up the courage to hear details. "What happened up there?"

She hesitates a few seconds. "Oh, screw the security protocol. I was towing a canvas target. That's what I've been doing since I got here. The gunners practice hitting it from the ground, to get them ready for combat."

"That sounds nuts. What if they hit you and not the target?"

"It's happened, believe me. One time I had to make an emergency landing. An engine blew and the plane was riddled with holes."

"Does the canvas ever get caught in trees?"

"Not here, but back in Delaware, yes. Trees, barns, phone lines."

I'm hugely curious about Helen's job, but I also know I'm avoiding hearing what happened to Sky. "So you were up there and then what?"

"There must have been an error with the radio tower because Sky flew into my airspace. The antiair gun hit his plane. The artillery went right through the window of the cockpit. The copilot was killed instantly. Sky lost control and crashed into the lake bed."

"We felt the explosion all the way over here on the main base. There wasn't a bomb on board, was there?"

She looks grave. "I don't know. From the air, all I could see was a sand cloud."

Arbocast storms in, his aide trailing after him, ghostly as the paper on the clipboard he's carrying. With his slight frame and Arbocast's large one, they remind me of Laurel and Hardy. "What the hell happened?"

The poor administrator behind the desk, a pockmarked young man, cowers. Helen stands and briefs Colonel Arbocast.

"Goddamn it!" he fumes. "Theodore Richards from Wichita?"

Helen nods grimly.

He turns to his aide. "You stay here, Morgan. Inform me the minute you hear anything. I need to go call this boy's parents."

The thin man salutes his boss, still unnerved.

Arbocast is about to tear out of there when he spies me. "Why aren't you in class? I need some good news, Schiff. Some good fucking news."

When he leaves, I look at Helen imploringly.

"Go," Helen tells me. "I'll come find you when I know more."

Of course I can't concentrate. My notebook remains blank. One trainee actually gets to "bombs away," causing much jubilation, but I barely register the sounds of excitement.

Two hours later, Helen pokes her head in the classroom.

I can't tell from her face. Is it good news or bad news? I drop my pencil and hurry to the door.

"He's out of surgery. He lost a leg. But he's alive."

Thank you, God. It seems there wasn't a bomb on board or else he'd never have survived. But oh, my poor Sky. Like that amputee I saw on the platform at 30th Street Station, the one from the battle of Midway. I'll never forget the way the young man looked as he hung his head over his father's shoulder. Sky has—had—a whole future of piloting ahead of him. He wanted to fly jets.

"Can I see him?"

"He hasn't woken up yet. We'll talk later. I have to get back to the crash site."

I have no appetite, but Carolyn and Ann force me to go to the mess and try to get something down. I pick at my beans and let the talk circle around me. Something about the Pacific theater. Why do they call it the theater anyway? As if it's some vaudeville act or a place to watch a movie and eat popcorn instead of a destination for violence. I don't want to listen to the voices of the men, of my roommates, but it's hard to ignore what they're saying. Light carrier USS *Wasp* was sunk by a Japanese submarine off Guadalcanal. The RMS *Laconia*, carrying civilians, Allied soldiers, and Italian POWs, was torpedoed and sunk off the coast of West Africa. And in Europe, Hitler delivered a speech to the German citizens, boasting that Stalingrad will be taken. Which is completely the opposite of what Anderson said.

What am I doing so far from home? What's the point of all this? Where is the fairness in this world? I don't wait for Helen to give me information about Sky. Immediately after dinner I go to the hospital myself.

I find him right away. There's only one bed occupied. His face looks the same except for a gash on his chin, but his lower body is like a mummy. His right leg is wrapped up with white bandages. It must have sustained serious injuries as well. His left leg is a white stub. I feel nauseous and my stomach convulses. I swallow down my bile, determined to bear witness, to look into the fire. God knows he's the one who will have to face worse. A medic takes his temperature, but Sky doesn't even budge when the thermometer is removed. The medic retreats through a swinging door and I pull up a chair next to his cot. I begin to stroke his forehead.

"You must really like me," I say. "You went and sacrificed your leg just so you could dance as poorly as I do." Sky doesn't react to my words or my touch. I keep going.

"We can invent a new dance, the wheelchair Lindy. All we need is something with a small turning radius. Like the dining chair and bicycle wheels that FDR fashioned for himself. It will become a smash across the country. Actually, my dad can learn it, too. All victims of war and strokes—"

I stop mid-sentence. I just told him about Dad. I wait for the crushing blow, the punishment I deserve. But it's just me and Sky, alone in this medical barrack.

I care about this man. I want him to know.

"You asked me how I got so smart? So good at math? It was because of him. He's a brilliant math professor. He was writing a book on transcendental numbers when he had a stroke. You and my dad are more alike than you can imagine. Only it's his right leg that doesn't work. Dad plus Sky equals one person."

Is that a hint of a smile? No. He's completely out.

"The thing is, I caused it to happen. Which is why I never wanted him to know I was good at math, too. Because it's not fair that I'm blessed with this brain when I'm the one who damaged his."

Sky breathes quiet and steady.

There. I said it. I shared my secret. But I know it doesn't count if the person I told it to can't hear me.

# 27.

It takes four days for him to wake up. When I walk into the hospital he's alert, sitting up with pillows propped behind his back against the wooden slats of the barrack wall. The ammonia smell fades to the background when our eyes meet.

"You're here," he says hoarsely.

"And you're awake."

He moves his arm toward me so I can hold his hand.

"Some dumb luck, huh?" he says.

"I'm so sorry, Sky." I will not cry. It's not about me. "Can I get you anything? Are you in pain?"

"Read me something, will ya? Take my mind off this crash that I keep replaying in my head."

I look around. There's nothing on the little side tables next to each bed but water glasses and clean washcloths. I do, however, see a copy of the *Antelope Valley Press* on the administrator's desk.

I scan the front page. Everything is war news. Who even knows if it's factual. I find a feature on the baseball team at the high school in Lancaster and read to him how the Antelopes routed the Bulldogs, 8–0.

Then a short article on the second-to-last page catches my eye. Despite the British RAF destroying Düsseldorf, three to four thousand Jews from Stanislau have been deported to a place called Belzec and killed in one day. Batja is from Stanislau! It happened on Rosh Hashana, which was a few days ago. I didn't even register the holiday. The chapel is mainly used by Christian soldiers, and no one talked about the Jewish New Year, so it passed me by.

Could this be real? I don't know what to believe anymore. But why would such a specific story like this be in a small local paper? Maybe that's exactly the reason. The national censors aren't paying attention to the little town of Antelope Valley.

"Why'd you stop reading?" asks Sky.

"Sorry. I was looking at an ad. Let's see if we can find some more scintillating local news." But my eye drifts back to the article.

There are no names of the victims. Just a statement from the German government that Stanislau is now Judenrein. Free of Jews.

I can't stop myself. Now the tears spill from my eyes.

"It'll be okay, Eleanor. They have these amazing wood-and-leather prosthetic legs for amputees."

"It's not that, Sky. I mean, this accident is so tragic and awful, and I'd be lying if I said it isn't adding to my feelings of despair, but I know you're going to walk again, maybe even dance. I'm just . . . Jews are being slaughtered. My cousin might be one of them. And I can't do anything about it. I—" I burst into sobs. "I want to go home."

I lift one of the cloths from a pile next to his bed and blow my nose.

"I could give you your hankie back, you know."

"You keep it."

"You can't go home, Eleanor. We need you here."

"You just want me around for selfish reasons. And believe me, I feel the same way about you."

"Not true." He shakes his head vehemently, then winces from the effort.

I look around for the medic to give him something for the pain. But he's nowhere to be seen.

"We need you here to troubleshoot the Norden," gasps Sky.

"You mean to supervise the boys learning how to use it, right?"

"I'm a second lieutenant, Eleanor . . . I've been briefed. There's something we've been missing. Some X factor that the Norden can't adjust for." He shifts in bed, trying in vain to sit up higher. He should save his strength, but he won't stop talking. "Maybe it's clouds that are obscuring things? Smoke screens from . . . enemy fire? Attack planes . . . that require us to move into defensive formations . . . so we can't . . . maneuver?" His voice peters out until it sounds papery thin. "I don't know. But if anyone can figure it out, it's you."

The medic comes over to us, glaring at me. "It's time to leave, miss. He needs to rest."

So Sky knew about my role here the entire time. Was that why he was so insistent on giving me practice time? Were all those private lessons just an excuse to help me troubleshoot faster so the US Army could take the advantage?

Maybe he doesn't have feelings for me at all.

My eyes burn and it's not the ammonia. Helen's right. I shouldn't have gotten so attached. I should have kept my emotions at bay. Serves me right. I'm so inexperienced that I ran headlong into boyfriend land. And now I'm a blubbering bundle of insecurity.

Outside the hospital, I start to cry. Eleanor Roosevelt's voice comes into my ear loud and clear. This is no way for a person to behave who has such an important job to do. Your country needs you. You need to keep your eyes on the goal. Fix the inaccuracies in the Norden. Then you can worry whether or not some boy likes you.

She's right. She always is.

I sniffle and push romance out of my mind. Sky said there's an X factor. Descartes decided that letters toward the end of the alphabet would be used to symbolize the unknown. So $x$ has always meant the one thing we do not conclusively know. But I can solve for $x$. I know how to do that. Maybe I've been focusing on the wrong thing—the small parts. I need to go back and look at the situation in its entirety. See the big picture.

In the middle of the hot and dry pathway, I close my eyes. No twitching occurs. It doesn't need to. I'm controlling the knowing now. I picture a globe, like we used to have in grade school, tilted at a perfect 23.5 degrees, which is critical for life here on Earth. I place imaginary red dots on the places where fighting has occurred. North Africa, the Atlantic Ocean, France, Greece, the Soviet Union, Hawai'i, the South Pacific, Norway, Poland, Bohemia, Moravia, the Sudetenland.

I hear Batja's voice. It's her writing voice, but the Yiddish comes floating into my ear. *Az mikh nit aumzist shtarbn.* I picked up enough of the language from years of correspondence, as well as listening to Uncle Herman and Aunt Jona, that I know what she's saying. *Don't let me die in vain.*

I shut my eyes tighter. The desert sun shrouds the back of my eyelids with orange. Sweat drips down my face, my neck.

The globe. The war. Global war. It's everywhere. Everything is connected. Including the Axis powers. If the Japanese can be stopped in the Pacific, then Germany and Italy will be weakened.

*Don't let me die in vain.*

I open my eyes. I'm trying, Batja. I'm trying!

Most of the planes here at Muroc have been deployed to operations in the South Pacific, whereas planes being sent to Europe leave from bases on the East Coast. I ask Arbocast's aide to give me site maps of all the island bombing runs where the Norden has been used up until now. I compare ballistics tables from each one of those missions and look at the point of impact as well as the geology of the region. This time my left eye does twitch. Volcanoes and vegetation and ocean and rocky terrain and rainforests all rise up from the map and dance in front of me. I drink stale coffee and don't go to sleep the whole night.

By the time the sun rises over the eastern part of Rogers Lake, I'm delirious with exhaustion. But also ecstatic.

Because I know what the problem with the Norden is.

# 28.

"It's turbulence."

"We've accounted for that," says the colonel. Arbocast isn't screaming, though he looks like he could at any minute. His head may be hanging and his eyes may be peering through tented fingers, but he looks ready to spring up and strike.

"If I may, sir. You haven't factored in the difference in air pressure that occurs when you approach from the sea and fly over an island."

"Go on."

"The air over the ocean, volcanoes, a flat island—it's all different. Vegetation or lack of vegetation will change dynamic viscosity. Also, the time of day, the amount of heat reflecting from the ground. At twenty-five thousand feet, as opposed to sea level, these factors are very different."

"But the stabilizer accounts for pitching and yawing. Turbulence shouldn't affect it," he says.

"I'm talking about the ballistic. Not the plane."

He's gobsmacked. "What do we do? Change the input numbers?"

"The problem with turbulence is its unpredictability. It can change on a dime. The calculations need to be done at the moment."

"You mean in theater."

I nod.

"Fuckin' A." He pounds his desk with a fist, sending papers flying. "I'm sending you to Pearl Harbor. I want you to explain your findings to the bombardiers there. Teach them how to compute for turbulence and adjust trail and drift accordingly."

"But what about my job here?" Don't think about Sky. About his recovery. About a future with him. That's not your priority.

"Your presence is mandatory. There's a target in the archipelago of the Solomon Islands we haven't been able to reach," says Arbocast. "It's high priority. The hit needs to be within a few feet. With this new information, we could actually do it."

"But don't you want to order some test runs to check my theory?"

"The brass at the air base in Hawai'i can order some trial drops if necessary. Wheels up at 0700."

It feels like my destiny is to leave places. Sunrise tomorrow. First things first. I need to sleep for a couple of hours. Then I'll visit Sky. Just as a friend.

"Oh, and Schiff? Good work."

I salute. "Thank you, sir."


I set an alarm clock for 1100, which gives me just over three hours to nap. I take a cold shower, grab a sandwich from the mess, and head to Admin for my appointment with Arbocast's aide, Morgan.

Without the colonel around, Morgan is at ease and efficient. I'm tempted to joke with him about our mutual fear of Arbocast, but of course you can't speak ill of a superior officer. Who knows how we'd get disciplined.

"You'll need to sign these," he says, handing me a stack of papers. It's a bunch of official forms having to do with insurance and army benefits. Standard procedure, I assume. But when I scan the first sheet, I get angry. "It says here that I'm not entitled to burial expenses or survivor benefits?"

"That's correct. You're part of WAAC, which is an auxiliary division of the army. You're a civil servant, not military. Officially, that is."

"So they're flying me to Hawai'i, a place that was attacked not even a full year ago, and my family won't continue to get my salary if something happens to me?"

"I'm sorry, Miss Schiff. My hands are tied." I shouldn't be taking it out on him. He has to face Arbocast every day and here I am getting mad at the poor guy. But what an unfair, imbalanced policy for all the Rosies doing their part. "I assume Second Lieutenant Samuel Muir will be getting compensation for his injury?"

"Of course."

At least Sky will be taken care of. My signature on the forms is wobbly, despite my bravado.

My next stop is the library. I want to find something to read aloud to Sky.

This time, Anderson is unloading books from a cardboard box that looks about to burst.

"You're just in time. Got some new donations in. Want to help me sort?"

"I wish I could." Especially with his arthritis. "But I'm shipping out tomorrow. Mind if I take a look?"

I kneel down next to him and pore through the box. "There's a bunch of children's books in here."

He shrugs. "I guess the good folks of the Antelope Valley don't realize this is a military base."

Maybe in the future, people like Ruby and her officer husband will raise families here. It's hard to imagine growing up in a place like this, but sadly, it's also hard to imagine a world without war.

A colorful cover catches my attention. It has a blue sky with gold stars and a lovely little house covered in snow. "It's by Eleanor Roosevelt!" I exclaim. "I didn't know she wrote books for kids."

The name of the book is *Christmas: A Story*. As I flip through the pages, it becomes clear this is a religious allegory of some kind, set in Nazi-occupied Holland in 1940. There's a big, bad wandering man, most likely symbolizing Hitler, a sweet little girl, and a lot of mention of the Christ Child, which is very foreign to me. But from what Sky told me about his Bible-focused upbringing in Utah, I think he'll like it. "Can I take this?"

"Be my guest."

"Thanks for everything, Anderson. Promise me you'll try that tea compress?"

He tips his hat to me. "Will do."

Before I head over to the hospital, though, I go back to my barrack and write a letter. I seal it in an envelope and slip it in between the pages of the book.

Sky's in good spirits. I hold up the book. "Don't laugh. It's for children. But it happens to be written by my guardian angel."

"You're my guardian angel," grins Sky.

"Don't say things like that." My voice comes out more harshly than I intend.

"Okay . . . So, tell me who wrote it, then."

I tell him about Eleanor Roosevelt and her growing up shy and me being called Nervous Nellie. It feels so good to share at least this part of my life with him. Especially because we'll probably never see each other again.

"I don't think of you as a nervous type at all."

"Ha! I've been tricking you this whole time."

"Well, speaking of tricks, I have a confession to make. I wasn't totally asleep when you came to visit me these past few days."

Oh no. All that talk about Dad. My heart is thumping so hard it's going to fly out of my chest. "Did you hear any of what I said?"

"Honestly, I couldn't make out words. Just the tone of your voice penetrated through the haze."

I exhale in relief.

"That's why you're my angel."

"What did you say?"

He takes my hand. "Your voice got me through the bad part, Eleanor. You really are my living, breathing angel." His smile is so sincere that it melts me.

"You like me, then?"

"What are you talking about? I more than like you."

I'm so relieved I kiss him smack on the lips, even with Mr. No-Funny-Business over there at the desk. I'm tempted to curl up next to him in his cot. But the bed is too narrow and the administrator is giving me the evil eye. Don't even think about it, he's thinking. That other leg needs to stay good and still.

I open the book. "Ready?"

"'The times are so serious that even children should be made to understand that there are vital differences in people's beliefs which lead to differences in behavior.' Eleanor Roosevelt.

"'St. Nicholas's Eve, 1940, was cold and the snow was falling . . .'"

When I finish the story, Sky is snoring quietly. I drift off in the chair, too. When we wake, the light in the windows has turned to slate and the administrator has set a kerosene lantern next to the bed. Maybe he's not such a meanie.

"So, I have some news," I begin.

Sky grins at me. "You solved it, didn't you?"

"I think I did. Arbocast wants me to train the bombardiers at Pearl

Harbor to adjust the Norden for ballistic turbulence when they're at twenty thousand feet up."

"Turbulence, wow! I knew you could do it!" A darkness comes over those normally bright blue eyes of his. "When do you leave?"

"First thing tomorrow morning."

He inhales and his eyes turn bluebird happy again. "Go get those Jap bastards."

We don't talk about when and if we'll see each other again. I suspect there are conversations like this happening every hour of every day. Our situation is different than most. I'm not the girl being left at home. He's not the boy going off to war. I know now that our feelings for each other are real. But I don't know if Sky and I have a future together. As Helen and my mom said, all we have is right now.

I take out the envelope I'd put inside the book earlier. It's a letter for Mom and Dad. I wrote that I'm going on an airplane for the first time. That I can't say where, but that I'm excited. I also told them about Sky so that they'll know I experienced the wonder of having someone who touched my heart. After reading that release of liability Morgan had me sign, I don't trust the army to even contact my family at all. Helen told me that she personally paid for the body of one of her downed female pilot friends to be flown home. "If something happens to me, will you see that this is mailed?"

"Nothing's going to happen to you. I took the fall for both of us."

I smile sadly. "Well, just in case."

"I'll get it delivered, don't worry."

"I'm not saying goodbye," I tell him.

"Neither am I."

We stay like that, not saying goodbye, our fingers intertwined, until the desert owl hoots and the coyotes howl and the imagined sound of the Pacific lapping against the shore drowns it all out.

# 29.

I tuck a lock of hair under my earflap. Helen has me so bundled up, I look like I'm ready for a snowball fight. Besides the hat, I've got on a shearling-lined leather jacket and thickly insulated leather pants. My boots are special cold-weather zip-up boots, so large that I had to put on three pairs of socks just to be able to walk without tripping over myself. Underneath all of this I'm wearing long underwear, a woolen shirt, and glove liners.

"I'm going to melt," I tell Helen.

"You'll cool off as soon as you're airborne," says Helen. "At fifteen thousand feet, it'll be twenty below zero."

"There *is* glass covering the windows in this thing, right?"

She laughs. "Of course. These cargo planes are just like commercial flights. Only they're not pressurized or heated."

Besides me and the two pilots, there are five male cadets being transferred to Pearl Harbor. We're also transporting a jeep. We watch as an ordnance technician carries the same Norden bombsight we used in the simulator onto the aircraft. He's flanked by two additional armed guards. Morgan told me that they don't have any extra Nordens for training purposes over there, so we're taking ours.

Arbocast asks the eight passengers to raise our right hands. "Since you're flying with the Norden, you all need to take the oath of protection."

One of the cadets sneers at me and whispers something to his pal. They both laugh.

"Is there some joke you'd like to share with the group, Cadet Captain Kennedy?" says Arbocast.

"No, sir."

"Good. Because without Schiff, that bombsight back there is worthless. Treat her with as much care as you do the Norden."

"Yes, sir," says the cadet.

"I didn't catch that," says Arbocast.

"YES, SIR!"

"Now then. All of you, repeat after me," says the colonel. "Mindful of the secret trust about to be placed in me by my commander in chief, the president of the United States, by whose direction I have been chosen for transporting . . . and mindful of the fact that I am to become guardian of one of my country's most priceless military assets, the Norden bombsight . . . I do here, in the presence of Almighty God, swear by the Bombardier's Code of Honor to keep inviolate the secrecy of any and all confidential information revealed to me, and further to uphold the honor and integrity of the Army Air Corps, if need be, with my life itself."

We're then told that in case of an emergency landing, the device is loaded with thermite, which will melt on impact. If that fails, the bombardier, or in this case one of us, has to shoot it with a .45 caliber pistol. Two rounds into the rate end and one round through the telescope. The pilot points to a metal box just inside the entrance to the plane where the gun is stored.

I get goose bumps on my neck, the one exposed part of my body. I remember Ruth running out of the room that first day at lab, my mental blackout when I got briefed by Arbocast and how I felt the same way Ruth did, fearful that my calculations might be wrong and innocent people would die. And now this: guarding a secret weapon with my life? The stakes keep getting higher. I think of the scientist A. Heinzmann, who conducted experiments with frogs in the late 1800s. His theory was that if you put a frog in boiling water it will jump out, but if you put him in cold water and gradually heat it, he will stay there until he kills himself. He gets accustomed to the temperature. I am not a frog. I will never get used to what I'm being asked to do.

It's time. Helen and I give each other a bear hug.

"How will I manage without you to show me the ropes?" I say.

She gives my puffy arm a squeeze. "You're a quick learner. You'll do great." She tilts her head toward the plane. "I'll see you in the clouds."

I take one last look at the Mojave Desert, wave to Helen, then step inside. I find a fold-down seat along the side of the plane and buckle my safety belt. If I stretch out my leg, I can touch the right front wheel of the jeep.

I turn to the cadet next to me, thankfully not one of the obnoxious laughing ones. "How long is the flight?"

"Fourteen hours."

Holy mackerel. I realize I brought nothing to read. I probably wouldn't be able turn the pages anyway with the gloves I'm about to put on. Good thing I didn't get much sleep yesterday. That might be the only way to pass the time.

The engine rumbles and we speed down the runway. Impossibly, we lift off. I know the physics of it, but it's hard to believe that this cargo plane, which must weigh fifteen tons at least, plus the jeep, the Norden, and all of us, can actually get airborne.

Sleep is impossible. It's so loud I can't hear myself breathe. But oh, what a thrill to look out the window from so high up! From my side of the plane, the right wing cuts through the clouds, its two propellers churning powerfully. Below me, whitecaps flip like little birds, benign from up here, but probably strong enough to capsize a small boat if you were sailing. After a few hours we hit turbulence. The plane pitches for a long while and I throw up my breakfast into a small bag next to my seat. I picture a ballistic falling through that bumpiness and hope I know how to calculate for it.

Just when I think I'm about to either freeze to death or lose my hearing, we land at Hickam Field on the south shore of the island of Oahu. As we disembark, the pilot, sounding just like a local, tells us that the Hawai'ians named this bay Wai Momi, or mother-of-pearl, because of the abundance of pearl oysters on the sea bottom. I want to ask him more, but the cadets are removing the cloth-covered Norden from the plane and handing it over to a pair of guards. I'm the only one who follows the men into a secure vault. I watch until the football is behind locked doors.

Only after that do I allow myself to examine my surroundings. First, I notice the briny smell of the sea, and underneath that, something sweet and flowery. I take off my jacket, feeling warm in a different way than I did at Muroc. Where the Mojave Desert is dry and thirst-inducing, everything here feels wet. It's like summers in Philly. I'm used to that feeling of stepping out of one shower and into another when you walk outside. But even though I'm on a military base, this still looks like a tropical paradise. Palm trees gently sway in the breeze and the moon reflects its trail to nowhere over the Pacific. I want to curl my toes in the sand, but it's dark out and I don't know my way around. The only lights are the ones lining the runways. Everyone carries their own lanterns around. I can see them bobbing in the distance like fireflies.

A woman with one of those lanterns is waiting for me outside the bunker. She extends her hand. "Eleanor, welcome. I'm Lieutenant Annie Fox, head nurse here at Hickam." She's in formal military attire, necktie and all, with short dirty-blond curls that pop out from under her cap. Unlike Mrs. Mauchly, she wears no makeup. She's also about ten years older.

We ride in her jeep, though I tell her I've been sitting for so long, I'd rather walk. "Don't worry. You'll get plenty of exercise here. It's four miles from one end of Hickam to the other."

The flowery smell gets stronger. "What's that beautiful fragrance I keep smelling?"

"Gardenia. They're everywhere on the islands this time of year."

As we drive, she points out buildings. "There's the new mess. The old one got destroyed in the attack. Obviously, rebuilding that took priority or they'd have forty-five hundred starving Marines on their hands. They're still working on the fire station, the guardhouse, and some barracks."

In the moonlight, I see bombing evidence everywhere—piles of wood and cement, charred foliage. I wonder if they salvaged any parts of the battleships that were hit. Sarah's at home collecting a few pieces of scrap metal, but the scale of this destruction is mind-boggling.

The men's barrack is pristine, though. It's L-shaped, three floors high with lean-out balconies. "It looks like a hotel," I say.

"You should have seen it on fire."

I remember the Japanese attacked first thing in the morning when men were eating breakfast or asleep. The element of surprise is a smart and evil strategy. Like killing the Jews of Stanislau on Rosh Hashana when they least expect it.

"How many nurses are on base?"

"Eighty-two. We have three medical facilities plus the *Solace*, a hospital ship."

I whistle in surprise. "At Muroc there are no nurses. Just an army medic."

"Eighty-two wasn't nearly enough," she says.

"What was it like that day?"

She turns off the jeep motor. "Here we are." Clearly, she doesn't want to speak about it.

We've pulled up in front of the women's barrack. It's more like a dormitory, actually, reminding me of Sigma Chi.

"You'll be rooming with Ethel, one of my nurses. She's expecting you. Take care and good luck."

Ethel Greenberg is a brown-eyed Jewish girl from Los Angeles. When she tells me her last name, I feel my throat tighten. I didn't realize how much I'd been missing someone of my own background. But she doesn't seem to care one way or the other that I'm Jewish, too. She just wants to talk about her boyfriend.

"Do you have a beau?" she asks me, combing out her short, light brown hair.

I stop unpacking for a second. "I guess you could call him that. He's back at the base in California." I leave it at that. I'm afraid if I talk about Sky's injury or think about him lying there all alone, I'll start to cry. I change the subject. "Did Annie Fox get wounded or something?"

"No, why?"

"She didn't want to talk about the attack."

"She's not a talker, she's a doer. She was awarded the Purple Heart, you know. But she'll never tell you that.

"You should have seen her that morning. Calmly doing triage, marking men's foreheads with lipstick if they could be saved. All while torpedoes and shells were raining down on us. The smoke was unbearable. She ordered us to put on gas masks and helmets, fearing there might be a chemical attack. Then she commandeered corpsmen to hold flashlights for us so we could operate in the dead of night. She didn't sleep for three days."

"I can't imagine how terrifying that must have been."

Ethel slides into her bed. "It was a nightmare. I went to swab alcohol on a burn victim and the skin of his entire forearm slid right off in my hand. I fainted and Annie caught me." Ethel shudders. "When I think I actually waved to one of those nasty Japanese pilots when he swooped down, mistaking him for one of ours. They were so close to the ground, I could see the expression on his face."

"Is it possible to hate someone even if you've never met them?" I ask her.

"I hate Hitler."

"So do I." Now's my chance to connect with her about our shared background. "Yom Kippur is in a few days. Are you going to fast?"

"I don't go for that kind of thing," she says. "But you should meet Rabbi Richmond. Maybe there will be a service or something."

When I finally put on my nightgown and slip into bed, my mind whirls with images. Plumes of black smoke. Nurses in gas masks. The determined face of a Japanese pilot. An enlisted man burning alive. Unspeakable horror. I was wrong. This may be a gorgeous Hawai'ian island, but it's no paradise.

# 30.

Reveille sounds, but this time I don't bolt upright. I'm ready. I shower quickly and put on my khakis. Hickam in daylight feels like a small city with its paved walkways and roads, landscaping, and white buildings. There are numerous uniformed men and women heading in every direction and I easily flag someone down.

"Can you direct me to Army Command Headquarters?" Unlike my first day at U Penn, I speak loudly and with confidence.

At the Schofield building, I'm shown into an air-conditioned conference-type room and told to sit at a long oval table. Shortly, eight military men enter. Commander P. V. Mercer, mid-fifties with a crooked nose, distributes folders to all of us. Introductions are made. In addition to him, there's Colonel H. A. Barber, Jr., from the War Department in Washington, Major General Frederick Martin from the Hawai'ian Air Force, and various lieutenant commanders of the Eighteenth Bomb Wing and Air Base Command. The last person is a captain. He's not as decorated as the rest and has broken blood vessels on his cheeks, making it look like he's wearing rouge.

I wait for the inevitable snide comments, the what's-a-girl-doing-here?

faces, but they don't come. Perhaps these men are ranked too high to be threatened by me.

Inside my folder are aerial photographs of an island.

"If you're familiar with Operation Snapshot," begins Commander Mercer, "you already know that we've been strafing various islands to confuse the Japanese so they won't know which one we're ultimately targeting to attack. Alongside these fighter planes we've deployed another plane with an F-24 camera for reconnaissance. The camera operator is secretly looking for tunnels, caves, outcroppings, camouflaged areas, anywhere the Japanese might hide equipment."

Though the photos are high resolution and perfectly clear, I can't tell what any of the shapes are.

"Four days ago we got lucky," says Mercer. "You're looking at Bougainville, the largest island of the Solomon archipelago. Point A on your photo is an airfield that the Japanese have built on the southern end. Find point B, northeast of there, on top of that peak. That dark shape hidden behind a ridge is a radio shack. Our plan is to knock out the Japanese communications system, so they won't be able to radio their planes or naval ships, specifically the ones near Guadalcanal, our main battle location."

"I assume we'll be doing a squadron box formation?" asks Martin.

"Not this time. It's a solo run. It's too hard to keep tight with twelve in a squadron. There will be one plane acting as both lead and defense."

"Escorts?" asks someone else. "AAF is still reeling from the losses over that German airfield in France."

"We don't expect surface-to-air fire. It's unlikely the Japanese will have antiaircraft in position as protection because that would be a giveaway that there's a radio tower there. But just to be safe, we'll stay at an altitude of twenty thousand feet."

"No saturation bombing, I assume?" asks one of the lieutenants. "It's random and ineffective." He doesn't hide his disdain.

"Actually, we will be doing some area bombing. The War Department has come up with an excellent strategy using both saturation and decoys. And the Norden isn't going to miss. Eleanor Schiff will see to that."

All eyes turn to me.

My eyes dart away. I find the door, hoping to see Mrs. Mauchly or Arbocast walk in and lend me support. Then I chide myself. They don't need to be here. They believe I can do this job. I smile briefly at the men.

"Miss Schiff has come all the way from Muroc, where she's been troubleshooting the bombsight. She's figured out how to adjust for turbulence due to air pressure changes between the sea and the mountain ranges of Duunaru."

He walks over to a chair where the red-cheeked officer is sitting. "Captain Haines here will be bombardier. He's our ace in the hole. Flown many successful missions so far. We'll let Haines and Miss

Schiff get acquainted. Math lessons begin at 1300 after lunch." He turns to the others. "Gentlemen?"

As everyone gets up to leave, they give backslaps to Haines and pepper him with encouraging phrases, most of which I've never heard before. "Duck soup, Haines." "Lay an egg." "Prang it."

The door closes and it's only him and me. I'd venture to put him in his late twenties, but the red cheeks and the small paunch rolling over his belt make me think he might even be older.

I lift my hand in a wave. "Hello."

"Howdy."

"Are you from Texas?" I don't know why I said that. Maybe it's the cowboy lingo or the way he's sitting with his boots propped up on the desk.

"No, I'm from Erie, PA."

"We share a state, then."

"Let's cut the small talk and get right to the math, huh? I have a grass-skirted baby doll and a tiki punch waiting for me downtown."

"But I thought the rear admiral said class starts at 1300."

"Seeing as I'm the only student, I say let's begin."

I'm so flustered that when I open my canvas satchel and remove the notebook, it slips from my hand. I think of Mrs. Mauchly the morning she came running out of the MathMeet. God, I miss her.

Although the table is wide and we're sitting opposite of each other in the middle, I can smell him. He's sweating and giving off a kind of sour, medicinal-like odor. I've perfected the art of breathing through my mouth from all those afternoons sitting by the latrine, but talking at the same time has its own challenges.

"So we know that the atmosphere is a viscous medium," I begin. "When a flow changes from smooth to turbulent, it's because there is some irregularity in there such as a disturbance in speed, wind shear, or temperature gradients between the atmosphere and Earth's surface."

I give up trying not to breathe through my nose and just bear the stench. "If you look at these graphs, you can see how the air over flat vegetation causes little turbulence." I pause to open my notebook. "But Bougainville is mountainous. Depending on time of day, encroaching storms, updrafts, or variations in air temperature, there will be pressure changes."

"You know this will be my eleventh mission, right?"

"Um, no, I didn't. That's . . . very impressive."

"So I know a thing or two about pressure changes."

"Of course. I didn't mean to imply . . . What I'm trying to say is this isn't about the turbulence effect on the plane or even the Norden. It's the bomb that won't perform correctly. Since there's no formula for predicting turbulence, we have to do a work-around. Using existing tables, you'll calculate the dynamic viscosity using the current air temperature. Then you'll quantify turbulence by using the Reynolds formula to find the Re number. From there, you'll set your trail arm on the sight."

"Do you know what the life expectancy is of a bombardier?"

He's having his own conversation, not even listening to me.

"Take a guess," he adds.

"I really have no idea. Let's just get back to the Reynolds number. There's a lot of math to review."

"It's eleven. Eleven missions. And then poof. You're gone."

I'm stunned into silence. I don't know how to reassure him. He's a human being. And he's going into harm's way. "I realize that's a frightening statistic, and the risk is real. But with this new turbulence adjustment, you'll have the best chance of getting in and out of there quickly."

"Cut the crap, will ya? Just show me what to do when I'm in the nose."

Is he always this rude? "It's not that simple. It might take us a few more sessions to get this sequence down. We have to run through different scenarios, different combinations of air temperature and ballistics. To achieve synchronization, it's crucial that—"

"Oh, come now. Your father would be able to do it in an hour."

My body goes rigid. "What did you say?"

"I said your father would be able to teach me in no time."

"I think you're mixing me up with someone else."

"Really? I figured with the same last name, it couldn't have been a coincidence. But I've been wrong before."

"What name is that?" My voice is a whisper.

"Schiff. Beryl Schiff was my math professor."

# 31.

Haines knows Dad.

I've been discovered.

What to do? What to do?

"Beryl, you say? I don't recognize that name." My voice sounds like I'm speaking inside a tin can.

Haines raises and drops one shoulder. "I guess I *was* wrong, then." He removes his boots from the table. "So, synchronization . . ."

I turn to a page in my notebook. Here's what I see:

$$\partial \div !\nabla\Delta\uparrow \forall\delta\mu \therefore \alpha - \cdots \zeta\eta\epsilon\mu\pi \leftrightarrow \therefore \vartheta\iota\lambda\nu\xi o\pi\varpi\rho\varrho\sigma\varphi\phi\chi \wedge\sqcap<\lessgtr\sim\cong \fff \Sigma \bowtie\|\neq\supseteq\notin\subset \prod \leqslant$$

and it's my handwriting on there, definitely. But it's gibberish, like the stuff I typed on Dad's typewriter when I used to pretend I knew how to read and that I was writing a book like he was.

"Pardon me, I just need a moment . . ." I turn some more pages. I can't make heads nor tails out of it. I shake my head and blink a few times, but it's still the same illegible math symbols.

Haines huffs impatiently. "Well?"

I lick my dry lips. Again, I examine my calculations. And again I can't make sense of it. "On second thought, why don't you go on and meet your date for that tiki punch and we'll resume at 1300, hmmm?"

"Suit yourself. But I can't promise I'll be back at 1300 on the dot."

He winks. "If you get my drift."

I mumble some sort of response and hightail it out of there before he stands up. Military personnel are everywhere. I duck into an empty women's bathroom. The girl reflected back at me in the mirror is unrecognizable. What's happening to me? I stick my face under the sink and gulp down water.

Two women in khakis walk in. My ears ring with the echoing sound of their laughter. They smile at me. I smile back and my mouth feels too big, as if hooks were on either side, pulling my lips up and apart. I leave before they start talking to me.

Down the corridor, I see an empty office with candy wrappers and discarded paper cups. Someone left in a hurry because there's a black radio telephone unmanned on a desk. That must be the only way to speak to the mainland from the islands. I remember Mrs. Mauchly had one in her office. I watch my feet walking into the room. Those are my boots, but then again, they're not. I can't feel my feet touching the floor. I have the sensation of looking down at the top of my head. I need to hear a familiar voice. Then I'll feel grounded. It's 11:30 a.m. here in Honolulu, which means it's 5:30 p.m. in Philadelphia.

I listen to make sure the channel is clear. Then I press the push-to-talk button. "Philadelphia Computing Section, Whiskey Three One Six Zero Foxtrot." I wait two seconds. "This is Hickam Army Airfield—" Shoot. I don't know the call sign here. I lift up the rectangular base of the radio. Someone has written the code on a slip of paper taped to the bottom. "This is Hickam Army Airfield Alpha Five One One Two Echo, requesting Alyce Sinclair, over."

The second I hear her voice, I start to sob.

"Eleanor? Is that you? What's wrong?"

There's a two-second delay between what she says and my replies, and I have to remember to push the talk button and not release it until I'm finished. But at least it's really her.

"Nothing. I'm just so happy to talk to you."

"How could I forget," says Alyce. "We're the people who cry when __ supposed to laugh. Where are __ right now?"

Words are dropping out. Mrs. Mauchly used shorter sentences when she made a radio telephone call.

"Honolulu. Left Muroc. Didn't have chance to write you," I say.

"You're ____ ballistics at Pearl Harbor?"

"Sort of. How are Lorelie and Margaret?"

"Who?"

No, that's not right. "I mean Louise and Marjorie." Why can't I remember these basic things?

"Louise has softened ____ bit, but Marjorie is as bad as ____. Another colored girl joined PCS."

"Don't become best friends," I tease.

"Never."

"How's Mrs. Mauchly?"

"Well. Dr. Mauchly is working ____ a new project. He brought in massive black cabinets to the basement and has ____ pushed against a wall. You wouldn't ____ all the cables he's got connected. It's some sort ____ electronic digital calculator. He claims it ____ plot a shell trajectory in seconds."

"Ha! That's what they said about—" I stop, unable to remember the name of the mechanical calculator we used back at PCS. I named it, I know that. I start to sob again.

"Eleanor, I can't hear you."

"This is Biggs Army Airfield in El Paso, Alpha Seven Zero Zero Nine Alpha. We have an emergency. Please get off this channel. I repeat. Please get off this channel."

I press the button to end the call. I broke a thousand rules anyway using it for personal reasons.

I'm still shaky, off-kilter. I should eat something. Food always helps. So I'll go to the mess, and get back to the conference room early, to prepare for my 1300 meeting with Haines. I won't think about the nonsense language in my notebook. I'll fill my body with nourishment and my brain will function properly.

At the mess, Ethel waves me over to sit with her and some other nurses, but I tell her I'm tight on time.

"You look peaky," says Ethel.

"Oh, stop trying to be a nurse," I joke. I take my tray and eat alone—a bowl of minestrone soup and a roast beef sandwich. The food is exponentially better here than at Muroc. Already I feel better.

With twenty minutes to go until 1300, I hurry back to command headquarters and sit down at the same conference table. Tempting though it is, I don't open my notebook. I'm afraid of what strange symbols I'll find in there. I'll just wait until Haines arrives, let the food digest.

But at 1300 he doesn't come.

Ten minutes pass and he's still not there. I wait twenty minutes, thirty minutes. Then forty-five minutes. No Haines. After an hour, I decide I've waited long enough. When he does come we'll be rushed. We won't have very much time. I'd better review the material. I take a breath and open the notebook. There's my crude topographical map of Bougainville Island. There's my Reynolds formula. The numbers start to come into focus. Thank you, God. Okay, I'm back.

Only I'm not.

My body is actually floating in the air right alongside the Reynolds formula. $Re = \dfrac{\rho u L}{u}$ . Reynolds equals density times flow speed times characteristic length of ballistic over dynamic viscosity. My ephemeral arm is attempting to grasp the numbers right out of the air, but they slip through my fingers. Before I know it, the symbols vanish and it's just me, outside my body, hovering like some sort of phantom.

And I can't put myself back.

# 32.

I make my way toward the exit of command headquarters, touching the walls like a blind person. Outside, the sky is impossibly blue, mocking my foggy state. I head to the beach. The sea will act like smelling salts and revive me.

But it doesn't.

Seventeen palm trees lined up in the distance. Each one with three coconuts. Fifty-one in all. But if two trees have four coconuts, then that's fifty-three, a prime number. It has exactly two factors. Yet it can never be divided into equal groups.

I look for more things to count.

I pass a white clapboard building. The chapel. What is the thickness of each piece of wood? How many slats from the ground to the first window? A chaplain works in a chapel. What was the name of that rabbi Ethel told me about? Richmond. If I ever needed spiritual advice, it's now.

There's a row of single-family residences behind the chapel, running parallel to the shore. I go slowly, reading the signs on each door. Twelve letters in the surname on the first door. Nine letters in the name on the second door. The next will be six letters. Then three. Tom or Jim or Bob. No, the pattern is wrong. Because the fifth house says Chaplain Harry Richmond. I pass it and turn back. That's the person I'm looking for.

My knock is answered by a little girl, maybe five or six years old, with her hair in two pigtails of brown ringlets.

"Mommy! There's a lady at the door."

"Who is it, Yonah?" calls a woman from another room.

The girl shrugs. "Who are you?"

This is a happy house. A mother and her child. Somehow, I find my voice. "My name is Eleanor."

A pretty woman with sideswept hair comes to the door, wiping her hands on an apron. She looks like she could be my schoolmate, not a mother on an army base. But then again, I'm on an army base.

"Can I help you?" she asks.

"Is the rabbi at home? I was hoping to speak to him." Once more, my voice is faint and far away.

"Unfortunately, my husband's conducting a funeral at the moment."

"Oh, I'm sorry to hear someone passed." My eyes dart around wildly. I don't know what to do now, where to go.

Yonah twirls one of her pigtails. "Mommy's baking treats."

The woman smiles. "I don't know when my husband will be back, but you're welcome to wait. I'm Judith, by the way."

The woman is so kind. I'm craving something—family?—so very much. "I guess I can come in. Thank you."

The barrack is small and decorated simply but comfortably. Seeing Yonah playing with her doll on the living room rug, I relax.

I linger in front of a framed quote on the wall near a side table. The words are legible, which is reassuring, given that everything written seemed foreign to me just thirty minutes ago. *He that preaches war is the devil's chaplain.*

Judith notices my interest. "Some people are surprised to see those words in a house on a military base. After Harry graduated Hebrew Union College, he volunteered for the draft as a protest. It's ironic, I know. But he wants to alleviate suffering for those who don't understand why they're fighting."

I picture Sky lying in that hospital bed with one leg and remember the doubt that I, too, felt about war.

Judith gestures to a dinette, covered with a flowered tablecloth. "Make yourself comfortable."

"How long have you been on base?" I hear myself go through the motions of proper etiquette, but those aren't my hands pulling out a chair. Those aren't my wrists resting on the tablecloth.

"Harry was called to duty in January of '41," says Judith. "It was fate that he happened to be here when we were attacked." She glances back at Yonah to make sure her daughter can't hear us. "He served in France during the Great War, too, but he said that the carnage on December seventh was like nothing he'd seen before."

"Did the rabbi work with Nurse Annie Fox?" I'm curious about her, about all the nurses, actually. But no one seems to want to relive their ordeal. Even Ethel clammed up after that first night.

"I can't keep up with all the people my husband works with. That's the price of being a rebbetzin."

"You speak Yiddish?"

She nods, pulling a tray of something sweet-smelling out of the oven. "A bissel."

"My family back in Philadelphia speaks Yiddish. Especially Aunt Jona and Uncle Herman."

"Where are they from originally?"

"Stanislau, in Poland."

Something dark passes over her eyes. "Are members of your family still there?"

I nod slowly. "You don't have any news, do you?"

"Other than the horror on Rosh Hashana, no. Harry managed to get a call through to Dr. Schwartz in Lisbon last week but no one has any specifics."

I recognize the name from the newsletters Mom got from the Joint. He's the director of European operations.

"If you hear anything, please let me know. I'm in the women's barrack."

Judith places three plates on the table. Yonah scrambles atop a chair that has two phone books stacked on the seat. I think of Dad and his special cushion. My eyes start to prick. I am so very close to losing it.

I blink a few times. "Something smells delicious."

"My mother's recipe. I was making it for break-the-fast, but I suppose we can sneak in a piece now. I hope you like brownies."

"I don't eat brownies," I say abruptly.

"Oh. Well, I'm sure we can muster up something else decadent for you."

"Get them away from me."

She stands there holding the serving platter, a confused expression on her face.

"I'll take two, then!" says Yonah.

The sound of the door opening takes our attention away momentarily. Rabbi Richmond walks into the kitchen.

"Daddy!"

The rabbi looks at least twenty years older than his wife. He has a kind face with large eyes and bushy eyebrows.

"Harry, this is Eleanor," says Judith, resting the tray on the table. Don't look at the brown squares. Don't look at the brown squares. "She'd like to speak with you if you have a moment."

He smiles at me.

"Daddy, Daddy!" Yonah is doing everything she can to catch her father's attention. But he's putting down his hat, loosening his tie, grabbing a brownie from the platter his wife is holding, and trying to still be polite to me, a guest in his house and someone in need of counsel.

Once he's seated, Yonah is still so excited that she spills a glass of milk all over his lap. The rabbi leaps up with a start, scaring his daughter. Yonah starts to cry.

"Don't cry, Yonah," I say. "You didn't mean to do it." I surprise myself by intervening in this domestic scene.

Judith places the plate of brownies next to the sink and comes back with a rag. Yonah sniffles and tries to help her mother sop up the milk, but she's just spreading the white liquid around more.

"Yonah. Let me," says Judith gently.

The rabbi turns to me. "I'll just go and change out of these pants and then we'll take a walk on the beach so we can speak privately."

Once the table is clean, Judith slides a piece of sponge cake onto the plate in front of me. I take a small bite and feel myself slowly returning to my body. "This is lovely, thank you."

Rabbi Richmond comes out of the bedroom quickly. "Ready to go?"

"Oh, Harry, one more thing," says Judith. "Do you have any more information from Dr. Schwartz? Eleanor's family is from Stanislau."

His eyes dart to me and back to Judith. "Why don't we walk first?"

"What do you know about Stanislau?"

"Come. Let's take a walk. I'd like to hear about how you ended up at Hickam," he hedges. "And what brought you to my house today."

I push my plate away. "Is there a list of names?"

He shakes his head. "Not exactly."

"Then what?"

He exhales.

"Please," I beg. "I can't stand it any longer."

"Very well." He gestures to Judith, who takes Yonah into her room. The rabbi grabs a chair. My knee is bobbing up and down under the table.

"It's been so hard to find any information in the papers," I say.

"Mainstream news is barely covering it," he says.

Sadly, Anderson was right.

"No one is able to believe there's a plan to murder every single European Jew."

I gasp. So there is a plan. That's what Szmul, the man on the radio, was saying.

"We're trying to get this up the chain, obviously. A report came out of Switzerland meant for the World Jewish Congress president, Rabbi Stephen Wise, but first it had to go through the State Department. They blocked it, saying it was just a war rumor."

The rabbi takes an envelope out of his breast pocket. "This came through the telegraph this morning." He unfolds a piece of paper.

From down the hall, I hear Yonah squealing with delight and the soft murmur of Judith's voice. "What does it say?"

He regards me closely. Maybe he's trying to judge if I'm able to handle the information, I'm not sure. "I'm afraid it's bad news. There are no survivors from the ghetto in Stanislau."

"I couldn't save her . . . I couldn't . . ."

Arms are around me, but I push them away.

"Eleanor, listen to me. Look at me," says the rabbi.

My tender hold on corporeal reality dissipates like smoke. I run from the kitchen, out the door, and don't stop until I'm at my barrack. Then I crawl into bed and pull the blanket over my head, shutting out my failed brain and the whole tragic world.

# 33.

The room is black. I feel black. Ethel comes and goes and leaves me food, which grows cold. She tries to get medicine down my throat, but I spit it out. I think I wet my bed. I don't know. I don't care. The light in the room shifts, becomes gray, and I don't get up.

Ethel changes the bottom sheet, rolling me over on one side to pull out the soiled one and replacing it with a crisp one. Still the food remains untouched. She gives me a sponge bath. I shiver, despite it being perpetually summer here.

Days go by. At some point, there's a knock on the door. "Ethel, is that you?" I murmur.

The knocking continues, insistent. Ethel would just come in. It can't be her.

"Go away," I croak out.

Whoever is there can't hear me. They continue to knock. The sound won't stop.

Somehow, I manage to find my robe, put my feet on the floor, and walk to the door.

Two men are standing there. One is Commander Mercer. The other might be from the War Department. There were so many men that first day, I can't remember. But a small voice from inside me tries desperately to be heard. Two high-ranking military officers are in your barrack! I salute, feeble though it is.

Mercer speaks first. "You haven't shown up at math class for the past three days, Schiff."

"I'm sorry. I . . . I haven't been feeling well."

"Don't worry. Haines didn't show up, either."

I seem to recall he was late coming back from a lunch. When was that? The details are blurry.

"I came to tell you he's gone AWOL," Mercer continues. "His commanding officer found bottles of vodka in his bivouac bag. Seems he's been numbing himself for over a year."

The red cheeks. The pharmaceutical smell. I should have recognized the signs of alcoholism. Trudie's mother had the same body odor. I just didn't think of it.

The other officer clears his throat. "This mission is crucial, Schiff. Our losses have been heavy, but we believe this can be the turning point in the Pacific. We've been at this for ten months now. We can't afford to wait any longer to get someone else up to speed."

Thirteen stars on each hat on their heads. Thirteen plus thirteen equals twenty-six. Half a deck of cards. Six claws on the eagle's talons. Six plus six equals twelve. Twelve months in a year.

"Your mouth is moving, but you're not speaking, Schiff," says Mercer. "Are you all right?"

Am I counting out loud? "Oh, um, yes, I'm fine, sir."

Mercer picks up the conversation. "Now that Haines is out, I radioed over to Muroc and asked Arbocast to send me another bombardier since they're further along in their training out there." He clasps his hands behind his back. "You know whose name he gave me?"

"I wouldn't know, sir."

"Yours."

Mine?

"That's impossible. I can't do it."

"I was against the idea," admits Mercer. "My chief of staff, too. There's a paper trail for everything we do around here, and we don't want to be seen putting a woman into harm's way." He frowns at the colonel next to him. "But the War Department has made a decision and I must abide by it. Colonel Barber, why don't you explain the rest."

"There are exceptions to civilians going into combat. And these are exceptional circumstances, Schiff. As a flag officer, Mercer can grant you permission and give you full army veteran benefits. We've added eleven escort planes for a twelve-aircraft squadron including the original decoy team to draw any potential air battle away from you. I'm not trying to underplay the risk. And we can't order you to do this, of course. Ultimately, it's your decision."

"No!" I scream. "You don't understand!"

"Excuse me?" says Colonel Barber.

"I can't do the math! I've lost my gift!"

Mercer is confused. "What are you talking about? What gift?"

My eyes fill with tears, and I turn my face away. "I'm not that girl, Commander Mercer. Please, leave me be."

They linger in my doorway a moment longer, then reluctantly leave the room.

More time goes by. Could be days. I lose count of the hours.

When the sun cuts a line through the middle of the blackout curtains, Ethel nudges me awake. "There's someone on the radio telephone for you."

"Tell them I can't talk."

"I think you're going to want to. It's your mother."

# 34.

The radio telephone is in a rec room on the first floor of the barrack. I'm still in my robe. I don't have it in me to even put on shoes. Barefoot, I slowly shuffle down the hall. The receiver is off its cradle, sitting next to the rectangle box. On the other end is the truth. If Mom's calling me, then she knows I'm here at Pearl Harbor. With an unsteady hand, I press the talk button.

"Mom?"

"Dad's here, too."

I want to flee.

"Eleanor?" Static interference is on the line.

She probably doesn't know how to use a two-way radio. I press the talk button again. "How did you get this call sign?"

"Your friend Alyce found us. She was worried about you. We're in Mrs. Mauchly's office."

That was loud and clear. Mrs. Mauchly is probably next to her, helping with the radio, concerned for me as well. Now my former teacher will know the truth, too. Guilt and burning shame battle for dominance in my chest.

"What's going on, Eleanor?" asks Mom.

I start to cry. "Please don't be upset with me."

"Why would we be upset? Other than the fact that you lied to us. Obviously, you're not at UCLA."

"Because . . . I'm . . ." I have to tell Mom the truth. If I don't, Mrs. Mauchly will. "Because I'm doing . . . math."

"That's incredible, Eleanor! You're helping our country."

"No! I shouldn't be doing math ever."

"What do you mean?"

"It's not fair. I don't deserve to have this brain." A great heat inside my chest erupts with brute force. "Because I took away Dad's!" I wail. "It's all my fault!"

"Oh, honey, no. Dad's stroke wasn't because of you. A blood vessel ruptured. It was weak from when he was a child. Maybe from rheumatic fever, the doctors aren't sure. But it was just waiting for the right time. It could have happened the day before or the day after."

My lungs are heaving. "But I begged him . . . to help me get the oven down. I made him . . . run upstairs. It's because of me that he collapsed."

"No. It was a terrible coincidence."

Static.

"I ruined your life, too!"

"That's not true. Oh, my poor Eleanor. You haven't been carrying this around your whole life, have you?"

I can't answer. Tears are streaming down my face.

"Wait, Dad wants to say something."

His slurry voice comes on the radio. "x plu one equ x."

$x + 1 = x$. It's the formula for infinity.

"I love you, too, Daddy. To infinity."

I'm sitting on the beach, my feet buried in the sugary sand. Finally, I get my chance to feel it between my toes. There's barbed wire next to me, erected after martial law was declared on December eighth last year. America won't let this territory be attacked by surprise again. Despite the wire, it's still so beautiful here. A seagull pecks at a piece of driftwood. All the battleships are in the harbor west of me, so nothing is blocking my view of the horizon. And I can see the dark shapes of shallow reefs under the aquamarine water.

The sun is nearly set. I've been here for hours, trying to figure out what happened to me these past few days and what the conversation with my parents all means.

"Eleanor!" It's Yonah, who breaks free of her father's hand and darts over to me.

"Hey there, cutie pie," I say.

She's carrying a tin pail with a shovel inside. "Daddy and I are going to build a sandcastle. Wanna help?"

Rabbi Richmond catches up to us. "Yonah, why don't you start collecting wet sand and we'll come help soon." He's barefoot with his pants rolled up at the bottom. He couldn't be further from the black-clad, hunched-over rabbi at Congregation Beth Sholom in Philly.

Yonah skips closer to the shore and begins to dig. Rabbi Richmond sits down next to me.

"I've been looking for you," he says. "I didn't think you wanted to be found."

"I'm not going to lie. It's been rough. And not just because I saw the rabbi's telegram, because I knew my cousin was gone."

"I regret part of our conversation at the kitchen table. I shouldn't have told you all that stuff about the WJC."

I shake my head. "The unknown is way worse. I'm glad you told me."

We watch as Yonah squeals, trying to outrun the gentle water.

"Earlier today I spoke to my parents back in Philadelphia." My eyes get teary again. "I didn't tell them about my cousin. I think my aunt and uncle are probably dead as well. I couldn't bring myself to say the words."

"It's probably best to do it in person anyway. Maybe by the time you go home we'll have a definitive answer on your aunt and uncle, too."

"I was crying too much." My voice breaks. "They told me that it's not my fault."

"What's not your fault?"

I shudder and sigh.

He waits for me to say more.

When I don't, he says quietly, "Why don't you start from the beginning, Eleanor?"

And so I tell him about my gift in math. About Dad's stroke.

About staying hidden most of my life. About my vow never to let my parents find out. About the terrible burden I've been carrying. All the way up to meeting Haines. "And then, when I was supposed to teach him the math, I couldn't stay in my body. I was crying for no reason. I couldn't remember names of friends, not to mention the formulas. It felt like I was melting down."

"It's called disassociation. No one in the medical field is really talking about this when it comes to trauma. Doctors still think there's something wrong with people's brains who disassociate. But I don't. I think it's a defense. Your mind did that to protect you. I've seen it happen over and over in wartime. Especially after the attack here. Soldiers will go outside their bodies in order to protect themselves psychologically. In a way, not recognizing the formulas was a way for you to hide your math skills from the people here at Hickam. Hiding is what's comfortable for you. Since you've been doing it all your life, it actually feels safe."

I just listen, crying quietly.

"It sounds backward, I know. But I think it was the only way you could cope once you were confronted with someone who knew your father."

"Except I didn't get attacked by the Japanese. Don't you think I overreacted with Haines?"

"You were a little girl. Your father collapsed in front of you. I'd say that's a pretty significant trauma."

"It's like a ballistic. Most of my life I've been moving on a certain trajectory and then boom, I fell out of the sky."

"Tell me more about the phone call with your parents. They told you it wasn't your fault?"

"Mom said Dad had a weak blood vessel from when he was young. That it could have happened at any point in his life. I guess that day in my room was the day his luck ran out."

Down by the water, Yonah waves happily at us.

"I was exactly Yonah's age when it happened."

"Remember in the house, when she spilled milk on me?" says Rabbi Richmond. "And you told her it wasn't her fault?"

I keep sticking the heels of my palms into my eyes but I can't stop crying.

"Six-year-old Eleanor would never do anything to hurt her father. Do you believe me?"

"I do now." I wipe my nose with my sleeve.

He hands me his hankie.

"Thanks. Believe it or not, I had two of my own, but I've given them both away."

"I'm sure those people needed it more than you."

It feels like I've received so much more from Alyce and Sky than I could ever give them.

I lift up some sand and let it fall between my fingers. It reminds me of an hourglass.

Time is running out.

"Thank you, Rabbi. From the bottom of my heart. I can't tell you how much meeting you, your whole family, has meant to me. I wish I could stay and build the castle, but I have to go."

"I'll tell Yonah goodbye for you."

I stand up, brush sand from my khakis, and go find Commander Mercer.

# 35.

Once again, I'm geared up for flight. Only this time, I feel like a Christmas tree in Jenkintown Square. I'm laden with electrical cords and attachments, though nothing as pretty as a shiny ornament.

Blame General Electric's heated flying suit, otherwise known as the Blue Bunny. Not everyone is lucky enough to get this light blue protective gear. The B-17 we're going up in only has charging power capacity for four heated suits, which usually go to the tail and ball turret gunners, since they sit in a cramped space and can't move about, and the waist gunners, since they stand by the open windows. One of the waist gunners, nicknamed Jacko, kindly gave his up for me.

The rest of the guys aren't as generous. They're not obnoxious with the innuendos like the men in the Norden training class were, but I'm definitely getting stares.

A female pilot was assigned to dress me. My five-feet-one-inch body must weigh over 175 pounds at this point. First, I have on summer khakis and a blouse. This is in case we get captured. I can't be marooned on an island in the Pacific with only heavy clothes to wear.

Over that is the Blue Bunny, a one-piece coverall-type electric suit. And then the third and final layer, consisting of a leather jacket and thick fur-lined leather trousers.

"Will I be electrocuted?" I had asked the woman.

She shook her head. "It's just like an electric blanket you have at home. The wires are sewn into the wool fabric so it never touches your body. You should be grateful it's 1942. Airmen and women didn't always have this heated suit. More than half of all combat casualties in the air used to be caused by frostbite."

How comforting, I thought.

On my hands and feet are wool felt inserts lined with moleskin cloth that contain heated wires. Over these we wear special boots and gloves, both brown, made of goatskin leather and shearling lining.

"Never take off these liners. Your skin will stick to the frozen metal inside the plane," she warned.

That was another comforting piece of advice.

The front of the Bunny has a small, zippered opening to the right of the crotch in case I need to relieve myself. I haven't had a sip to drink except when I brushed my teeth this morning. I'd like to avoid that embarrassment if possible.

My head alone must weigh fifty pounds when you add up the helmet, goggles, radio intercom, and oxygen mask. We have to use the masks once we hit 10,000 feet above sea level or else we'll suffer from anoxia, which will impair efficiency and judgment.

I plan to use it well under that altitude. I've already had enough mental confusion for a lifetime.

There's a black AAF patch with white letters on my left shoulder. On my right chest is a four-inch-long leather name plate. It's stamped with my name, E. Schiff.

I'm holding a parachute pack, which I'll stow near my Norden station. It's made of silk, thanks to all us women who've given up our stockings. The female pilot showed me where the two-pin, short cable ripcord handle is, on the right end of the rectangular pack. Hanging just below my rear end is a raft case. This is required for all flights taking an overwater route. I'm not sure how I'm going to sit for such a long flight with this bulky thing behind me.

I'm thankful for the precautions, but if I think too much about them—the khaki pants and white blouse for capture, the parachute if the plane is hit and we have to bail out, the raft to survive on the water (never mind the sharks), the oxygen mask so I don't go unconscious—I turn into Nervous Nellie. Then I won't be good to anyone. In the letter I dashed off to Sky explaining my decision to replace Haines, I admitted I was scared. But I couldn't have anticipated any of these details.

I'm about to board when I hear my name. It's the captain—call sign Viking. He looks it, too, with his chiseled cheeks and big hands. "You have to kiss the painted lady, Schiff. For good luck."

In all my gear, I hadn't noticed the name of the plane. *Rosie's Riveter.* How fitting.

A gunner shakes his head. "It's gonna take more than that, Captain. I'm telling ya, I have a bad feeling. I ain't never flown with a girl before."

A bunch of other crewmen from the 5th Bombardment Group nod in agreement. So that's why they were staring at me. They're all superstitious.

"Shut up, Branson. With her talent, she's our lucky charm." Viking sweeps his arm out gallantly. "After you, Schiff."

I touch the scantily clad pinup girl, then kiss my hand. Just like a mezuzah.

As the rest of the ten-man crew climbs aboard, they each do the same thing. Branson does it twice, then makes the sign of the cross.

Because I'm so short, I can walk upright to my spot at the nose, whereas the rest of the crew has to crouch. We settle into our positions. I've got my clipboard tied to my chair by an elastic cord. The pencil is also attached with a string. If we had enough fuel, the flight would take just over seven hours. But we'll be stopping at an island in the Midway Atoll halfway through the trip to refuel. We also have to load up the bombs once we're there. B-17s can't land on a runway with armaments inside. The weight of the bombs would crush the landing gear.

The ground crew move like worker bees, pulling fuel lines, unblocking wheels, signaling to the control tower. The four engines roar to life, Viking gives a thumbs-up to the flag man, and we're off. If I crane my neck to the side of the bubbled nose window, I can make out the V formation of the escort planes behind us, with *Rosie's Riveter* in lead position. Six of the planes are decoys and will veer north when we get to Bougainville to draw the Japanese away in case an air battle ensues. The other five bombers behind *Rosie's Riveter* will break formation and fly at 15,000 feet, carpet-bombing around the bottom of the mountain range first. This is to trick the Japanese into thinking we don't know where their radio tower is and also to prevent them from questioning our strategy to fly at such high altitude. We don't want them guessing that we have a high-precision bombsight on board. Once the carpet-bombing is complete, I'll locate the target visually through the Norden and drop the final bombs.

The time passes more quickly than I imagined. There's plenty for me to look at, whether it's the view of Earth out the nose or the crew behind me. Joe, the radio operator, sits at the desk listening for enemy communication. Jacko and the other waist gunner stand up occasionally, but mostly sit in their seats, keeping watch out their respective sides, alert as owls. I can't see the other gunners, but I can hear them talking with Viking and the copilot through the interphone.

As the clouds drift by, I think of Eleanor Roosevelt. If there was ever a time for her to watch over me, it's now, but she's probably otherwise occupied. I've heard the president's health is failing. I wonder if she's really the one pulling the strings at the moment. I wouldn't be surprised.

About twenty nautical miles from Midway, I take down the barometer reading of the air temperature: 41 degrees. I'm going to time myself finding the Reynolds number. It will be a practice run before we get to the real drop over Bougainville. With Haines going

AWOL, we never got to do a proper test flight to see if my math actually worked. Now, it doesn't make sense to drop a bomb over the ocean with only moving whitecaps for targets. The place to do it would have been at Muroc, but of course, at that point, we had no idea I'd be the one actually doing this.

I set the military stopwatch mounted on the wall next to me and begin. First step: Check the table and find the air viscosity number and density for 41 degrees. Second step: Determine the flow speed. Since the bomb will start out slow and pick up speed as it heads down to the target, I need to use calculus to approximate what the velocity will be at various points in the trajectory. It's similar to what we did at PCS, except I'll use the velocity equation and the basic formula for projectile motion. Third step: Plug those numbers into the Reynolds formula. Fourth step: Take the Reynolds number and find the corresponding correction to the drag coefficient due to turbulence effects. Fifth step: Adjust the drift knob and trail arm on the Norden accordingly. On this final step, I just pretend to turn the drift knob and trail arm. I don't want to mess with the dials more than necessary.

Done. Stopwatch reads three minutes, twenty-three seconds. Not bad. Combine that with the regular Norden input requirements and I should be fine.

When we touch down at Midway, I'm struck by how important each and every battle is. That girl I saw at the train station on my way from Philadelphia to California held up a sign for her brother, Dusty. She wrote that he was their Midway Hero. Dusty helped secure this island so that we can land here safely right now and refuel. So that we don't have to use an aircraft carrier and risk an attack by a Japanese sub. Everything is connected.

The rest of the crew gets out to stretch their legs and empty their bladders, but I stay in my chair, running the practice Reynolds numbers again, trying to shave seconds off my total time. The ballistics information is already entered. I practice with different altitudes, various TAS numbers. My body is in action mode, its basic needs forgotten. Nervous Nellie hasn't shown herself. My pulse feels calm and steady.

I watch as the Midway crewmen load the bombs from the trolley and strap them in. Eight thousand pounds of destructive power. How far I've come since Sky first took me inside *Flamin' Mamie* and I couldn't even look at where the bombs would have been stored.

The second leg of the trip goes faster. I don't let my focus wander even for a minute. I run through the formulas in my head, doing mental math over and over. Just a few more hours to go now. As we get farther southeast, we ascend to 20,000 feet. Freezing air streams into the plane and never leaves. My body is plenty warm, though.

"Target nine nautical miles south," says Viking through the interphone. "Tighten up the formation."

It's go time. Bougainville is beneath me. From up here I can make out green patches and beige lines and waterways. Of course, I can't locate the radio tower from up this high. But I can see the mountain range and I know where the ridge is from the Operation Snapshot photographs. Then I set the stopwatch. Temperature −2 degrees. I go through the steps of the formula and finish in under three minutes. Now altitude and TAS. Then check the ballistics tables for disc speed and trail. Finally, adjust the drift knob and trail arm for the new disc speed.

Except I can't work the dial. It's too tiny and my gloves are too thick! I have to remove them, using just the heated liner. There's no other way.

"We're over the target," announces Viking.

I exhale, seeing condensation in front of me. I remove the right outer leather glove. The cold is immediate, biting. I move the dial to 50 mils. It goes past to 52. Steady, Eleanor. There. 50. Quickly I put my glove back on. I can't feel my hand. I use my left hand to force my right into a fist. Then I pry it open again. It takes a few openings and closings, but finally some sensation comes back in. It hurts like the devil. At least the pain means I have feeling in it.

Then, *POP, POP, POP*, far below the plane. Out my window I see black puffs of smoke.

"Antiaircraft flak!" says the pilot through the command setting. All twelve of our planes can hear him.

They know our path. The Japanese are here. Don't panic. Keep your eye on the sight.

"We're too high for them to reach," says the copilot.

"Decoy planes, move into position," orders Viking.

More popping.

"Starting evasive action."

We turn. We wait. It seems to have worked. I can't see any smoke below on the island. Have we even carpet-bombed yet?

"Coming back over the target," calls the pilot. "Transferring to autopilot."

I'm flying the plane, controlling it through the bombsight. No changing course now. We can't dodge fighters or flak.

"You got it, Schiff."

"Bomb bay doors open," I call.

"Zeros coming around, three o'clock!" yells a gunner.

From the top of *Rosie's Riveter*, our ball turret gunner fires back. Rounds of bullets come nonstop. I can't tell if it's us or the Zeros, the Japanese fighter planes. Then everyone starts talking at once through both the interphone on our plane and through the radio of the other planes.

"Two more divers, nine o'clock!"

"Decoy plane three is hit. One engine's on fire."

"Keep your eye on 'em, boys."

"Come on, you sonuvabitch."

The noise is deafening. The plane is shaking. My chair is swiveling. It's hard to keep still. Ignore the battle. Keep your focus on the crosshairs. This is what the stabilizer is for. The sight isn't moving, we are.

"There he is. Breaking at eleven!"

"I can't get him!"

An explosive sound.

I fall off my chair. Have we been hit? My mic is loose. I smell smoke. It's black and the cold air turns hot.

"Our oxygen tank's on fire!" yells Jacko.

I hear the sound of air whooshing. An extinguisher? Have to get back into my seat.

"Schiff, you there?" It's the pilot.

I'm talking, but he can't hear me. My mic. It's not on properly. I can't see a thing. I have to do it by feel. I fumble with my thick gloves and somehow manage to get the mic back in position. "I'm okay."

The smoke starts to clear and I can see the bombsight again. The indices are off. I turn the rate knob to slow it down. Okay, I'm back on the target. There's still time. I level up just a bit. I move the automatic release lever ever so slightly. No big corrections now.

Crosshairs centered on the target. This is it.

"Bombs away!" I call into the mic.

I can see the six bombs floating down below me. I pray my turbulence adjustment did the trick.

Smoke erupts on the island, obscuring everything. Where there was green and beige, there is now nothing but gray. Doubts creep in.

"Bombardier to pilot," I say. "I need one more attempt. Can we come back around?"

Viking takes back control from the autopilot. "That's a negative. We couldn't even carpet-bomb. We're taking heavy fire. Oxygen tank is still smoking."

"But I can't be sure the target's been hit," I protest.

"Mission is complete," says the pilot. "I repeat, mission is complete."

God, I hope it worked. I look out my window. Are the Japanese still up here, hiding behind a cloud? In the pathway of the blinding sun so we don't see them coming?

"Zero, six o'clock!"

It's a speck in the sky. It seems impossible our gunners can hit that. More rounds of ammunition are fired.

"He's coming in on a half roll!"

"Pull her up, Viking!"

"Got him! He's bailing out."

Finally, the only sound is our own four engines. The radio voices stop, and I realize that we couldn't have survived just now without our wingmen. They were crucial. Now *that's* the kind of wingwoman I wouldn't mind being.

I fill out my bombing flight record and less than an hour later, we land at Henderson Field on Allied-occupied Florida Island in the Solomons. Miraculously, all twelve planes made it here safely. Only one engine was destroyed on the decoy plane, and aside from numerous flak dents and holes, and the fire damage inside *Rosie's Riveter*, the B-17s are in fairly good shape.

I stand up for the first time in over eight hours and my legs feel like jelly. I take off two layers of clothing, walk slowly to the latrine, and only when I'm alone in the small shed do I weep.

Once the stress has been released, I join the others to wait and hear if our mission was a success.

# 36.

The ten crew members of *Rosie's Riveter* are sitting in a small hut next to Henderson Field. Airmen from the decoy planes and the other bombers are scattered in various huts nearby. Stiff legs are stretched out; thirsts are being quenched. Some of us close our eyes, but swatting the mosquitoes keeps me awake.

A tall man in khakis and a white naval officer's cap strides toward our hut.

We all stand and salute.

"Rear Admiral Daniel Callaghan here," he says, saluting back to us. "Good news, gentlemen and lady. The radio tower on Guadalcanal has been destroyed."

We burst into cheers and the other crewmen come running over. I'm lifted up by nine pairs of hands. I'm like an airplane, horizontal, flying through the sky.

"Let me down, you guys!"

They don't listen. They zoom me in and out for a long while, making engine sounds like little boys playing with toy airplanes.

When my feet finally touch the ground, Jacko says, "Ready to go again, Schiff?"

I smile. "One is good enough for me, thanks."

"Are you kidding?" teases Viking. "You were ready for a second bombs away up there."

I can't believe I actually did it! A feeling of warmth washes over me, like the smell of lemon bars, like Alyce's smile, like Sky's lips on mine. Actually, I'm wrong. This is better than any feeling in the world. The only thing that comes close is when Dad told me the formula for infinity.

Someone hands out shot glasses and Viking pours us each some whiskey.

"Ready, one, two, three, shoot!" says the ball turret gunner.

After a meal of real eggs, they hand out sleeping rolls and foldable cots. We're told to sleep in all our clothes to keep away chiggers. I try not to think about what diseases they carry. At least we have a bed net to keep away the mosquitoes. In the morning, when *Rosie's Riveter* is topped off with fuel, we head back to Midway and then home.

Over the next few days at Hickam, I sleep through reveille. I get my hair cut. I swim in the ocean. I go shopping in downtown Honolulu and buy dumb souvenirs for Mom, Dad, and Sarah. Then I buy myself an oyster guaranteed to have a pearl inside. A young woman reaches into a large tank and grabs the shell I point to. She opens it carefully, then gives me a toothy smile.

"Hurry up!" calls a brusque voice behind me.

It's a sailor, low-ranked, based on his white uniform and black scarf tied in a square knot around his neck. "These coolies are so damn slow," he adds.

Flustered, the cashier wraps the tiny pearl in tissue paper and rings up my purchase as fast as she can.

As I move out of line, I stop next to the sailor. "You remind me of someone."

"Your boyfriend back home, honeycakes?"

"No. A girl named Marjorie."

At the bus stop back to base, I look around, wondering if that sailor is catching a ride, too. He's not, but I would have welcomed the chance to glare at him. Once I board, there's a group of WAACs seated near the front. "It's her! The Numbers Girl!"

I blush and move past them toward some empty spaces in the back.

"Wait!" calls one of the WAACs, a bright-eyed girl with a snaggle-tooth. "What was it like? Were you scared?" They may not know the details of the mission, but clearly they've heard something about it.

I stop and turn around. "It was the scariest thing I've ever done."

"Oh, come on. You're giving us a line. Growing up, everyone in school probably called you Cool Cathy or something. What's your first name anyway?"

I just laugh. Then I take a seat right next to them and listen to all their stories instead of telling mine. I'm closing the book on Nervous Nellie.

That afternoon, Mercer requests a meeting.

In the lobby of command headquarters, I'm met by a young aide in a crisp uniform. "Please follow me."

I've only been on the second floor, where the conference room is located. The first floor is a large open space. Male aides and female secretaries sit at desks, clacking typewriters or receiving telegraph messages. Metallic cabinet drawers squeak open and snap shut. People yell directives to each other. This is the business of war. No one pays attention as we pass through the room.

The aide leads me down a quiet hallway, the only sound our shoes on the linoleum. I spot Mercer's door and stop automatically.

"Over here, Schiff." The aide continues down the corridor. I have to do a half skip to catch up to him. Finally, he pauses in front of a closed door with a sign that reads ADMIRAL CHESTER NIMITZ, COMMANDER IN CHIEF OF PACIFIC FLEET.

"There must be some mistake . . ." I stammer.

"Oh, you're in the right place," says the aide, sweeping open the door. The admiral is on the phone. He waves us in and holds up his index finger for us to wait one minute.

The aide whispers to me to take a seat, then leaves me alone with the God of Pearl Harbor. On the one hand, Chester Nimitz looks like a grandpa with his white hair and veined hands. But on the other hand, his chest candy and four stars on each point of his collar assure anyone in his presence that he's no ordinary relative at the holiday table. I recognize some of the people in the framed photos hanging on the wall of his office. Arbocast had pictures taken with many of the same folks. Hap Arnold, commander of the AAF, with his leprechaun grin; Queen Elizabeth; President Roosevelt.

He hangs up the phone. "My apologies for the delay."

He's apologizing to me?

"I suppose you're wondering why you're sitting here in my office?"

I nod.

"Mercer tells me you were a real pro up there," says the admiral. "I'd like to give you this." He opens up a small box. Inside is a medal dangling from a red-and-blue ribbon. "It's the Distinguished Civilian Service Award."

"It was an honor to serve, truly."

"Arbocast wants you to know the medal is for your work at Muroc as well. He sends his very best congratulations. We can't give you a proper ceremony because the mission was classified, but it's yours to wear on your uniform."

I grip the box in my hand, overwhelmed. "Thank you, sir." I push out my chair, not wanting to take up any more of his time.

"Before you go, Schiff, I'd like to know something. How long did it take you to figure out what was wrong with the bombsight?"

I go back to those eight hours when I pored over the maps at Muroc, thinking about fluidity and air pressure and volcanoes, drinking stale coffee and staying up until the sun rose. But I don't say that. "My whole life."

He nods. "Hard work is the secret to everything. Nothing happens overnight."

Even when it does, it doesn't.

"My aide, Lieutenant Lamar, will instruct you further."

I'm led by the young aide into a small cubicle. He informs me that I'm to stay here at Pearl Harbor for a few more days and teach one of the noncommissioned officers how to do the turbulence math. That way they'll have someone on staff who can train subsequent bombardiers.

"And after that?" I ask.

"Mary and John Mauchly want you to return to PCS. Something about a new top-secret computing project they need your expertise on."

It'll be nice to work with Mrs. Mauchly again, and to reunite with Alyce of course, but part of me was hoping I'd be sent back to Muroc so I could see Sky. By now he must know that our mission was successful. Where does this leave us, going forward? I haven't let myself think about a future with him. Mom and Dad would never accept me marrying someone who wasn't Jewish. But not seeing him ever again? A chasm in my chest opens up when I picture a life without him. Is this what love feels like?

Back in my room, I carefully store the small box from Admiral Nimitz in the zipper pouch of my suitcase. I won't be wearing the medal. Now I understand why Annie Fox doesn't talk about her Purple Heart. It's not about the recognition. It's about what led up to it.

Two days later, after a math session with the noncommissioned officer, there's a letter waiting for me on my bed. It's from Sky! His prosthesis is installed. He's walking around with a cane now. He'll be going back to Provo. He wants me to visit him there.

It's not a marriage proposal. It's just an invitation. Maybe our different faiths don't have to be an obstacle, but rather a commonality. I don't know. For now, I'm just happy to be able to see him again.

I write him back with one line:

*We have a date to go see some hoodoos in Utah.*

The trip home isn't as long as the train ride out West. I fly from Honolulu to San Francisco and then to Philadelphia as part of the Army Transport Command, which has taken over most of the commercial flights. My plane is a plush T&WA airliner with sleeper berths and something called a "charm room," where I can freshen up. Despite the heated cabin, one thing's for sure: The view isn't nearly as good as from the nose of a B-17.

By the time I land, it's 10:00 p.m. Mom, Dad, and Sarah pick me up at the airport. I sink into their arms, their familiar smells. Then, careful not to put too much weight on him, I sit on Dad's lap right there in the wheelchair so I can give him a proper hug. I know I have to tell them about Stanislau. But bad news is always easier to take in the morning. They've waited this long. It can wait one more night's sleep. As for Sky, it's going to take some time for them to get used to the idea of me having a non-Jewish boyfriend. I need to take baby steps. But rather than taking one step forward and two steps back, which is the way my life used to feel, I'm only moving in one direction.

"You look different," says Sarah.

"She looks tired," says Mom.

"No," says Sarah. "That's not it. She looks like—"

Dad interrupts her. "A mathema."

I translate for him. "A mathematician."

## AUTHOR'S NOTE

Though this is a work of fiction, many of the plot points are from true events.

Nat Segall's night club, the Downbeat, got raided several times for "serving alcohol to minors." But some journalists believed this was a way to pressure Segall into segregating his popular establishment. Rather than give in to political forces, he sold the club in 1948.

On the holiday of Rosh Hashana in 1942, out of the remaining Jewish population in Stanislau, between three and four thousand were deported to the concentration camp Belzec, where they perished. Over the next several months, the rest of the Stanislau Jews were shot. About one hundred hid and managed to survive, along with a few engineers and technicians who had been in the central prison.

From August 1942 through February 1943, the Allies fought a series of land and sea battles against the Japanese in the Solomon Islands. The ultimate victory at Guadalcanal was a large morale booster and marked a turning point in favor of the Allies in the war in the Pacific.

Pancho Barnes and her Rancho Oro Verde became known as the Happy Bottom Riding Club, an oasis for airmen, captains of industry, and Hollywood stars until 1953.

By the end of World War II, seven and half million bombs were dropped from an average altitude of 21,000 feet, with only 16 percent falling within 1,000 feet of the aiming point. While this did not meet Norden bombsight expectations for precision, it did stop German oil production and destroyed 20 percent of the German war machine in the last sixteen months of the conflict.

Between 1942 and 1945, more than one hundred young women worked as junior human computers, calculating firing tables for the Philadelphia Computing Section. At least one was asked to go to Muroc Army Air Base and compute ballistics in the desert. Six other PCS women went on to become part of the team that built the first digital computer, the Electronic Numerical Integrator and Computer (or ENIAC), under Dr. John Mauchly and J. Presper Eckert at the University of Pennsylvania. Mary Mauchley was also a gifted mathematician. Alyce McClaine Hall, a public school math teacher, was the only woman of color to work at PCS. Later, her sister, Alma, joined her to help program the ENIAC.

Before and immediately after World War II, women played a leading role in operating computing machines for national security applications. This included highly mathematical codebreaking programs run on the Bomba machine in Poland, the Turing-Welchman Bombe and the Colossus in England, and the Desch Bombe in the United States.

Most of the women never told their families about the computing work they did.

# ACKNOWLEDGMENTS

A thousand thank-yous to:

Mr. John Murphy, Chief Historian, Edwards Air Force Base

Jeannine Geiger, Archives Specialist, Edwards Air Force Base

Rodney Bengston, Director, Pearl Harbor Aviation Museum

Taigh Ramey, Vintage Aircraft

Jacob Ham, PhD, Clinical Psychologist

Chris Damiani, Historical Society of Pennsylvania

Jack McCarthy, Archivist and Philadelphia Historian

Sharon Ann Holt, PhD, Coordinator of Public History Program, Penn State

Chidinma Ikonte, Student Research Assistant, UCLA Powell Library

Diana King, Librarian, UCLA Powell Library

Joan and Herman Rush, Philadelphians and dear friends

Catherine Wyler, producer of the film restoration of *The Memphis Belle: A Story of a Flying Fortress*

LeAnn Erickson, Filmmaker, *The Computer Wore Heels*

The brilliant mathematicians Gurleen Bal, PhD; Felicia Dalton; Austin Totty; and Jude St. John

My perspicacious agent, Steven Chudney

The lovely and masterful Lisa Sandell at Scholastic, who first asked for a story set during World War II

Elizabeth Parisi, Amanda Trautmann, Rachel Feld, Daisy Glasgow, Erin Berger, Seale Ballenger, David Levithan, Janell Harris, Emily Heddleson, Maisha Johnson, Sabrina Montenigro, Lizette Serrano, and the entire Scholastic sales team

And last, but never least, my esteemed writing mentor, Barbara Bottner, and the talented critiqueniks: Denise Doyen, Jim Cox, Juniper Ekman (extra points for you beta readers!), Hillary Perelyubskiy, and Cynthia Baseman

If you're experiencing panic attacks from trauma, you can find help at the National Child Traumatic Stress Network: www.nctsn.org/audiences/youth

# ABOUT THE AUTHOR

ambria Gordon is the author of *The Poetry of Secrets*, which *New York Times* bestselling author Ruta Sepetys called an "epic, poetic journey," nd coauthor of the award-winning *The Down-to-Earth Guide to Global Warming*, winner of the Green Earth Book Award. She has written or *Los Angeles Times Magazine*, *Boys' Life*, *Parent Guide News*, and the *wish Journal* of Los Angeles. She lives in LA with her husband and youngest son, and as close as possible to her two adult children, without annoying them.